Praise for *Love's Deception*, by Kelly Nelson

*This book is one of the best books I've read in years I fell in love
with both Ty and Cat and honestly* go on for
another 200 pages. I con way past
my bedtime two nights Nelson
writes more novels just li. r

*Such a heartwarming story. . ιυved it. It is so nice to read a sweet
love story that is clean and has great morals.* —ADCollins

*I loved the whole concept of this book—which kept me on my
toes with unexpected twists. It's a sweet love story that I didn't
want to end!* —Jenn Hough

*The author is an excellent storyteller, and this quality kept
me turning the pages. . . . Ms. Nelson writes her characters
sympathetically and with credibility.* —Amazon Reader

*I loved all of the characters in this book and how their lives
changed as they prayed and worked through problems, trials
and successes in their life. I fell in love with Ty and the changes
he made in his life. I look forward to reading more books from
this author.* —Donna C.

*I really loved this clean, uplifting, and very nicely written love
story. It was perfect from start to finish. ... Thank you Kelly
Nelson. You have a fan for life.* —Dkmax

*Such a good book! It was a great reminder of forgiveness and
how we should forgive others . . . and ourselves! Have faith—
everything happens for a reason. The Lord answers our prayers.
It may not be on our timetable but he DOES answer, on His
timetable and in His way.* —Amazon Customer

I could not put Love's Deception *down. It is a beautiful story of a somewhat unlikely match.* —Sarah Nielsen

A tender story. I couldn't put it down! It felt very real to life and I appreciated the gospel connections and themes of faith, forgiveness, and enduring to the end while striving to rejoice in all things. The book definitely had some tear-jerking moments, but it was written in such a way that it was uplifting, though also being poignant. This is well worth your time, and I encourage you to take a chance on it. I look forward to more gospel-related novels by this author. —SurvivorMama

Great book. Wonderful love story that keeps your interest from the beginning and has just the right amount of suspense to keep a person intrigued. Really loved it!!! —Amazon Customer

I enjoyed both the story line and the characters. With the title Love's Deception *I was a little concerned with what the "deception" might be because I hate it when characters I love end up not being what I think. Thankfully the deceptions in this story did not lessen my love for these characters.* —Kathy Habel, Top 1000 Reviewer, Amazon

The Woman
WITH NO NAME

HOPE YOU ENJOY!

Kelly Nelson

Kelly Nelson

WALNUT SPRINGS PRESS

Other Novels by Kelly Nelson

Inspirational Romance
Love's Deception

Young Adult Fantasy
The Keeper's Calling
The Keeper's Quest
The Keeper's Defiance
The Keepers' Council

For my husband Greg and his cousin Dave

Cover design by Tracy Anderson (TracyAndersonPhoto.com)

ISBN-13: 978-1-59992-145-7

Acknowledgments

I'm grateful for all the amazing people who made up my support team for this novel. I couldn't have done it without you. Thanks to Dave Clemens, who critiqued the hunting portion of my manuscript while he waged a fierce battle with ALS. He dedicated precious time to help me, and though his advanced illness made it difficult for him to write, he made an audio recording of his feedback. Dave's strength, bravery, and resourcefulness in the face of such a debilitating disease was truly inspiring.

I express gratitude to my mom, Kristin, who is always the first to read my work and give encouragement. To my critique partners Laura Johnston, Susan Dayley, and Wanda Luce, thank you for deleting my dumb sentences and pointing out what I missed. Thank you to my editor and friend Linda Prince; publishing with her feels more like fun than work. Thank you to Garry Mitchell for establishing my career as an author. Credit for this amazing cover goes to Tracy Anderson, the most creative and talented person I know.

Without my police procedure squad, I couldn't have finished this book. Thank you to Officer Dave Morse, who knows I'm not contemplating a life of crime when I ask crazy questions. Gratitude goes to Lieutenant Carl Johnston, who sat in his office with me for hours while I researched Utah law and how it might feel to spend a night in a county jail. Special thanks to former FBI special agent KC Johnston, who read the manuscript and tutored me on the Federal Bureau of Investigation's typical involvement in cases like the one in this story. I made every effort to accurately portray law enforcement procedures, and the fault for any errors in that area is my own.

Thank you to my handsome husband Greg, who is the inspiration behind Colt's character and who can spin a hunting or fishing tale that makes people laugh so hard their stomachs hurt. Life with Greg is never dull. And finally, I would be remiss if I failed to express gratitude to my loving Heavenly Father, from whom all blessings flow.

One

Colt Murdock patted the spotted neck of his appaloosa. "Duke, old buddy, we've gone pretty far. We'd better beat it back to camp. Looks like it'll be another soaker."

Stalks of wet grass brushed the horse's belly, and before Colt could stop him, Duke grabbed a mouthful. Colt raised his eyes to the darkening sky. Nightfall would come early, and from the looks of things, it wouldn't be a peaceful one. A low rumble of thunder rolled over the Manti–La Sal mountain range. Hours earlier, the sky had wrung out her skirts, probably soaking every tree, flower, and bush in the high country of Central Utah, and turning dirt roads into slippery water slides.

Colt knew he should continue in the direction of camp, but instead he reined his horse toward the hilltop. Lightning forked the sky, and the air felt eerily still. Ignoring his gut, Colt said, "But first, what do you say we take a look at Pine Creek meadow? The elk might be on the move with this storm rolling in. I'd risk getting caught in the weather, if we could find the big boy. Wouldn't you?" Colt shook his head. *Talking to my horse as if he might actually answer. I've spent too many days alone.*

Still, the mere thought of taking a monster bull elk sent Colt's pulse racing and drove him forward. The elk were here—somewhere.

Several minutes later, he raised his binoculars and brought the meadow across the ravine into focus. Methodically, he scanned the expanse of grass rimmed with groves of pine trees and quaking aspens and bisected by a narrow, rarely used Jeep road. The road appeared on the map, but in Colt's earlier scouting trips he had discovered it was rutted and overgrown in places and could be more accurately classified as a four-wheeler trail.

Three cow elk entered the meadow and stopped, then raised their heads and tested the air with flared nostrils. The grass beneath the animals' bellies bent under a gust of wind. Colt felt a stir of excitement in his veins. Where there were cows, there had to be bulls. For a sportsman like him, nothing could compare with the thrill of big-game hunting. All year he lived for the elk hunt.

Through the high-powered binoculars, Colt saw the elks' ears prick forward. The lead cow barked a warning, and in unison, the three animals whirled and retreated to the safety of the trees.

I wonder what spooked them, Colt thought. On the second Tuesday of a three-week archery hunt, he didn't expect to run into many hunters. Plenty of guys had hunted on the weekend, but he'd been the only one on the mountain for the past two days. "What did you see, girls? Or is it just the storm?" he muttered.

Duke stamped his hoof as Colt panned the hillside before them, focusing on the direction the elks' ears had pointed. A splash of bright blue interrupted the earthy hues of the road.

What the . . . Colt leaned forward, as if those few additional inches would answer his question. He peered at what looked like the outline of a slender shoulder on the edge of the meadow. It didn't move, except for what he hoped was the rise and fall of steady breathing, but at this distance, he couldn't be sure. Roadside weeds obscured the rest of what looked like a person, maybe a girl, although after being alone in the mountains, Colt realized his mind might be playing tricks on him. Could be just a lost piece of clothing brought to life by the storm.

Either way, he had to see for himself. He dropped the binoculars onto his chest, then wheeled his horse around and trotted off. Duke shook his head at the unplanned detour as Colt urged him down the ravine. Without slowing, the horse splashed through the creek and then scrambled up the muddy bank onto dry ground. Colt had glassed this hillside earlier in the morning, but had never ridden it. Studying the lay of the land, he picked his way up, hoping to emerge near the right location.

Duke stumbled over deadfall so thick it looked like someone had spilled a box of oversized matches on the forest floor. Colt jumped down and pulled aside enough branches to make the trail passable. Not clear by any means, but hopefully not a leg-breaker for his horse. They negotiated the downed timber until Colt could mount again.

If he'd calculated correctly, the meadow wasn't much farther. The wind swirled down the hillside, plucking leaves from trees. He breathed deeply, smelling the coming rain — good for hunting tomorrow, bad considering how far he was from camp tonight.

A tickle moved across the young woman's arm. She wanted to open her eyes, but the awful thumping in her brain seemed to get in the way. She shoved back the pain and pried open her eyelids. A fat spider explored the fine hairs of her forearm. Shrieking, she batted away the eight-legged intruder and scrambled to her feet, then shut her mouth and ran. But she wasn't running from the spider. Something had happened. Something terrible. But what? Her mind stood before her like a blank whiteboard. Her only emotion was fear, her only thought to flee.

The majestic trees wobbled before her eyes, and the ground rocked beneath her feet. She reached for a branch on the fallen tree next to the road, hoping to steady herself, but her fingers grasped only air. Black emptiness overtook her once more.

Colt kicked his horse into a trot and left the dark forest behind. He scanned the meadow, searching out the clump of weeds near the road where he had seen something blue through his binoculars. No luck. He urged Duke into a gallop and they flew across the open space. At the road, Colt pulled the horse to a stop, vaulted from the saddle, and looked around. Nothing.

He jerked off his cowboy hat and ran his fingers through his sweaty hair. Then Colt listened. Even the meadow seemed to hold its breath. He dropped to his haunches and touched a dark spot on the grass. His fingers came away sticky with blood. An occasional footprint and blades of grass told the story. The girl, or whoever he had seen, had walked down the road, then had lain here injured, but in the time it took him to cross the ravine she had gone. But where? Something didn't feel right.

Dark clouds brought a premature twilight. Before long Colt wouldn't be able to see a thing. Duke trailed behind him as he searched the area. One drop of blood at a time, one footprint at a time, Colt tracked her. She walked a crooked line, weaving from the grassy shoulder onto the dirt road.

A sigh of relief escaped his lips when a hint of bright-blue fabric appeared near a downed tree. Colt broke into a run. "Hey," he called out. She didn't answer.

"Hey . . . miss."

Still nothing.

He crouched next to her and frowned. Blood covered the right side of her head and stained her sweater. Duke crowded in, his muzzle nearly knocking the hat off Colt's head. He pushed the animal's face away. "Get outta here." The last thing he needed was his horse stepping on this poor lady. But Duke ignored him, rubbing his face across his owner's back. Colt marched the horse away and tied the lead rope to the nearest tree, then hustled back to the woman and dropped to his knees. He slid his finger under a lock of blond hair streaked red with blood. "Are you okay?"

She didn't respond.

Colt's heart raced with the worry he felt for this stranger. He moved the hair away from her face. *Pretty,* he thought. He picked up her wrist, noticing a good-sized cut across her palm that still oozed blood, and felt for a pulse. Her manicured fingernails hung limply in his hand. Unable to detect a pulse, he moved his hand to her throat and worked his fingers into position. He let out a sigh of relief when he felt the steady drumming of a heartbeat. Without warning, the woman shoved Colt's hand away and hit him.

He reached for her flailing hands. "Hey, it's okay. You're hurt. I'm—" No sooner did he get hold of one hand than the other raked across his face. "Ouch!" Colt managed to grab her other wrist while the sting of those pretty nails burned his cheek. The woman opened her eyelids and captured him in the depths of the bluest eyes he'd ever seen. He held both her wrists while she kept up the futile struggle.

A look of terror flashed across her face. "Let go of me," she said in a quivering voice. "Just leave me alone."

Colt loosened his grip but didn't release her. "Only if you promise not to try anything. You almost scratched my eye out, you little wildcat. I'm trying to help you. You're hurt."

She looked him over. Her lip trembled, and she bit down on it before nodding.

"Okay then." He slowly released her hands.

When she tried to sit up, Colt wrapped his fingers around her arm to help.

"Don't touch me." She yanked her arm free. "Please go away."

He lifted his hand and stood. "Sorry. I was trying to help." Deciding to give her a minute to come to her senses, he backed up and stood next to Duke.

The woman leaned against the fallen tree and drew her knees to her chest. She looked at her dirty, bloodstained hands as if seeing them for the first time. Her fair complexion seemed to pale as she saw her own blood.

Colt waited, expecting her to get up, or at least say something. When the first raindrop cooled the scratch on his cheek, he approached the woman again and asked, "What happened?"

"I . . ." She shook her head. "Just give me a second."

He frowned at what appeared to be the beginning of a bruise on her face. "How did you get way out here?"

"I was . . . um . . . This is so weird. I'm not sure." She met his gaze, and the confused look on her face turned to annoyance. "I thought you were leaving. This is really none of your business."

A gust of wind threatened to steal the hat off Colt's head, so he tugged the brim down lower. "Not after the way my mama raised me. She'd tan my hide if I left you alone out here. Let me help you get somewhere safe, and I promise I'll be on my way. Now, what's your name?"

The girl's expression softened as he mentioned his mama. "I'm . . . wait . . . I know my name," she said. "It's . . ." She shook her head once more, a frustrated huff escaping her lips. "I can't believe this. I don't remember."

Colt grunted in disbelief. "You don't know your own name?"

Her big eyes stared up at him like those of a frightened child. "I know I should, but I guess not."

Colt glanced over his shoulder at Duke and then turned to the woman again. "All right then," he muttered. "So, lady with no name, what *do* you know?" He tried to stop the sarcasm before it rolled off his tongue.

"I'm scared," she answered so quietly he barely heard her voice over the whistle of the wind through the pines.

The fear on her face broke through Colt's tough-guy exterior. He dropped to his haunches and said softly, "It's okay. I'm sure you'll remember soon. Looks like you cut your head, so you probably have a concussion. My brother had a few of those playing high school football." He extended his hand. "Why don't you come with me? I can help you."

She raised her brows and tilted her head, pinning him with a look of defiant disbelief. "Where? I don't even know you, and you expect me to blindly follow you?"

Colt pulled his hand back and scratched the stubble on his chin. "You got a better idea, Miss High and Mighty?" He pointed to the sky. "In a minute those storm clouds are going to dump buckets. Already the temperature's dropping. Once you get wet, it'll be hard to stay warm out here. Ever heard of hypothermia?"

She seemed to deflate and her expression turned pensive. "Of course, but it isn't winter. You're being overly dramatic."

"Doesn't have to be winter to get a freeze in the high country. So unless y'all got a tent nearby that I don't know about, your smartest move would be to let me help you."

The gentle pitter-patter of rain escalated to a downpour, and the clouds spit lightning. The woman exhaled, and again Colt offered his hand. Wind tossed her hair across her face, so she tucked the locks behind her ear. She glanced up at Colt, then dropped her gaze to his outstretched arm. Cautiously, she set her small hand in his. Smiling, he extended his other hand and pulled her to her feet. Thunder echoed through the valley like a shot from a high-powered rifle. The woman raised one hand to her forehead and took a step to the side.

"Are you dizzy?" Colt asked.

"A little."

"I'll hold your arm to steady you, if that's okay."

She nodded, letting him lead her. Dark water spots covered her blue sweater by the time they reached Duke. Colt dug through his saddlebags and pulled out a camouflage rain jacket. He held it open for the young woman. "Put this on," he said, then tugged it over her shoulders and zipped the front. He grinned at his coat dwarfing her. "You're a petite little thing, aren't you?" He untied Duke and then shrugged out of the pack on his back that held his bow.

"What's that?" she asked.

"A compound bow. I'm elk hunting."

"Oh, I see. Are you a cowboy or something?"

Colt swung onto the saddle, then kicked his left foot out of the stirrup. "Something like that." Clasping his bow in one hand, he offered her the other. "Put your foot in there. I'll pull you up."

She raised her foot, clad in a black leather dress shoe, and wrapped her fingers around his wrist. Anxious to be going, Duke tossed his head as she climbed up behind Colt. A loud crack sounded in the trees, and the horse lunged forward. Colt jerked back on the reins as a branch, broken by the wind, fell to the ground nearby. "I'd feel better if you held on," he told the woman, surprised she had remained seated.

She wrapped her arms around his waist. He glanced down at her slim fingers. He may never marry, but he did enjoy feminine company now and again. With his free hand, he slowed Duke to a manageable pace. Holding the bow was a pain, but riding double didn't leave any room to wear it on his back.

Icy rain pelted their faces as the last of the day's light faded. By the time Duke crossed the creek, Colt couldn't see farther than ten feet in front of him. "Can you reach in the left saddlebag and get my headlamp?" he asked the woman.

Soon the light dangled from her fingers. Colt hooked the reins around the saddle horn, then grabbed the headlamp and flipped it on. "Thanks. Now take my hat, will you? It'll keep the rain off your head."

She pulled off his cowboy hat, and he tried to work the elastic strap of the headlamp onto his head with one hand. Her fingers brushed past his ears as she reached up to help him. "Thank you," he said.

"You're welcome. What's *your* name?"

Colt turned in the saddle and could see her curious expression in the glow of the light. She blinked, and he quickly faced forward, not wanting to blind her with the glare. "I'm Colt. Colton Murdock."

"Colt—I guess that's a good name for a cowboy."

He chuckled. "I reckon so."

Colt seemed kind, the young woman thought, and although she knew nothing about him, somehow he made her feel safe. But whom had she been fleeing from? Why couldn't she remember what happened? *This guy must think I'm crazy.* The utter blankness of her memory frustrated her. She didn't understand how a person could forget everything about herself and yet still know that three times six is eighteen. Surely only an idiot would forget her own name.

They rode up and down hills and across two creeks. After a while, the woman's legs began to ache. Rain dripped from the jacket onto her black slacks, soaking them. A chill worked its way up her spine, reminding her of her rescuer's hypothermia comment. She leaned closer to his back, thankful for the protection. A bit later she peered around his broad shoulders and asked, "Do you even know where we're going?"

"Yeah, my camp is over yonder. But even if I didn't, Duke knows the way back."

"Duke?"

She could hear amusement in his voice when he said, "My horse."

Ludicrous, she thought. "A horse is our GPS? Are you sure you can trust him?"

"In ten years of hunting he hasn't let me down yet. Six years ago in Idaho, the fog set in so thick I couldn't see the ground from up in the saddle. I dropped the reins and let old Duke have his head. He took me up and down draws, in and out of trees, but when it was all said and done, we ended up back at camp."

The woman smiled, soothed by the confidence and the slight Southern twang in his voice. "What's at your camp?"

"A bag of grain and Duke's buddy—an old horse named Charger. Don't know where the name came from, though. I've never seen him move faster than a trot."

"Any people?"

"Not right now, as I'm the only one who drew a tag for this unit. My brother Sam put in, but he didn't have enough points. My dad and my other brothers put in for the rifle hunt. Jared, my oldest brother, was going to try to come up over the weekend, but he didn't show, so he must have been too busy with his family."

"Oh," said the young woman, figuring tags, points, and draws must have something to do with this hunting business.

"Do you remember anything yet?" Colt asked her. "About how you got hurt, I mean."

She thought for a moment, recalling only the spider that woke her, then running. It felt as if she'd been dropped from heaven onto the side of that mountain, as if life had begun when the fat spider crawled across her arm. "I wish I did, but I don't remember a thing before I woke up in the woods."

"You should probably see a doctor," Colt said.

Her head shot up. "I don't want to." She couldn't explain the reason for it, but she had no desire to be prodded and questioned by some physician.

Seeming surprised, Colt looked over his shoulder. "Well, lucky for you I'm not breaking camp in this kind of weather to go find one."

Lightning splintered the sky in a display more resembling fireworks, with thunder cracking like a whip on its heels. The girl jumped, squeezing Colt's middle. The storm was gaining momentum. Towering pines creaked and groaned under another burst of wind as the horse climbed upward.

"Isn't this dangerous?" the woman heard herself ask. "With the lightning and whatnot?"

Colt shrugged his shoulders. "Probably. I'd rather not be out in this, but camp is on the other side of that ridge, and there's no way I'm staying over here all night. The lightning is still miles away, but we'll hold to the trees and pray the storm moves off to the north before we have to crest the hill."

The woman's backside felt like a basketball in a dribbling contest, when hours later the horse finally trotted over the open ridge. They dropped down the other side and entered a grove of a different kind of trees. With their white trunks standing like sentinels in the night, they were a stark comparison to the dark pines. "Are these aspens?" she wondered aloud.

"Quakies—quaking aspens," Colt answered.

Duke raised his head and sent a shrill whinny down the mountain. Nearly lost in the rustle of the leaves, another neigh echoed in the distance. Eventually, a camp appeared within the perimeter of the headlamp. The horse stopped next to a tent that flapped in the wind. Colt swung his leg over his horse's neck and hopped to the ground. He leaned the bow against the tent, then turned to the woman and helped her dismount. Once he had unzipped the tent flap, he placed his hand on her back to urge her forward. "Go inside. I'll find you something dry."

Peering into the darkness, she hesitated. His headlamp lit the interior when he stuck his head through the opening. Gear sat against one wall, a lone sleeping bag against the other. The next icy gust of wind finally drove the woman inside. Even in the waterproof jacket she shivered, and if she relaxed her jaw, her teeth chattered.

She stepped into the tent and crouched next to the door while Colt rummaged through a stack of clothes. He offered her a pair of sweatpants and a sweatshirt. "Put these on. They'll be way too big, but at least you can get out of those wet clothes. Then climb in the sleeping bag and you'll warm up in no time."

She took the sweats and he turned to leave. "What are you going to do?" she asked.

He paused. "I'm going to take care of my horse." He zipped the tent flap closed, leaving her in darkness.

The woman dropped the dripping coat onto the floor. Her frozen fingers fumbled with her sweater as she worked her wet hands through the soft cashmere sleeves. She pulled the sweatshirt over her head, then added her black slacks to the pile of wet clothing. Fatigue flooded her entire body, and her head still throbbed. Vaguely she wondered if she should think twice about wearing some strange man's clothing and climbing into his sleeping bag, but the sound of driving rain and the numbing pain in her frozen toes and fingers made her toss the worry aside. She stumbled through the darkness and crawled inside the bag.

Two

Colt turned away from the tent and the mysterious woman. Steam rose from Duke's back, and his head hung low. They had been up long before dawn and covered a lot of miles that day. Colt loosened and unfastened the cinch, pulled the saddle off the horse, and tucked the wet gear under the tarp in front of the tent. He dug out the grain feeders and filled them, then anchored the billowing tarp with rocks. With another person in the tent, he would have to store more of his gear outside tonight.

He led Duke to the highline, and with fingers stiff from the cold, he clipped the horse's halter to the dangling rope. Next, he held a grain bag under Duke's nose and fastened it to the halter. He turned toward his other horse. The animal nickered, and Colt rubbed his brown nose. "Want some dinner, Charger?" He attached the second grain bag to the halter as the horse dug his muzzle into the feed. Colt glanced at the water bucket—half full and filling—and then stood surveying his camp.

The temperature had plummeted at least fifteen degrees since sunset. Cold rain dripped off Colt's neck and trickled down his back. He shuddered involuntarily. It would just be MREs—the freeze-dried meals he'd ordered off the Internet—for dinner tonight. But before he could even think about food, he had to warm up and get dry.

He rubbed his hand along Duke's side as he passed, letting out a long sigh. "Thanks for the ride, buddy. Maybe tomorrow we'll find the big boy."

The wind roared through the quakies, and rivulets of water ran off the tarp tied over the tent. Colt ducked under it and climbed through the flap. Standing hunched over, barely inside the door, he panned the interior with the headlamp. The woman's wet blond hair showed above the top of his sleeping bag. She hadn't moved since he stepped in, so he figured she was asleep. He grabbed a pair of fleece pants and a T-shirt, then clicked off the headlamp. *This could be interesting,* he thought. But considering how cold he felt, he wasn't about to stand around shivering while he analyzed the situation. Goosebumps raised the flesh on his arms as he stripped down in the dark. Hopping on one foot then the other, he pulled on clean pants. He worked his wet arms into a dry shirt and closed the distance to the sleeping bag in one step.

He ran his fingers through his hair and sniffed his armpit. *Whew.* He knelt beside the woman and unzipped the bag. "Forgive me, but it's freezing and I'm coming in," he whispered.

She started to sit up. "I can get out."

If he weren't so doggone cold, he would have thought twice, but he said, "No, stay. I need your body heat. Please." Before she could move, he climbed in and blocked her exit.

Except for the bottom where her feet didn't reach, the bag felt warm. Colt's left shoulder stuck out above the zipper. Luckily he'd packed the oversized sleeping bag or they both wouldn't have fit. He folded his arms, trying to make himself as small as possible. The woman lay so still he wondered if she was holding her breath. "How's your head?" he asked, trying to ease the awkwardness between them.

She turned slightly, as if to look at him when she answered, but the bag was too constricting to allow her to roll over. "It's not pounding like it was earlier."

"That's good. After I warm up, I'll make you some dinner and find the first-aid kit. We should take a look at that cut and get some medicine on it."

In no time at all, it was downright toasty with the little heater next to him, and Colt closed his tired eyes. The alarm had gone off at five that morning. He'd glassed more hillsides than he cared to remember, since none of them had produced the big bull he was after—the *muy grande,* as the sheepherder had called him. *Maybe tomorrow.*

The woman tried to roll over but ran into Colt's shoulder. Inch by inch she shifted her body. Only once did the steady rhythm of his breathing falter—when the oversized sweatshirt twisted and she yanked it back into place. She froze, fearing she had awakened him. But the cadence of his breathing fell into step, like the sound of well-trained foot soldiers.

The night was too dark to see anything except the shadowy outline of his form, but her very short memory filled in the details. It wasn't like there were a lot of faces bouncing around in her mind from which to choose. There was only one—his. She remembered the eyes: deep-set and bluish green, like the sea. They were serious eyes, but then she had yet to see him smile. Everything about Colton Murdock exuded confidence, and he had quickly gained her trust. She imagined his hair to be strawberry blond, because his beard was, but with the cowboy hat he had worn and then the darkness, she couldn't be sure. She smiled at the memory of his coat nearly drowning her. He was tall and broad-shouldered.

How strange, she thought, *to be here with a complete stranger, and yet feel perfectly safe.* Her stomach growled, but she tried to ignore it and focus on his warmth. She yawned once, then closed her eyes and surrendered to sleep.

She slept peacefully until Colt rolled into her. The way he scrambled out, a person would think a snake had bit him. "What the—" he said, then flipped on the headlamp and turned to face her. "Dang! You scared me." He laughed, the light casting shadows across his face. Rain still battered the tent. "I forgot you were here. Guess I'm not used to sharing a sleeping bag."

Startled, the woman cleared her throat and softly said, "I'm sorry. You fell asleep. We both did."

Colt knelt on the floor of the tent and ran both hands through his hair. "No, don't be sorry. I'm sorry. I just—hey, are you hungry?" He looked at his watch. "I can fix you an MRE. It's almost ten. We slept through dinner."

She sat up, cross-legged, and watched him. *If nothing else, he's interesting to talk to.* "A what?"

He turned and dug through his gear. "An MRE—meal, ready-to-eat. They're military style freeze-dried meals. A high school friend who ended up joining the army turned me on to them a few years back. I ordered these online, but you can pick them up at any sporting goods store or army/navy surplus store. They taste pretty good and they're fast. You just add water. Lightweight, too, so they're easier for the horses to haul up here than a bunch of canned food." Colt dropped a stack of packets on top of the sleeping bag and picked up the headlamp. "Your choices are grilled chicken, chicken and noodles, beef brisket, chicken and dumplings, beef meatballs and sauce, or vegetable lasagna." Even with the dim lighting, the good-natured grin he flashed her was unmistakable.

The woman smiled back. "Vegetable lasagna, please."

"These are single-serving packets, so what's your second choice? That way I can make sure I don't eat it."

She shrugged. "I guess the chicken and noodles."

"And your third?"

"Oh, I don't care. They all sound edible."

"Okay, I'll eat the meatballs."

Her bladder felt like it would burst. "Is there a bathroom around here?"

Colt chuckled. "Thousands of them. They're called trees."

"Seriously?" she muttered, realizing the folly of her question. She was, after all, sitting in a tent in the middle of nowhere.

He stuffed all but two of the packets back into the bag and stood, his head and shoulders hitting the roof of the tent. He picked up the rain jacket and headlamp and offered her his hand. He pulled her to her feet, helped her into the jacket, and stuck the headlamp on her forehead. "Don't go very far, though," he told her. "I don't want you getting lost out there."

The woman slipped her feet into her wet shoes, wishing they were boots. Did she even own a pair of boots? The memory had to be in her brain somewhere. At least she had a practical pair of flats, wet as they were.

Colt held the tent flap open, and she stepped out into the icy rain. She pulled the hood over her head and followed the glow from the headlamp. She hadn't gone far before she stopped. The forest closed in around her, isolating her from the safety of the tent. Not to mention, she was getting cold again. She turned in a 360-degree circle, making sure no one could see. The creak of the trees bending in the wind had her darting furtive glances over her shoulder. Her wild imagination conjured up scary animals, their eyes boring holes in her back and making her nervous.

Not the most comfortable bathroom, she thought as she started back toward the tent half a minute later. A shiver shot down her spine, and her heart rate accelerated when she didn't see the camp at first. She didn't particularly like the dark, or being alone in it, she decided, breaking into a run.

Colt was sitting on his haunches inside the tent when she rushed in. "You okay?" he asked, looking up at her.

She stopped short and exhaled, glad she hadn't run into him in her haste. "Yes, of course." She slipped out of the wet jacket and stepped past him. "Just trying not to get too wet."

Wearing a headlamp of his own, he looked down at a small piece of equipment at his feet. "Another minute and this water will boil. There's a fork and a spoon on the sleeping bag. You can take your pick. And I found the first-aid kit."

The woman sat near the utensils and pulled off the headlamp. The strap had worked its way over the cut on the side of her head, irritating it. She winced as she probed the tender skin with her fingertips. A large lump framed the cut, but at least the wound had quit bleeding and the awful thumping in her skull had dwindled to a dull ache.

She ripped open an antibacterial wipe from the first-aid kit and worked it between the layers of her hair. Colt poured water into one of the pouches and set it in front of her. She glanced down when the light from his headlamp hit her eyes.

"Do you want some help?" he asked.

"Do you have a mirror?"

"Uh, no."

She had no idea how the cut looked or if she was even close to getting it clean, so she handed him the wipe.

He pulled her hair back and gently cleansed the wound. "Someone's probably pretty worried about you tonight," he said. "We should get you back as soon as we can."

"Mmm-hmm." *Back? Back where? Who might be worried about me? I don't have a clue.* She wondered if there could be anything more dreadful than having a loved one and not even remembering the person. The throb in her head returned. All this thinking was doing nothing but giving her headache. Tomorrow she would sort it out.

Colt tossed the used wipe on the floor. Before the woman could thank him, he ripped open another. His fingers tipped her head to the side, and he cleaned the blood off her face and neck.

"Let me see your hand," he said. He tore open a third wipe and took her hand in his. After cleaning the deep cut across her palm, he spread antibacterial ointment on the wound and covered it with a butterfly bandage. His gaze met hers, and in the glare of the headlamp he seemed to scowl when he turned her head and gently touched her cheek. She shivered, but this time it wasn't from the cold.

She felt her face where he had a moment before. "Ouch! What do you think happened to me?"

Colt poured boiling water into the second MRE pouch, then turned back to her. "I don't know. It could be any one of a lot of different things."

"Like what?"

Ignoring her question, he squeezed antibacterial ointment onto her scalp and gently worked it into the cut with his fingertip. Then, he sat next to her with his MRE and picked up the spoon. He pulled off his headlamp and set it on the sleeping bag. "Do you care if I say grace?" he asked.

"Not at all." She folded her hands in her lap. The foreign feel of the motion made her wonder if she ever prayed on her own. Colt's voice, softened by reverence, stilled the rise of panic in her heart at realizing how lost she truly was.

He said a simple prayer, pleading for the return of her health and her memory, for their safety and protection from the storm, and for their food to provide the necessary nourishment and strength. A peaceful calm came over the young woman—something she hadn't felt all day. Colt said amen and then scooped a meatball onto his spoon.

She picked up the fork and her MRE and held the first bite in front of her mouth. "You never answered me."

He stopped chewing. "I'd rather not say. Maybe you should take a guess at it. What do you think happened?"

"I already told you, I can't remember."

"I know, but take a random guess at some of the possibilities. Maybe it'll help jog your memory."

She finished chewing and thought for a moment, letting her imagination loose. "Perhaps I went skydiving and bumped my head when I landed. I climbed out of my parachute, found that poor excuse for a road, and wandered onto your mountain."

The sound of Colt's laugh filled the tent. "As unlikely as it seems, especially considering that outfit you were wearing, I suppose it's a possibility. What else?"

"Maybe I rolled my car off a narrow mountain road and walked away in search of help."

He lifted his spoon in acknowledgment. "That sounds a bit more realistic. We know one thing for sure—you've got a great imagination. And nice clothes, too. But although you had the good sense not to wear high heels, what would you be doing in the mountains dressed for a day at the office?"

She glanced at her clothing piled near the tent opening. Dress shoes, lightweight turtleneck sweater, and black slacks. "Hmm. You bring up a good point there, Colt Murdock." She tried hard to remember something, but once more came up with nothing. The weight of confusion left her fatigued and discouraged, which didn't help the nagging headache. It was extremely frustrating knowing the answer lay hidden in her mind, yet being unable to access it.

Colt finished his MRE and set a bag of Peanut M&M's between them. "Lady, I wouldn't worry about it yet. Whatever happened, happened recently. Give it a day or two, and I'll bet it all comes back to you."

While he organized his tent, clearing more floor space, she ate a handful of the candies, wishing they were Peanut Butter M&M's instead. How frustrating that she could remember her favorite flavor of M&M's, yet she couldn't for the life of her recall her name. Hopefully, Colt was right and she wouldn't need to wait long for her memory to return.

When she yawned, he looked at his watch. "Almost midnight. Should we hit the sack? I was thinking if we spread out the two pads and unzipped the sleeping bag, we could use it as a blanket. You know, make it like a little bed. We might be more comfortable tonight."

"I'm sorry for the inconvenience."

"It's no big deal. Thankfully, I brought the four-man tent so I could store my gear and have room for my brother if he made it up here. It'll sleep both of us easy enough."

The woman moved out of Colt's way and watched him transform the sleeping bag for one into a makeshift bed for two. He smiled at her when he finished. "The cushion won't be as thick and we'll get a little draft on the edges, but at least you'll have room to roll over."

Wind still shook the trees, and rain battered the tarp and tent above them. What if he hadn't seen her? She'd be alone . . . in this. The horror of it made her shiver. "Thank you, Colt. You're a lifesaver—literally. I don't know what I would have done if you hadn't found me. I'd still be out there waiting for a search and rescue team, I guess."

He paused briefly, as if thinking, then said, "You're welcome. But I'm sure the Lord had a hand in it. He's the one you should thank."

The Lord? She hadn't even considered that God could have had a hand in the day's events. But if He did, why had He withheld her memories from her? Why had He left her to flounder in the darkness?

Colt drew back the sleeping bag. "Which side do you want?"

Pulled from her thoughts, the woman met his gaze. "The left, I guess." She crawled into the bed, content within the safety of the hunter's tent, but more curious than ever about what tomorrow would bring—more absentee memories, or a rush of information answering all her questions? Because no matter how hard she tried, she couldn't find the answers. *Who am I? Where did I come from? Do I have a family? Friends? What would I be doing right now if I weren't hurt and lost?* If only she knew.

Colt didn't climb into bed as she expected. Instead, he pulled on a headlamp and shoved his feet into his boots. "I'll be back in a minute, after I check on the horses." He put on his jacket and left the tent.

Three

Colt zipped the tent closed and stepped into the wind and rain. He wanted a minute to clear his head, and he should put away the grain bags. No need for Duke and Charger to wear them all night. He walked toward the animals, which stood with their tails to the wind and their heads lowered. When he unclipped their feeders, both horses nickered as if begging for another scoop of grain. Water dripped from every hair on their bodies. It would be a long night for them. "Hang in there, boys," Colt told them.

He leaned against a quakie. Staring through the darkness at the tent, he thought through his questions. *Is this woman for real? Does she truly not remember her name, or what happened?* If she didn't have the goose egg, he would wonder if she was trying to hide something. *And how did she get hurt?* He had a theory on that one, but didn't want to talk to her about it. The bruise on her cheek looked like it came at the end of someone's fist. Somebody Colt guessed was a lot bigger than her. That somebody better not come within his radar. Beating up on girls wasn't tolerated in his family. If his dad had taught him one thing, it was respect for women. Hopefully, Colt was wrong about the cause of the injuries. If not, at least the woman didn't wear a ring, so maybe she wasn't married to the guy who had hurt her.

Her comment about waiting for the search and rescue team also made Colt think. No one would purposely head into the high country dressed as she was. All things considered, the likelihood of someone thinking to send S&R units to the Manti–La Sal unit seemed remote at best.

Colt shoved his hands in his pockets, reluctant to return to the tent. Falling asleep by her earlier was the closest he'd been to a woman in six years. The last one had been his fiancée. Oh, he'd dated plenty, but he'd kept it casual. And now he faced a night of either standing in the rain or sleeping next to the pretty blond again.

He chuckled to himself. *If my mama could see me now.* On how many occasions during those years had she chastised him for spending all his time hunting and fishing? "Colt, honey, you're never gonna meet anyone tromping around those mountains," she would say. "It's high time you got serious about dating. You'll miss your window of opportunity if you don't. You know, you can't live with your father and me forever."

Colt smiled at the memory. His mother, raised in the Deep South, knew how to speak her mind. A couple of years ago he had taken the hint and gotten his own apartment, and now he had met someone. Not someone to possibly marry, even if he was looking for a serious relationship, which he wasn't, but at least he'd have fun telling his mama how wrong she'd been about his hunting. Now whenever she complained, he could remind her of today — finding a pretty blond in the mountains during his Manti elk hunt.

A gust of wind swirled the rain into his face. In weather like this, he couldn't afford to get chilled. He left the protection of the tree and jogged back to the tent. Inside, he stepped over their wet clothes. They wouldn't stand a chance at drying if this storm didn't break. Hopefully, tomorrow would bring some early-fall sunshine. Colt added his dripping jacket to the pile and stepped on the heel of his boot to pull out his foot, and then removed the other boot the same way. "Hey," he whispered.

Silence answered him. He exhaled in relief. He was tired, and it would be easier to ignore the woman if she wasn't awake. He carefully slid under the edge of the sleeping bag.

Hours later, a sigh escaped her lips when Colt's arm rubbed against her. Startled, he woke up and checked his watch—a little after three. Her even breathing told him she still slept. But if she had a concussion, he should probably wake her every few hours. He clicked on the headlamp, pointed it toward the ceiling, and rolled onto his side. She looked peaceful. If he could have gotten her to a hospital they might have stitched up her head, although maybe the cut wasn't deep enough to need it. He wasn't sure, but at least her hair would hide any scar.

Leaving the mountains during a storm like this would have been stupid, not to mention Colt would've needed to contact his dad or one of his brothers to bring a truck up to the trailhead. He shook his head in frustration. Of all the bad luck, his truck's transmission had gone out two days before the opener. His older brother Jared had hauled the horse trailer with all Colt's gear up the mountain. The plan—Colt would call if he shot something and needed to be picked up. Otherwise, Jared and their little brother Sam would bring the Dodge on Friday, after the transmission was fixed, and leave the vehicle by the trailer.

Until last night there hadn't been a reason for Colt to think about his cell phone, packed away in the duffle bag. Or at least that's where he'd thought it was. But when he had rearranged the tent, he hadn't seen the phone. Come daylight he would find it and call the police. The best thing would be to get the woman off his hands, and fast.

Now, his conscience nagged at him with renewed fervor. He was no doctor, but it didn't take a PhD to know the woman had a concussion. He really should wake her, just to be safe. "Hey, lady."

She had her back to him. When she didn't move, Colt touched her shoulder and rolled her toward him. "Hey, wake up, sleepyhead.

She stretched her arms. "What time is it?"

"Three in the morning."

She started to sit up. "What's wrong?"

"Nothing. I just wanted to make sure you're all right."

She flopped down on her pillow—his sweatshirt—and kneaded it into a different shape. "Are you kidding me? At three o'clock in the morning you're waking me to ask if I'm all right?" Despite her grumbling, her lips curved in a small smile.

"You've got a concussion. Aren't you supposed to wake up people with head injuries?"

She finished her sweatshirt-sculpting and gave him a wide smile. "How would I know? I'm the one with the head injury, remember?"

"Right." He clicked off the headlamp and lay down. Obviously she was fine.

Two hours later, the alarm on Colt's watch beeped. He had set it to go off every morning an hour before first light. The lady lay next him, still sleeping. He sat and rubbed his eyes. Normally, he'd grab something to eat and hit the woods to look for elk, but today wasn't a normal day. He needed to call the authorities. Someone would be looking for this woman. Maybe they could send the state police to pick her up so he didn't have to leave the mountain and cut his hunt short. But if not, he'd have Jared pick them up so he could get her back to civilization.

If Colt left the mountain today, it might not be worth it to come back in. He could road-hunt the lower elevations, but this might be it for the high country. Again, he looked at the woman's slumbering form. Maybe he'd have time to hunt the meadow above camp before she got up. After their 3:00 AM encounter, he didn't want to wake her again, and the lure of the hunt was strong. A quick jaunt through the woods wouldn't hurt anything. Colt pulled on his boots and coat. He stuck his head through the strap to his binoculars and picked up his bow, then glanced back at the woman before leaving.

Sunlight illuminated the front of the tent when the woman opened her eyes. She sat up and found herself alone. Most likely Colt was outside with his horses. The mysterious events of the day before had left her muscles tied in knots, like she had a bad case of whiplash. She kneaded the back of her neck between her thumb and fingers and tilted her head from side to side, trying to relieve some of the stiffness. Hopefully, once she got moving, those muscles would loosen a bit.

After rolling up the legs of his sweat pants, the woman put her feet in her damp dress shoes. Again the call of nature beckoned— time to visit one of those thousand bathrooms this mountain was famous for. She climbed through the tent flap into a brilliant sunrise. The storm clouds of the night before had fled the scene, leaving a sparkling wooded wonderland. Birds serenading in the treetops filled the air with music.

Unsure where Colt was, she carefully chose her bathroom spot. Both horses whinnied at her when she walked by, and she wondered where their owner would have gone. Probably not far, since he didn't take a horse. She stopped to rub her hand across the animals' sides. The fur felt stiff from the dried rain.

She saw no sign of Colt when she returned to camp. Her growling stomach begged for food, but since she didn't feel comfortable helping herself to his supplies, she waited. Raindrops glistened in the sunlight as if someone had sprinkled glitter from heaven. There didn't seem to be a dry log or spot of ground to sit on, so the woman pushed up the sleeves of the oversized sweatshirt and decided to have a look around.

She found water not far from camp. A small creek meandered along, filling a pond and then spilling over a beaver dam. The owner of the dam surfaced and slapped the water with his wide tail. Everywhere the woman looked, dead trees and branches littered the ground. She wondered if all forests were this messy. Still, after what she'd heard from the wind last night, it was no surprise trees fell down around here.

At the sound of a voice in the distance, she turned and listened. "Hey, lady. Where are you?"

She smiled. *Colt.* She hopped over tree trunks as she hurried back. Fully decked in camo, he paced the campsite. He looked grumpy, like he'd woken up on the wrong side of the bed. "Hi," she said, her arms folded across her chest.

He had traded the wet cowboy hat from the day before for a camo baseball cap, which he readjusted on his head at least three times before asking, "Where were you?"

She pointed behind her. "Looking at the beaver, in the pond."

Seeming to relax, he nodded and then turned to the tent. Methodically, he began emptying his packs and rummaging through his clothes. He muttered under his breath and threw a canvas bag behind him.

She stepped closer. "Did you lose something?"

He got up off his knees and kicked a pile of clothes back into the tent. "My phone. My truck is in the shop, so I've got to call my brother if I want to get off this mountain before Friday. The problem is I'm starting to wonder if my phone is still plugged into the charger in his truck. I can't remember seeing it since then." Colt paused and stared down at the packs. When he lifted his eyes to meet her gaze, he said, "Do you want to eat something, and then I'll pack up camp and we'll head out?"

A sudden fear sank its talons deep into her chest. "Head out where?"

"It's a full-day's ride down to the trailhead where I left the horse trailer. It's a long shot, but we might find another hunting party or someone camped along the road who has a phone. If we do, then you can call your family, or a friend. If not, we'll keep riding Duke down the road until we find someone who does have a phone."

The woman stared blankly at Colt, unsure what to say.

"If you still don't know what happened or who you are, I can help you," he said. "We'll call the police, find out if they know anything. I'm sure someone is out there looking for you. Plus, I think you should see a doctor about that bump on your head, although when my brother got those concussions playing football there wasn't a lot they could do for him. The doctor told him to rest and take it easy."

Colt's plan sounded like a wild-goose chase with an end result she didn't particularly like. Irrational fear transformed into desperation. Were people wondering where she was? Were they talking about her—the helpless victim? The idea repulsed her. What if she showed up and didn't remember a single one of them? Nameless faces flitted through her imagination, demanding answers she couldn't give.

A random memory came to mind. The woman stood before an elderly lady . . . her grandmother, she realized. There it was—a memory. Solid and tangible. She could remember. She just needed more time. Gran stared back with vacant, unrecognizing eyes. Alzheimer's had set in, giving the elderly lady's normally kind voice a sharp edge. "Who are you? What are you doing in my house?"

The woman refused to be like that. Whoever her family and friends were, she couldn't face them yet. Not like this. How could she be with people who knew her when she didn't even know herself? It would be so awkward. "I don't want to call the police, and I don't need a doctor, not yet anyway," she told Colt. "I may not remember everything, but it's coming back. I remember my gran had Alzheimer's. I remember being in her house, and she didn't recognize her own granddaughter. I don't want to be like that. Can't we wait a while longer? I just need more time—I know it will come back to me."

Again Colt adjusted his hat brim, and when he didn't answer, she forged ahead. "What about you? Aren't you supposed to be hunting? Couldn't I stay here, at your tent, while I try to remember? Then you wouldn't have to pack up camp to go search for someone with a phone. I'll bet you don't even want to leave yet, do you, Colt?"

He ran his fingers through his hair and clenched his jaw. "No, but I've got this feeling I should do something. There has to be a reason you were in the woods, and I've got a responsibility to report it."

She lifted her head. "I'm not a child you have to babysit. I am perfectly capable of deciding what I'll do and where I'll be. You don't have to feel it's your responsibility." She exhaled, then walked to him and placed her hand on his arm. "Colt, please, let me stay here. I promise I won't be any trouble. Just for a day or two. I may not remember much, but I know I don't like doctors or cops. And I can't stand the thought of other people knowing more about me than I do. Anyone could tell me anything, and I'd have no idea what to believe. After a couple of days, if I don't remember who I am, we'll do what you said."

Colt's eyes held hers. *Feisty,* he thought. *Crazy, too.* He figured any normal person would want to be with her family, or someone else who might help her remember. But maybe she was different. Maybe she hadn't grown up in a loving environment like he had. He would give her the benefit of the doubt—for now. Perhaps there was family baggage her subconscious knew about.

It didn't thrill him to think of riding his horse down the road in hopes of running into someone who might have a phone he could borrow. Especially when the alternative was hunting big bulls in a primo elk unit. Not to mention, as wild as it sounded, spending time with this woman would beat sitting around camp all alone. He might actually enjoy the company. If she got on his nerves, he'd pack up camp and haul her out of here. "Okay, we can stay for a day or two. But if we see anybody, I'm asking to borrow a phone and will make the call. Deal?"

She smiled. "Deal."

"Either way, we're pulling out on Saturday. I've got to be back for church on Sunday and work on Monday morning."

"That's three days from now," she muttered. "Thank you, Colt. I'm sure I'll remember by then."

He nodded. Unsure of whether he'd made the right decision, he failed to return her smile. "What should I call you?"

"I told you, I still don't remember my name."

"Then pick one. Because if we're going to be spending time together, I can't keep calling you *lady*."

"Why not?"

"That was my dog's name." Colt pictured the hyperactive yellow lab he got on his twelfth birthday and raised from a pup.

The woman bit down on her lower lip and furrowed her brow. "I can't name myself. That's ridiculous. Nothing is coming to mind anyway."

"Then I'll call you Skye."

She laughed. "Sky isn't a real name."

"Yes, it is. Spelled S-K-Y-E. I have a cousin with that name, in Franklin, North Carolina. She's eleven and cute as a button."

"Why that name? Do I look like your cousin?"

"Not at all. She has brown hair and green eyes."

The woman folded her arms and pouted. "What? You're saying I'm not as cute as a button? Am I ugly? These trees you use as bathrooms aren't exactly equipped with mirrors, and after yesterday, I must look like a drowned rat, hung out to dry."

Colt lifted his hands. "Hang on. That's not what I meant," he said, trying to dig out of the hole he'd accidentally stepped in. Truth be told, she was the prettiest girl he'd seen in years, maybe ever. "You've got nothing to worry about there. You're more than cute . . . in fact, you even look good in my camo." He dropped his eyes to his boots, embarrassed. *What a lame compliment.*

"Then why Skye?" she asked.

He met her gaze. "Because of your eyes. They're the bluest blue I've ever seen. Like the mountain sky on a summer afternoon." Anxious to change the subject before she pried any more sappy comments out of him, he turned toward the tent and said, "So, are you hungry? Because I'm starving."

With the Jet Boil, it didn't take long to heat water and make oatmeal for breakfast. Colt handed a bowl to her. Lowering himself onto the jacket he'd spread over a log, he inadvertently brushed her shoulder with his. Out of the corner of his eye he watched the woman—Skye—eat her breakfast. Her manners were impeccable. City girl. Probably well-educated and used to living a refined lifestyle.

In the light of day, he looked over her injuries. Her chin-length hair hung in loose ringlets over the cut on her head, hiding most of it. Near her temple on that same side of her face, the top of her cheekbone had turned dark purple. It matched the shiner under her other eye. Good thing there were no mirrors here; she probably didn't even know about some of her bruises.

He shook his head at the irony of this picture. Colt, the ultimate loner, sharing breakfast with a lady in the high country during the archery hunt. Again that niggling feeling that he should be doing something more knocked on his conscience. While walking back to camp this morning, he had figured it all out. Find his phone. Call his brother or the cops and then get rid of her. If his cell phone didn't turn up, he would pull camp and find someone with a phone he could borrow. Regardless, he'd solve the mystery of her and be done with all this nonsense, even if it meant taking her to the police station. If she truly didn't remember her name, there was undoubtedly a reason for it, and someone out there who did know her identity. Colt had a feeling that person would be looking for her.

Yet, within minutes of returning to camp, Skye had shot down Colt's well-thought-out plans with those compelling blue eyes and sweet voice. Granted, he hadn't exactly been a hard sell. He had looked forward to this hunt all year. He had a history of grabbing at any excuse to hunt, fish, or otherwise spend time in the outdoors, even at the expense of more important things. Without a doubt, it was his biggest weakness. Because of hunting ducks at the slough, he'd been late to school so many times during his senior year of high school that he'd nearly failed first period. Sometimes he wondered if he had been born in the wrong century. He would like to have explored this country with Jim Bridger and the other mountain men. Instead, Colt's explorations were limited to the national forests and whatever land he could find that hadn't been posted with No Trespassing signs.

Skye turned her head to look at him, interrupting his musings. "What do you do for work?"

"Construction management—mostly commercial jobs," Colt replied. "I work with my dad and my older brother."

"Do you build stores?"

Today he'd given her the spoon and the bowl, so he worked his fork across the plate, scraping the last of his oatmeal into his mouth. One fork, one spoon, one knife, one bowl, one plate—that was all he had. He hadn't exactly planned on anyone joining him for meals, unless Jared rode in, and his brother knew to pack his own gear. Colt lifted his head and smiled at Skye. "Retail stores, office buildings, warehouses, church buildings—whatever people pay us to build."

"Are you married?" she asked, her voice dropping a notch.

He glanced down at a line of ants marching past the toe of his boot. "No."

He'd answered the same question a hundred times before, but for reasons he couldn't explain he kept talking this time. "I was engaged once. A girl named Janna. About six years ago.

I thought life was perfect. I had it all planned out. We'd get married, finish school, buy a house, have four kids, and live happily ever after. But I learned the hard way things don't always go like we plan. She was driving to spend Thanksgiving with her family when a car sped past her. It happened north of Malad, Idaho, on I-15. The car hit black ice and slid into the semi-truck in front of her. The truck driver lost control and wiped out the speeding car. They piled up in front of Janna. She never had a chance. They said she died instantly—that she didn't suffer. But the rest of us sure did."

"I'm so sorry," Skye said softly.

He glanced at her and recognized the empathy in her eyes. But Colt didn't want her feeling sorry for him. Didn't want her to pity him. Because even though he feared the sting of that day would never fully leave him, he had learned to live with it. He shrugged his shoulders. "It was a long time ago. What about you? Do you think you're married?"

Seeming to ponder the idea, she chewed her oatmeal. "This is so frustrating—the fact I can't remember. But I don't think so." She raised her left ring finger.

Colt stood. "I imagine as time passes you'll start recalling things. Once it took my brother three days to remember the football game that gave him a concussion. I'll go wash the dishes, and then we should hang out our wet clothes to dry while we've got some sun."

It didn't take him long to wash their few dishes in the creek. When he got back to camp, Skye was spreading the wet clothes across logs and hanging them from tree branches. She stopped and eyed her sweater with a furrowed brow.

"How did you wash the dishes?" she asked.

"In the creek. Above the pond."

"Is there dish soap down there?"

He set his cowboy hat in the sun and picked up his wet T-shirt. "No, I just used water."

Her eyes widened. "You didn't use any soap?"

Smiling, he spread the shirt next to his hat. "Nope, just water. Trust me, that's all you really need."

"Do you even have soap?"

He flung a button-down shirt over a branch above his head. "Yeah. Do you want it?"

"If you don't mind. I want to try to get the blood out of this sweater. After it dries, I can give you back your clothes."

Colt dug through his bags and produced a hotel-size bar of soap. "Here you go." He handed it to her. "But you are welcome to use my sweatshirt as long as you'd like."

She took the soap from him. "Thanks."

With raised eyebrows, he watched her leave, wondering what he was doing with a girl in elk camp. When she disappeared below the hill, he pulled his topographical maps from his pack, spread them across his lap, and studied the lay of the land. He'd scouted this area a month ago and met a sheepherder—a humble man with a family of five still living in Peru. The sheepherder had regaled Colt with tales of the *muy grande*—very big—elk, with a rack so wide that the short, stocky, South American claimed he couldn't touch both tips at the same time. According to him, the big bull called this valley home. That was why Colt had left his horse trailer and ridden in to camp here. But after hunting the valley hard the first weekend and finding no sign of the bull elk, he had ridden across the ridge to try somewhere else. What he'd found there was the farthest thing he could imagine from a *muy grande* bull. He'd found a pretty blond—Skye.

With her to worry about now, the thought of riding very far didn't appeal to him. He'd seen elk sign early this morning when he hiked through the ravine below his camp. Maybe he'd stick close. Hunt this valley at sunrise and sunset, the prime hunting times. That way he could come back to camp and check on her midday. If he got lucky, the big bull would wander back onto this side of the mountain. Or maybe he'd been around here all along and Colt just hadn't found him yet. But if not, on Friday he'd pick off the best bull he could find and call it good.

When Skye returned, she wrung the excess water from her sweater, shook it in front of her, and hung it on a low limb. "This may never recover," she said. "Did you know it says Dry Clean Only on the tag? I just put it through the roughest version of a wet clean I can imagine. One thing is certain—I obviously didn't have this type of activity in mind when I got dressed yesterday. I never would have chosen to wear something I liked this much, if I'd known the abuse it would take."

Colt smiled as she straightened the fabric. "I think that sweater is the least of your worries."

She stood and rested her hands on her hips, then let out a big sigh. "I suppose you're right. Losing one cashmere-and-silk-blend sweater to the brutality of an old-fashioned washing is nothing compared to losing one's mind."

He chuckled, then gestured to their clothes fluttering like flags in the breeze. "If the sun holds out, everything should be dry by nightfall." He paused. "Do you want to help me graze the horses?"

Skye shrugged. "Uh, sure. What do we do?"

He clipped a lead rope to Duke's halter, then handed her the rope and pointed up the hill. "Why don't you take him up there and let him eat grass while I move his highline."

She took the rope and led Duke away. Colt had expected her to flinch at the responsibility of such a big animal. Most novice horse people did. He watched her until she stopped walking and let the horse lower his head to eat. Skye turned and met Colt's eyes, reminding him he had a job to do. He reached above his head and untied one end of the rope, then walked in a different direction, pulled the rope taut, and tied the end to another tree. Now Duke would have good eating for the rest of the afternoon.

Colt unclipped Charger, setting him free to roam while he adjusted the other highline. The horse sniffed at Colt's pockets for a minute before trotting up the hill toward Duke.

He was busy with the highline when Skye called down the hill, "Colt?"

Smiling at the sound of her voice saying his name, he looked up at her. "Yeah?" Charger stood, nudging her pockets, probably hoping to find a bit of grain or a carrot.

"Shouldn't someone be holding onto him?" Skye asked.

Raising his eyebrows, Colt chuckled. "You mean me?"

"Of course I mean you."

"Nah, he won't go anywhere as long as you've got Duke. Just shoo Charger away if he gets too close to you. Pick up a stick if you have to."

She waved her arm at Charger and ordered, "Shoo!" The horse only stared at her.

"I'm almost done here and I'll come get him," Colt told her. Once he finished retying the highline, he grabbed a lead rope and hiked up the hill, where he clipped onto Charger's halter and pulled the horse away from Skye. Then Colt sat down on a log, holding Charger's rope, and watched her work her fingernails through a tangle in Duke's mane.

"Do you want to go for a ride tonight?" he asked.

She turned to look at him. "A horseback ride?"

"I thought we could ride up the ridge and glass the meadows on the other side for elk."

"Sure."

Four

After they fed the horses, Colt and Skye collected firewood. He yawned at least five times before she said, "If you're so tired, maybe you should take a nap."

He took off his watch and handed it to her. "Please don't let me sleep longer than an hour or we'll be late."

"Late? I didn't realize you were punching a time clock out here."

Colt chuckled softly and then disappeared into the tent.

Skye wandered around camp doing odd jobs for nearly an hour. When she glanced at Colt's watch for what felt like the hundredth time, five minutes remained. Once those minutes slowly ticked away, she lifted the tent flap. For the first time she saw him with his hat off in the daylight. His hair wasn't strawberry blond like she'd thought; it was more of a dark blond. Right now it stuck out at all the wrong angles, causing her to put her hand over her mouth to keep from giggling. But then who was she to laugh at his bed-head and turkey tails, when undoubtedly her hair was horrendous. The rain had undone her straightening job and now she could only imagine the state of her stringy curls.

She cleared her throat. "Colt, it's been an hour." He didn't answer. His breathing was deep and even.

Skye reached to touch his tanned arm, pausing as her fingers skimmed across his firm bicep. "Colt, wake up."

He yawned then mumbled, "Is it time?"

She pulled her hand away, suddenly aware that her fingertips had lingered on his arm. "It's been an hour, like you said."

He rolled over, and for a moment he simply looked at her. When she glanced away, he grabbed his hat and climbed to his feet. After caging his unruly hair beneath the camo baseball cap, he bent to put on his boots. "Thanks for waking me. That was a good nap. Are you ready to go hunting?"

"I guess."

Colt crisscrossed and tied the bootlaces. Then he hooked a knife to his belt, smiling at Skye. "Good. I'll saddle up old Duke and we'll leave." He pulled a sweatshirt over his head and left the tent. She followed him and watched as he threw the saddle on Duke's back and tightened the cinch. He attached the saddlebags and filled them with water bottles, granola bars, and jackets. Finally, he retrieved his bow from in front of the tent and mounted the horse.

As he'd done the previous evening, he kicked his boot out of the stirrup and offered his hand to Skye. She climbed behind him and wrapped her arms around his waist. Being in his company felt surprisingly comfortable, and she wondered what this hunting business was all about.

Colt's excitement was like a can of soda pop rolling down a hill. Duke tossed his head and pranced through the trees, acting just as excited. Colt pulled back on the reins. "Walk, buddy."

They rode along the ridge top before dropping down to a clearing. Colt hopped off the horse and brought his binoculars to his eyes. Skye gazed across the valley, trying to see what he might be looking at. She didn't recognize anything more than grass, trees, and bushes. "What do you see?"

He still peered through his binoculars. "A herd of cows. A spike. A couple of smaller branch bulls."

"Oh, really?"

After a moment he turned to her. "Here, take a look." He handed her the binoculars.

She put them to her eyes and looked at the opposite hillside. A maze of trees came into focus. She panned the expanse before her, but failed to see a single animal. She lowered the binoculars and frowned. "I can't see anything."

He stepped closer to where she sat on Duke and pointed. "See that rocky ridge? Come down and to the right of that. Do you see the meadow there?"

"Yes."

"Now find it with the binoculars. The elk are at the top of that meadow."

Again she searched the hillside, eventually finding the rocky ridge and then the meadow. She gasped when light-brown bodies popped into view. But they were so far away that even with the binoculars they looked small. The loud, guttural call of an animal echoed through the valley. She lowered the binoculars and listened while Colt pulled something camo-printed from his saddlebag. Another animal answered. "What was that?" Skye asked.

"An elk bugling. The rut should be starting any day now." He handed her the reins and started moving away. "Wait right here for me. I'm going to get a closer look—see if I can call them in and find the big boy."

"When are you coming back?"

"When it's too dark to see, if not sooner. Stay with Duke and you'll be safe."

Within seconds, Colt disappeared into the shadows beneath the trees. When Duke started following his owner, Skye scrambled forward into the saddle and pulled on the reins. She tried to get her feet in the stirrups, but her legs weren't as long as Colt's. She turned Duke in a tight circle and halted him. The excited horse seemed to have his mind set on doing anything except standing still. What had Colt said? "Wait right here?" *He should have told that to the horse,* she thought, pulling him to a stop for the tenth time.

She gave up trying to make Duke stand still and resorted to walking the impatient horse in circles as he grazed the clearing. She liked the rocking cadence of the horse's movements. It felt natural, like maybe she had done this before. The last of the sun's rays sank behind the western horizon. The chorus of bugling from up and down the valley escalated as night fell. Her frustration mounted each time Duke grew antsy and tossed his head, refusing to stay in one place. "It's too dark for *me* to see," she said to the horse. "So where is that hunter of yours?"

A shiver ran down her spine. The darkness seemed to invite her fears to join them. For the third time, Skye looked over her shoulder, imagining cougars, bears, or even one of those big, loud elk barging into the clearing. Her eyes darted from side to side. She wanted to at least see what was coming before she got eaten. A light bouncing off the trees caught her attention. She froze, waiting.

"Skye?"

"Colt," she whispered. "Right here!"

He jogged into the clearing, breathing hard. "You okay?"

"Yes, but you should have told your *horse* to wait here. He wouldn't hold still. We probably wore a track around this clearing with all the circles he paced."

"I'm sorry. I assumed you'd tie him, but I guess I should have done that for you."

"He's not very patient, you know."

Colt laughed. "Patience isn't usually one of a horse's virtues."

She breathed deeply, feeling herself relax. "Did you see anything out there?"

"A bunch of cows and the smaller bulls. I called a three-hundred-inch bull in to forty yards, then he circled around and winded me. I might have heard the big one, though. I ran out of daylight. I'll come back here first thing in the morning and try again."

He stuffed his gear into the saddlebags and extended his weapon toward Skye. "Can you hold my bow for a minute? I'll ride behind you for a while."

She took the bow and leaned forward, giving him room to climb onto the horse. Colt's arm went around her and he lifted the bow from her hand.

"Why is it your horse stands perfectly still now that you're back and it's time to leave?" she asked.

"Guess he knows who the boss is. Come on, Duke." He clucked to the animal.

The horse took a few steps then broke into a trot. Colt's hand shot forward and grabbed the reins, his fingers brushing Skye's. "Walk, buddy, walk," he said softly, the whiskers of his beard tickling her cheek. "He'd better walk or he'll end up bouncing me off his back on this hill."

Relishing Colt's closeness behind her, she used his line from the night before. "You might need to hold on if you don't want to fall off."

He chuckled. "I might have to." But they rode all the way back to camp and he didn't once wrap his arm around her. When Charger's whinny heralded their imminent arrival, Colt said, "I'll put Duke away and then make something to eat. Is chicken and noodles still your second choice, or do you want to look at the other options?"

"Chicken and noodles sounds good."

After they dismounted and Colt unsaddled the horse, he put his gear away and went into the tent. Moments later, he emerged with two MREs and the Jet Boil. He started the water and looked up at Skye. "I'll build you a fire, then we'll eat."

She sat on the log and watched him take a handful of dried moss and several small sticks. He arranged the sticks over the moss and pulled a book of matches from his pocket. He struck a match, lowered it to the moss, and blew on it to spread the flame. He added more sticks, graduating to larger and larger ones, until finally he added the logs he'd split with the hatchet that afternoon.

She listened to the friendly crackle of the fire as she watched Colt. She couldn't stop thinking of the story about the death of his fiancée. Skye wanted to know more, but hadn't worked up the courage to ask. She stretched her hands toward the warmth. Above her head, the sky twinkled with the light of a million stars.

"Colt, look at the sky. I don't think I've ever seen so many stars at once."

He looked up and nodded. "Yeah, they're amazing up here."

"It's so beautiful, like someone scattered stardust."

By firelight, Colt stirred boiling water into the MREs. "You did pretty good with Duke tonight," he said, glancing at her. "I'd guess you've ridden horses before."

"Perhaps. I do like them."

He handed her the fork and her chicken and noodles. "Me too."

They ate in silence. When she finished eating, he took their dishes, donned his headlamp, and headed for the creek.

Skye stared into the glowing embers. One popped, sending up a spray of sparks. In her mind, she reviewed the events of the day. It had been good, but other than the snippet of memory regarding her grandmother, not one of the locked doors holding her past hostage had opened. *Maybe tomorrow.*

Colt returned from washing dishes and sat by her. "How's your head feeling tonight?" he asked, watching the flames.

"I have a little headache, but it's not as bad as yesterday. How does it look?"

She squinted when he turned on his headlamp and pulled her hair back. She felt the warmth of his fingertips touch her face. Being this close to him and feeling his gaze on her sent her heart racing.

Colt lowered his hand. "It doesn't look infected. And your goose egg is shrinking. I'll get the first-aid kit and put some more medicine on it for you."

After retrieving the kit from the tent, he sat next to her again. He lifted her hair with one hand and carefully spread ointment along the cut with the other. "Am I going to have a scar?" she asked.

"If you do, your hair will cover it." When he finished, he let her hair fall onto her cheek. The breeze blew it across her face, and she reached up to push it behind her ear. "How's your hand?" he asked.

Skye looked down at the dirty bandage covering the cut on her palm. "It's sore."

"Here, let me look at it." Colt picked up her hand and tugged off the bandage. Pink rimmed the edges of the wound. He cleaned it with an antibacterial wipe, applied more ointment, and covered the cut with a clean bandage.

Skye noticed he didn't let go of her hand right away, and his gaze lingered on her even after he'd flipped off the headlamp. "Thank you," she murmured, wishing for a mirror. She didn't like to imagine how awful she must look. She tucked a lock of hair behind her ear. "You don't by chance have a brush anywhere, do you?"

He turned to fasten the clasp on the first-aid kit. "Nope, sorry. I figured I could get by without one."

"You probably can, with that hat on your head all the time. But I feel like I'm wearing an old mop."

Laughing, Colt waved his hand dismissively. "Don't worry. This is elk camp, not a fashion show. It's not like there are a lot of people around here to impress."

But there's you. "Maybe you're right."

"I am right. Don't fret about it. You look beautiful."

Feeling her face warm, she focused on anything but him. Her scuffed shoes. The white trunks gleaming in the faint moonlight. *Is he teasing me?* He had been laughing at her not five seconds earlier. Skye tilted her head in his direction. He now stared straight ahead into the fire, which had burned down to a pile of hot coals. The faint glow showed his serious expression. He stood suddenly and asked, "Hey, do you want to roast marshmallows?"

She smiled up at him. "Love to."

He rummaged around the tent and produced a plastic bag, half full of marshmallows. "Hold these, please."

Skye took the bag. Colt carried his hatchet to the nearest tree and hacked off two slender branches. He buried the hatchet in a log and took the knife off his belt while he walked toward her. After whittling the end of each stick to a sharp point, he handed her one. "Now for the marshmallows."

She opened the bag and he stuck a marshmallow on the end of her stick. "You're going to need more than one," he said, then pushed a second marshmallow into place. "There you go."

She held her stick over the hot coals while he skewered three marshmallows onto the end of his. When the first hint of brown darkened the edge of his marshmallows, Colt stripped them off one by one and plopped them into his mouth. He sucked air, obviously trying to cool the gooey mass. Skye giggled and he turned his head to say, "What's so funny?"

With a mouth full of marshmallows, Colt's words came out in a mumbled slur, making her laugh all the more. "You. Couldn't you wait five seconds for them to cool? You'll burn your tongue and then you won't be able to taste a thing for the rest of the night."

Colt reloaded his stick with marshmallows and hunched over the coals. "Point taken. I promise to let the next batch cool."

Skye's marshmallows drooped on the end of her stick, the toasted exteriors holding the melted centers captive. She sat up straight and slowly turned her stick, trying to keep the marshmallows from sliding off.

She caught Colt staring at the end of her stick. "Would you eat those already?" he said. "The suspense is killing me. They're about to fall in the fire."

"Patience is a virtue one should strive to master."

"Who told you that?"

She smiled, still turning the stick to hold gravity at bay.

Nothing ruined the taste of food like a burned tongue. "I have no idea." She pulled off the first sticky glob and blew on it for a minute before taking a bite. Once she had finished both marshmallows and licked her fingers, she said, "Mmm, I don't remember these ever being so tasty."

He chuckled. "I suppose you wouldn't remember marshmallows, if you don't even remember your name."

She gave his shoulder a playful shove. "Colt! That's not fair."

"You asked for it with a comment like that." Still laughing he added, "Sorry."

"Are you really sorry?"

He held out two more marshmallows as if making a peace offering. "Nah, probably not. You're too fun to tease."

Skye smiled and took them, wondering if she regularly had this much fun. They finished off the last of the marshmallows, and Colt tossed the bag on the coals. It shriveled before briefly bursting into flames.

"You know, we could ride out of here at first light," he said. "We'd reach my trailer around noon. That would give us the afternoon to find someone with a phone. Who knows, maybe my brother got my truck out of the shop and it will be there waiting for us."

She shook her head, not ready for this to end—not ready to face real life and whatever that entailed. For the first time she wondered if it might also have something to do with her growing attraction to Colt.

"You sure?" he asked.

"Of course. Didn't you say you thought you heard that big bull? If you leave now you might never find it."

He stirred the coals with the tip of his roasting stick and fell silent as if thinking. "The last two mornings there's been a breeze coming off the ridge from the east," he finally said. "I think I'll try a new route tomorrow. See if I can sneak up on them from the west while they're feeding in the meadow. Might get a better look at the herd that way." Skye smiled, realizing her simple statement had completely changed the subject for him. Here she thought his silence meant he had set his mind on leaving, when in reality he had been preoccupied with hunting strategies.

A while later Colt kicked dirt over the remaining embers, submerging them in darkness. "I should get some sleep, if I want to be in place at first light." He offered her the headlamp. "Do you want to use the bathroom before we hit the sack?"

She took the light and stood. "I hope I can find a good one. Whoever designed this camping facility went heavy on quantity but definitely cut corners when it came to quality. I could sure use some basic bathroom amenities—like a toilet." Colt's warm laughter followed her into the darkness.

Like a faithful guardian, he stood waiting when she returned. He held open the flap and she darted into the tent, thankful for its protection. With no fanfare, Colt unlaced his boots and set them inside the door. He dropped his hat on top of them and picked up a pair of sweats. "I'm going to change." When he undid the top button on his jeans, Skye spun to face the wall. About ten seconds later he said, "I'm done."

She stepped out of her shoes and climbed under the sleeping bag, still wearing his baggy sweatpants and camo sweatshirt. Her clothes had finally dried; she would put them on tomorrow.

Colt lifted the corner of the sleeping bag and sat down. He held the headlamp and one of the smallest books she'd ever seen. "What's that? It's tiny."

He turned the front of the book toward her. "A travel-size copy of the Bible. I usually read a chapter before I go to sleep. With the storm and everything, I skipped last night."

She grabbed the book from his hand and studied the cover, trying so hard to remember . . .

"Did something come back to you?" he asked.

Skye shook her head and frowned. "I don't know. Of course I recognize the Bible, but I can't recall why it feels so familiar."

Colt held out his hand. "I'll read to you. Maybe something will come to mind."

She lifted her eyebrows—a religious cowboy, then. She returned the book and plumped up the sweatshirt that doubled for her pillow.

"We'll start from the beginning," he said. "See if that rings any bells."

He donned his headlamp, opened the book, and read: "'In the beginning God created the heaven and the earth. And the earth was without form, and void; and darkness was upon the face of the deep. And the Spirit of God moved upon the face of the waters. And God said, Let there be light: and there was light.'"

Skye listened to the soft cadence of Colt's voice rising and falling as he spoke. She rolled onto her side and watched this man who was redneck-tough one moment and as gentle as a pastor the next. The words felt familiar and safe, but she couldn't recall any more details than that.

Before long, Colt's voice lulled her into slumber. She slept soundly all night, and woke in the morning to the song of birds in the trees. A new day, but a quick mental search left her frowning. No miraculous return of her forgotten past.

She rolled onto the empty spot next to her. Colt must have already left to hunt elk. The warmth of the sleeping bag made her reluctant to wander through the trees in search of a suitable spot to relieve herself. If not for that major inconvenience, Skye could say she genuinely liked elk hunting. She had slept so comfortably wrapped in the tent's cocoon of safety. But she would be lying if she didn't admit the real reason she enjoyed it—Colt.

The call of nature finally drew her from the sleeping bag. Duke was gone, but Charger nickered hopefully. She made two trips to the creek, hauling water to fill both horses' buckets. With nothing else to do she clipped a rope to Charger and walked him up and down the hillside to graze. There had been enough rain over the summer that the grass was still green and sprinkled with yellow flowers. Skye imagined it wouldn't be for long. There was a definite chill in the air, signaling the imminent arrival of fall. She pulled the hood of Colt's sweatshirt over her head and tucked her hands under her arms.

Waiting for him, she got so hungry she thought her stomach would gnaw a hole in her insides. Rummaging through his bags she found an energy bar. Not the best breakfast, but she would make do. It seemed he'd been gone longer than the day before, but perhaps she had simply awakened earlier this morning. Not having her cell phone was driving her crazy. Skye did remember one thing—her cell phone doubled as a watch. She had reached for it at least twenty times in the last forty-eight hours or so. But it was never where her hand expected it to be. *The phone and my memory probably ran off together. Those traitors!* she thought.

She sat on the log, staring at the charred remains of their fire. When Charger's whinny brought her head up, she followed the direction he so intently watched. Colt rode Duke at a trot down the hillside toward camp. Smiling, Skye stood and walked to the highline he would tie the horse to.

"Good morning," Colt greeted her. "How do you feel today?"

"Good. Not as sore as I felt yesterday. How about you?"

He dismounted. "Cold, but good."

It sounded like his teeth rattled together when he spoke. Skye stepped closer. His hair looked wet beneath his hat, and a drop of water trickled down his neck. She wiped it away. "You're wet. What happened?"

His smile remained, but his teeth were definitely chattering. "I took a bath."

She raised her brows in disbelief. "You took a bath? Outside?"

Colt laughed as he pulled the saddle off Duke. "Yup, in a creek. When your own smell reminds you of the locker room after a high school football game, you know it's time."

"That's crazy, Colt. I could see my breath this morning."

He dropped the saddle on the tarp and made a beeline for the tent. "Yeah, so could I."

Skye followed. He hopped on one foot and then the other as he stripped off his boots. Then he threw back the sleeping bag, dropped onto the pad, and wrapped himself up. Looking at her with a puppy-dog expression, he said, "You know, if you're not busy you could climb in here and let me borrow a little warmth."

She folded her arms. He had the sleeping bag tucked under his chin, grinning and shivering all at the same time. The honesty she read on his handsome face left her no doubt of the innocence of his plea. He'd been a perfect gentleman the two nights before. "Oh, I suppose my busy schedule will allow me to spare a few minutes."

She climbed under the sleeping bag and felt Colt's strong arms encircle her. As he pulled her close, a garden bloomed inside her, complete with butterflies. Skye breathed in deeply and smiled. He smelled so clean. At that moment, even the chill of fall didn't stand a chance at chasing away the warmth in her soul. Then she realized his shivering was more like shaking. *What a foolish thing to do for a bath,* she thought worriedly. But before long the temperature under the sleeping bag became sweltering, at least for her. Colt finally relaxed, his shivering subsiding, and he fell asleep.

Skye tried to wiggle out of his arms, but each time she moved, his muscles tightened in reflex, trapping her in his embrace. She wiggled her legs and arms out from under the bag, trying to cool off. Colt stirred once, his fingers seeking out hers when she tried to move his hand away. With their fingers entwined, he let out a contented breath, almost a sigh. Skye inhaled deeply, trying to calm her racing heart and fluttering stomach. Holding a guy's hand hadn't invoked a reaction like that since her first high school dance.

Five

It felt like someone had thrown Colt into a furnace. He kicked off his sleeping bag and opened his eyes. Next to his face was Skye's blond hair. She tried to move, making him acutely aware that he held her firmly against his chest. Her fingers were interlaced with his, and he wondered how they'd gotten there. He released her and rolled onto his back. "You're a good little heater," he said, hoping to cover his embarrassment with humor. "I'm about to break out in a full sweat. If that happens, I'll have to take another bath."

She sat up next to him, drawing her knees to her chest. "We don't want that. You're bound to catch a cold if you go bathing in the creek again."

"How long did I sleep?"

She shrugged her shoulders. "A while. Do you feel better?"

Colt sat up and draped his arms across his knees, then lowered his head. "Yeah." *What am I doing?* The face of his fiancée—the image that had haunted his memories for years and had popped into his mind whenever he'd tried to date other girls—was strangely absent. He hadn't seen her in days. Now he had come awake holding Skye in his arms as if she was his.

Her hand touched his arm. He glanced up and lost himself in her vivid blue gaze. She touched his face, his forehead. "Are you sure you're all right? You look flushed, and you're burning up."

Dragging himself out of the daze Skye had left him in, Colt slapped a smile on his face and climbed to his feet. The height of the tent forced him to stoop like an old man. "I'm fine. Just got too hot. How about we eat something? I'm famished." He put out a hand and pulled her up, then stepped into his boots and walked outside to lace them. He sucked in the fresh mountain air and waited for his head to clear.

Following him, Skye said, "Can I ask you something?"

"Go ahead."

She sat on the log next to him. "If I overstep my bounds, please tell me. But I can't stop thinking about what you told me—about your fiancée. You seem so happy now. How did you get over something that tragic? Aren't you angry? I think I would be so mad I wouldn't know what to do."

Odd that she should dredge up that awful experience on a day when he'd been enjoying the absence of it from his mind. Colt tied a double bow in the laces on his boots and turned to look at Skye. "I was angry for a while. I tried being angry with the driver who was speeding. With the truck driver simply because he'd lost control. I was mad at God for the weather. I even tried being mad at Janna. I had wanted her to stay and spend Thanksgiving with my family, but she insisted it would be her last Thanksgiving with just her family. Unfortunately, she was right. But all my anger did nothing to change what happened. It didn't ease the sting of it, either. My dad said something that made me realize what a burden all that anger was. Not only did I carry around the pain of losing Janna, but I'd heaped a heavy pile of anger and resentment on top of it."

Colt paused as a rush of memories flooded his mind. As long as he lived he would never forget the day he'd shed that burden. "I came home from school late one night to find my dad sitting at the kitchen table waiting for me. I dropped my books across from him and said, 'What?'

"My dad, all straight-faced and serious, said something like 'Son, you've been chewing on a mouthful of bitterness for months now. It's poison. If you don't spit it out, it'll kill you.' With that my dad stood. He shoved his open Bible across the table toward me and went to bed.

"I ate a bowl of cereal and two pieces of toast before humbling myself enough to even look at the page. Finally, I read what he had underlined — Ephesians 4:31–32: 'Let all bitterness, and wrath, and anger, and clamor, and evil speaking, be put away from you, with all malice: And be ye kind one to another, tenderhearted, forgiving one another, even as God for Christ's sake hath forgiven you.'"

Colt lowered his head in thought. His faults had glared at him with the same clarity as the sharp red underlining in his dad's Bible. Being active in his faith, Colt knew all the right answers. But knowing them hadn't necessarily made it easy to live by them. He'd gone back and reread those verses so many times that he now had them memorized. He glanced at Skye, who asked softly, "What did you do then?"

"I put Christ's atonement to work for me. He's already paid the price to cover everyone's sins — even those of the speeding driver who caused Janna's death. And Christ is willing to carry our burdens, if we let Him. All I had to do was come to Him. I needed to follow His example and forgive the driver I so badly wanted to hate. So I prayed. I prayed harder and longer than ever before. When I finished, my load was lighter. It took some time to completely shed the burden, but I'd finally started in the right direction."

Skye gazed at Colt with rapt attention. "And now, do you still want to hate the driver?"

He half smiled and shook his head. "No, I feel only sadness for him. He died that day too — his mistake cost him his life. So,

I try to follow Christ and His example and look for happiness where I can. Like up here in these mountains, hunting."

She bit down on her lower lip, a furrow creasing her forehead. "There's a guilty pit in my stomach. Like your story was meant for me, but . . ." She rubbed her eyes and then her temples, as if trying to make sense of something. "I don't know. I can't remember anything substantial. Bits and pieces of trivial childhood and high school memories have come back, but nothing concrete."

Colt had quickly figured out one thing—Skye was strong-willed. So while he knew asking would be futile, he did so anyway. "We could always pack up camp and go do a little research . . . try to crack the case of your missing memory."

In her eyes he saw her defenses go up. "No. Not yet," she replied. "I really want to remember on my own. Have you ever forgotten the title of a movie or an actor's name and it about drives you crazy? Like it's right on the tip of your tongue, but for the life of you, you can't remember? And you don't want anyone to tell you, because you're saying, 'I know this!' That's what this is like. I want my brain to do its job."

Frustration had laced her every word, so Colt guessed she would take offense at his next statement as well. "Maybe seeing a doctor would help. What if your skull is fractured or something?"

Her pointed gaze felt like the tip of his buck knife. "Now you're being dramatic. My skull is *not* fractured. I may have forgotten my name, but that bump on the head didn't knock me completely silly."

Colt exhaled and turned his gaze to the leafy canopy. While he had a differing opinion on the whole situation, he had no desire to turn that into a point of contention. He honestly didn't think her skull was fractured, but she certainly had all the classic symptoms of a bad concussion. Based on his brother's experience, the doctors would likely tell her to rest, avoid computers and television, and basically give it time—all things she could do right where she sat now. Colt nodded, dropping the subject for the time being.

They ate together and then grazed Duke. Skye held the horse's rope, while Colt gathered armfuls of dead branches. A smattering of yellow leaves mixed with the green ones above him. In the next month, the mountainside would erupt into a kaleidoscope of fall hues.

He didn't realize he'd been monitoring his watch so closely until Skye said, "Are you afraid you'll be late again? I swear you've looked at your wrist a hundred times. I'm not a hunter, but I don't think elk stick to an eight-to-five work schedule."

At the realization that she'd been observing him so thoroughly, Colt felt his face turn red. "I should probably throw the saddle on Duke and get up there if I want a chance at finding them before dark. If I promise to tie Duke up, do you want to come hunting with me?"

Skye smiled at him, her blue eyes bright with a hint of mischief. Other than the purplish bruises, her skin glowed with a healthy hue. The observations eased Colt's conscience. She was probably right. Nothing too serious could be wrong with her. "Sure," she said. "There isn't much else to do."

"That is why I'm here, after all."

He tacked up his horse and got on. Then, holding his bow in his other hand, he pulled Skye up behind him. Riding Duke up the ridge with her warmth pressed against his back and her hands around his middle made him grateful for the company. Even for a habitual loner, a week of solitude in the mountains got old after a while.

Skye leaned around his shoulder and said, "Tell me about your family. I know you have a brother you work with, and your dad, but what about everyone else?"

"I've got four brothers and one sister. And of course our mama's the glue that holds everything together."

"Wow, six kids. Where do you fall in the lineup?"

"I'm second. I work with my older brother, Jared. He's married with three kids. Jacob's after me. He's married with a baby on the way. They live in Oregon. Then there's Bo. He's at Utah Valley University. The youngest two are twins, Sam and Lizzy. They're seventeen, though I swear Lizzy acts like she's going on twenty-five."

Skye sighed. "How nice. I'll bet you had fun growing up together."

"Yeah, when we weren't chasing each other around the house and getting grounded for it," Colt said, chuckling. "You put five boys together and it gets pretty wild."

"How long have you lived in Utah?"

"I grew up in Jasper, a little town in southern Tennessee. Work was scarce in the mid '90s, so our family came out west. My uncle, who owns an electric company, said the building industry was booming along the Wasatch Front. My dad moved out here and worked the winter I turned twelve. The next summer he brought all of us to Utah."

"That explains the touch of Southern drawl I hear from time to time."

Colt turned his head and saw her easy smile, and the twinkle in her eyes—a far cry from what he'd encountered two days ago. Then, she'd had a look of fear and was as jumpy as a handful of jacks hitting concrete. "Yes, ma'am. I suppose it does," he said, accentuating the twang in his voice.

She laughed. "Your family sounds wonderful. I'd like to meet them sometime."

Without thinking, he said, "I can only imagine the look on my mama's face if I were to bring you home from the hunt. She loves telling me I'll never meet anyone if I spend all my time hunting and fishing."

Skye wrapped her arms tighter around his waist. "That settles it, then. When we leave the mountain we'll go to your house first."

Surprised, he glanced over his shoulder at her. *Hmm,* he thought, wondering how long she would delay the inevitable. His conscience gave him another nudge, and he looked down at his hands. *What am I thinking, keeping this girl all to myself—not telling a soul? What if there is a mother out there, worried sick?* Or Skye could be hiding something. There had to be answers, and somehow Colt needed to find them.

She rescued him from his musing by reaching over his shoulder to point her finger and whisper in his ear. "Colt, look!"

His head snapped up. Duke's ears were already pricked forward and he'd slowed to a snail's pace. Ahead on the trail stood a mule deer—a four-point buck, in fact. It bounded into the trees, leaving Colt to wonder what Skye had done to him. He hadn't even spotted the game standing directly in his path. "Good eye," he muttered. "Too bad we're not hunting deer."

Colt stopped in the same clearing as the night before, hoping the herd hadn't moved out of the area. This time he tied Duke to a tree and set up his spotting scope. He adjusted the focus and glassed the clearing, then said, "Skye, look. That's where I'll be."

Watching her peer through the scope, he admired the way her long fingernails held her hair out of her eyes. "I see one."

"You do?"

She lifted her head, and Colt peered through the eyepiece. A line of cows were entering the meadow. "I'd better get over there," he said. He grabbed his bow and darted into the trees. He ran down the hill, jumping the deadfall and weaving between the aspens. When he came to the creek, he left speed behind and switched to stealth mode. He worked his way up the opposite hillside toward the meadow. In the distance, random elk bugled their challenges to the herd bulls. Colt stopped and listened. When the deep, throaty call of the herd bull echoed off the hills he crept forward, moving farther up the canyon. The bull's cows grazed in the meadow above him.

Colt paused behind the brush, then raised his elk call to his lips and sent a challenge to the herd bull. An immediate answer came back. The bull he wanted to get a look at was holding to the safety of the trees above the draw. Grinning, Colt pulled his camouflage facemask into place. After testing the wind, he advanced again. A slight breeze blew his scent away from the bull—perfect. As long as no cows circled below and raised an alarm, the bull would have no reason to suspect Colt wasn't just another young bull.

The setting sun graced the valley with the last of its rays. Colt was running out of daylight. His stomach growled impatiently. Hopefully, the elk's hearing wasn't keen enough to catch that. It seemed Colt was destined to always be hungry on the elk hunt. He had hoped to avoid that this year with the MREs, and he had brought extra, but then he'd found Skye and started rationing.

He placed each foot with care, not making a sound as he moved closer, constantly monitoring the cows above him. Minutes turned into an hour. In rut, the bull, confident in his supremacy and driven to protect his cows, exercised no such caution. Branches snapped as the huge animal moved closer. Colt raised his call to his lips, again challenging the bull. Crashing through the underbrush and trotting along the top of the draw, the bull boldly answered.

Colt switched calls. He placed the small cow call between his teeth before sliding an arrow from the quiver and knocking it into place. With his tongue he moved the call in his mouth. He hooked the release to the string and slowly raised the bow. The thundering of his heart felt like a herd of galloping horses.

Relax, Colt, breathe. No bull fever, he coached himself. *You gotta make a clean shot.* He caught sight of a flash of tan moving through the trees. The bull trotted toward him, lifting his nose to the wind. His antlers caught the low-hanging branches, leaving them swaying in his wake. In the fading twilight Colt smiled. The sheepherder had been right—*muy grande*.

The bull angled downhill. Colt adjusted his grip on the bow, his palms damp with sweat. He had to stop the animal before he came in below him or it'd be over. Once the bull was downwind, he would raise the alarm and the whole hillside would erupt in a stampede.

Colt drew back the bowstring and settled his hand against his cheek, the string skimming the edge of his nose just like he'd done thousands of times in practice. Fifty yards away the bull walked into an opening between the trees. At full draw, Colt blew once on the cow call, making a high-pitched mewing sound. The bull whipped his head to the side and froze, ears pricked forward as he searched the trees for a cow. With a perfect broadside shot, Colt released his arrow.

Skye sat on the ground, occasionally peering into the spotting scope Colt had left for her. The animals on the other side of the valley were always on the move, taking a bite of grass here and there. A couple of the elk sported antlers. But no matter where she looked, she never saw Colt. She imagined he'd be hard to see, wearing full camo.

The sun dropped behind the horizon, taking the mercury in the thermometer with it. Skye dug a coat out of Duke's saddlebag and wrapped it around her. All evening the elk had bugled, their eerie calls echoing in the stillness. Skye sat next to the scope and watched the hillside. In the last bit of light she saw one cow and then another raise their heads and scatter into the trees, as if something had startled them. Suddenly, the hillside lay vacant before her.

Hopefully, Colt would return soon. It didn't look like there was anything left to hunt. Twilight made way for nightfall, and Skye stood, reluctant to sit on the ground in the dark. She packed his scope in the saddlebag and then leaned against Duke. With her hands shoved under his mane and her cheek against his neck, she shared the animal's warmth.

"Skye?" a voice echoed from the darkness.

She raised her head and managed to make out the shape of Colt in the faint moonlight. "Over here," she said.

He strode across the clearing. "You had me worried. I didn't see you. Are you and Duke okay?" Clearly in a hurry, Colt leaned his bow against a tree and pulled the gear off his head. He touched the small of Skye's back as he leaned next to Duke to load his saddlebags.

She smiled. "We're fine. How are you?"

Breathless, Colt dug through both saddlebags and finally pulled out the headlamp. "I'm great. But I sure could have used this an hour ago." He turned on the light.

"What happened?"

With the headlamp on, he picked up his bow and untied Duke. "I've got a bull down. But he rolled into a draw. It was too dark to climb in there after him. I think he's big, Skye—real big. A *muy grande*."

"A what?"

Colt mounted his horse and held out his hand. He laughed. "It's Spanish. *Muy grande*—very large, very big. That's what the sheepherder called him. And he was big. Man, I am so excited. I can't believe what I just shot. He's got to be at least a 350 bull."

"That's great, but you just left it there?" Skye exclaimed. "What if it's gone when you get back?"

Colt laughed. "I don't think he can get up and walk away, but if he did, that would mean I didn't get him after all."

She grabbed his hand and put her foot in the stirrup. "Oh. Are we going over there?"

"Yeah. I need to gut it and get the meat cooling. We'll come back at first light with Charger to pack him out."

She climbed behind the saddle and wrapped her arms around Colt's waist, pleased to see him so happy. Shadows bobbed in the light from his headlamp as Duke wound his way through the trees. When they reached the bottom of the hill, the horse splashed through a trickle of water and began climbing the other side. Gravity tugged on Skye as the horse lunged upward, and she tightened her hold on Colt. After spending the past two nights studying this ridge she imagined they were nearing the large meadow. But Colt veered left, keeping to the trees. Suddenly, he pulled Duke to a stop and jumped to the ground. "We're here."

Skye looked within the radius of light but saw nothing even remotely resembling an elk. Colt tied Duke to a tree and ran off with his bow. "Wait there. I'll be right back," he called over his shoulder. With Colt gone, the darkness closed around her and a chill worked its way through her bones.

In the distance, Colt whooped for joy and yelled, "Skye! I found him. He's big, real big. This is going to take a few minutes. Are you okay up there?"

Other than the darkness totally creeping her out, she was fine. She stayed on Duke, feeling safer on his back. As time passed her eyes grew heavy, and she let them close for a moment.

Suddenly, a pungent odor intruded on her senses. Startled, she gasped. "Oh! What are you doing sneaking up on me?"

Colt set the headlamp on the back of the saddle and pulled his T-shirt over his head. "You weren't hard to sneak up on."

Skye caught herself studying his well-muscled chest as he stuffed the dirty shirt in the saddlebags and got out a jacket. But the offending odor eclipsed all else. "What is that awful smell?" She sniffed. "Is that you?"

"Sorry. Elk innards don't have the best scent."

"Ugh! That's the understatement of the century."

Colt looked up at her, smiling. "Do you want to hike down and see my bull tonight or wait for morning?"

Pursing her lips, she weighed the options.

"It's steep and I'm starving, but I'll take you down there if you want," he said.

"I'll see it tomorrow."

Once they got back to camp and Colt had visited the pond with his bar of soap, he started heating water for their MREs. While waiting for the water to boil, he emptied his packs and pulled them from the tent. "We'll need the game bags and the bone saw," he told Skye as he repacked those items. "And maybe some rope. Definitely the camera. I can't wait to see this elk in the daylight. We've got to get some good pictures of him." Colt stood, pulled the hat from his head, and ran his fingers through his hair. "I want to get back to the bull before daybreak — get it quartered and out of there. It's good it's been so cold at night. That way the meat won't spoil."

He was all business, talking as fast as he could, and Skye stifled a chuckle, amused by the intensity of his every action. "That sounds like a good plan, Colt." She tried to keep a straight face as he went back to his packing.

Six

Colt checked his watch. He'd been awake for an hour, listening to Skye dozing next to him. Like a child on Christmas Eve, he couldn't sleep. He wanted to see his bull again. But he planned to take Skye with him and it was too early. If they left now they'd be sitting at the top of the draw waiting on the sun. No, it was better to wait here and let her rest a little longer.

He folded his arms across his chest and stared into the darkness. He wasn't sure when, but sometime in the past two days, he'd quit thinking in terms of *I* and *me* and now it was *we* and *us* and *her*. But Colt was no fool. This little dream world couldn't last forever. And truthfully, he didn't know if he wanted the responsibility of a relationship right now. It would end, and Skye would return to her own life.

It was Friday, so he expected to be out of the mountains the next day. Maybe he could stall. Take her to meet his family like she wanted. He'd get a real kick out of seeing his mama's reaction. But he would have to report his Jane Doe to the police, so they could figure out her identity. The initial thought that maybe Skye had run away from a mental hospital just hadn't stuck. She was too levelheaded for that, unless she was also a really good actress. She could be hiding from someone or something, but what? Colt shook his head. If she wouldn't confide in him, or if she really didn't remember anything, he had no choice but to contact the authorities.

When he checked his watch again, he decided it was time. He could saddle both horses and get everything ready before he woke Skye. He rolled out from underneath the sleeping bag, laced his boots, and pulled on two sweatshirts. Both horses got a generous amount of grain; they would definitely need the extra energy today.

With the horses ready, Colt stuck his head into the tent. "Skye, do you still want to come with me?"

Yawning, she rolled over and stretched her arms above her head. "Is it time to get up?"

"Yeah."

She threw off the sleeping bag and climbed to her feet. "Okay, I'm up."

She must have been tired, because she didn't say anything else for a long time. During the ride, she rested her head against Colt's back. He held the reins in one hand and Charger's lead rope in the other. They passed through the clearing and descended to the bottom of the hill. Once they'd crossed the creek, Colt turned the animals up the canyon. It was barely light enough to see when he said, "That's the meadow I showed you in the spotting scope. Where the elk were last night."

"Is that where you shot your bull?" Skye asked.

"No. He kept to the trees."

A few minutes later, Colt pointed. "See that big tree? That's where I was. And down by that dead tree is where the elk was. When I shot him, he rolled over the edge there."

Colt swung his leg over Duke's neck and jumped to the ground. He tied the horses' lead ropes to trees.

"Everything looks different this morning," Skye said.

"Come on. I can't wait to show you this bull." After he helped her dismount, he dug through his saddlebags for the camera, game bags, and bone saw.

At the edge of the drop-off, Colt groaned at the sight before them. *What a nasty hole to get an elk out of.* Just as he'd suspected the night before, there'd be no riding the horses into there. "I'll take this stuff down and come back to help you," he told Skye.

As he descended, he sent a spray of rocks ahead of him on the steep hillside. He grabbed oak brush and tree limbs to slow his slide. A grin as big as Texas hit his face at the sight of his bull propped against the stump of a splintered tree. In the dark, Colt hadn't been able to see how lucky he was. He sent up a silent prayer of thanks. Thanks for the big bull, and thanks for the tree that had stopped its fall. Otherwise, the elk would have rolled all the way to the bottom of the draw. The prospect of pulling the animal up from there made this look like a cakewalk.

The first rays of sunlight seeped into the valley. Colt left his game bags and camera by the bull and scrambled to where Skye waited. "You gotta see it," he said, holding out his hand to her.

She set her fingers in his and took a step off the edge. Almost immediately, her feet started slipping in the loose rock, so she clutched Colt's arm with the other hand. Spouting out the first thing that came to mind, he said, "Next time we need to get you a good pair of hiking boots."

She laughed. "Next time? When is next time?"

Colt wondered what to say. There likely wouldn't be a next time for her, he realized, surprised that the idea didn't sit well with him. He settled on a generic answer. "Can't hunt elk again until the end of next summer at the earliest."

Skye gasped. "You're going to do all this *again*? It's not a one-time thing?"

"Every year that I'm lucky enough to get a tag. Wouldn't miss it for the world."

When they reached the elk, Colt grinned proudly.

"It's dead," Skye said.

He turned to catch her staring at the elk in what appeared to be a mild state of shock, her face pale. Until that moment, she'd probably never seen a dead animal bigger than a fly. "Yeah, that's kind of the point of hunting," Colt said with a chuckle.

She hemmed and hawed a moment before replying, "I guess you're right. Do you eat it?"

Colt stepped behind the animal and lifted its heavy head. "Always. Elk meat is the best. Tastes a lot like beef." At the sight before him, adrenaline pumped through his veins. The bull looked even bigger up close. "Would you look at these whale tails. And see the width of this bull? It's got to be over fifty inches. Come feel this main beam of his antlers. That's good mass. The fronts could be a little longer, but still. I'll bet it scores over 350."

Through all of this, Skye watched Colt, her mouth curved in a smile. "Is that a good score?"

"Heck yeah. It's a real good score. It'll probably be high enough to get me in the Boone and Crockett record book." Colt clicked his camera on. "Come stand by the antlers and I'll take your picture with the bull."

"Why don't I take yours?" Skye said.

She reached for the camera, but he held it above his head, out of her reach. "Not until I get yours. I want a picture of you with the elk."

The light from the rising sun revealed the roll of her eyes just before she stepped behind the antlers. He snapped the picture. "Don't move. Stay there."

He was fiddling with the camera settings when she asked, "What are you doing?"

Smiling, Colt balanced the camera on a decaying log and peeked through the lens. "Get ready to smile. I set the timer so it'll automatically take our picture. On your mark, get set, go."

He pushed the button and scrambled across the hillside toward the bull. Skye laughed as he slid into place next to her and dropped onto one knee. But so near her and those big blue eyes, he forgot about the camera. Forgot to look at it when she was gazing so intently at him. Instead of taking hold of the impressive antlers, Colt wrapped his fingers around the back of Skye's pretty neck. He tipped his head and kissed her just as the camera clicked.

Stunned at his own boldness, he dropped his hand. "Sorry."

Her surprised expression softened as she smiled at him. "Don't be."

"Let me try that again." He adjusted his cowboy hat, got up to reset the timer, and rushed to take his place next to Skye. He smiled at her before turning to pose for the photo. After that, she snapped pictures of him and the bull from every possible angle.

Then, anxious to get working on the meat before the temperature rose, Colt drew his knife. With the blade poised over the animal, he looked at Skye. "You might not want to watch this part."

She grimaced. "Good idea." She walked over to the log and sat facing the opposite direction.

Colt removed the skin and trimmed off the backstrap, occasionally glancing up at her. Thankfully for the meat it had been another cold night. But he imagined the chill in the air made the wait miserably cold for Skye, who had the hood pulled up over her blond hair. Working fast, he quartered the elk and caped out the head. This bull was a trophy—no doubt about it. If the mounted head and antlers didn't fit in his apartment, he would be begging his mother to let him hang it in her vaulted family room. Colt's smile hadn't left his face since he'd found the bull. He'd be calling the taxidermist first thing Monday morning.

Gradually, Skye must have grown braver. Or maybe boredom set in. It started with a glance over her shoulder at Colt and ended with her turning to watch. About the time he finished carving the meat into manageable pieces, the sun blazed through the trees, warming everything in its path. Colt shed his sweatshirt, and Skye dropped the hood on hers. Once he'd loaded all the meat in game bags, he cleaned the blade of his knife with his shirt and said, "While I shuttle this meat, do you want to wait here or at the top?"

She stood. "I'll go up."

He climbed just behind her, carrying a front shoulder. Four more times he climbed down the hill and carried up a section of his elk. Two hours of Stairmaster at the gym couldn't have made his legs burn any worse. Sweat dripped from his face by the time he reached the top with the head and antlers. He dropped them next to Charger, then staggered to the saddlebags and drained a water bottle without coming up for air. "That was hard work," Colt muttered.

"How heavy are they?" Skye asked.

He motioned to the antlers and shrugged. "Pick them up and see for yourself."

Smiling, he watched her grasp the antlers and try to lift the head off the ground. Her jaw dropped. "Holy cow! Those *are* really heavy. And here I thought maybe you were exaggerating."

Stuffing the empty water bottle in the saddlebag, Colt laughed. "Back to work. Now we load the horses and head for camp. We've still got a long way to go today."

"Do you realize it would be a lot easier to visit the butcher at the back of the grocery store?"

Colt shook his head, lifted one of the hindquarters, and tied it to Duke's saddle horn. "Where's the fun in that?"

It wasn't until the horses were loaded and they were walking back to camp that Colt had time to reflect. Kissing Skye had definitely not been on his to-do list for today. But the excitement over his bull, combined with her irresistible smile, had been too tempting. And he didn't necessarily regret it. The sensation of his lips on hers passed through his mind, bringing a smile to his face. Kissing her did make him more vested in her past as well as her future. He only hoped what he found out about her wouldn't change everything.

Seven

Colt had never felt more relieved to see his tent. He and Skye walked into camp leading Duke and Charger, who were loaded with the meat and antlers from the big bull. Colt's every muscle ached from butchering the meat, hauling it up the steep hill, and then hiking out. He clipped the horses onto their highlines and threw one of the game bags over his shoulder.

"I'm going to cook you elk steaks for dinner," he told Skye.

She picked up Duke's empty water bucket. "You are?"

"Yup, I'm so hungry I could eat the whole elk."

After taking off the meat they would need for dinner, Colt hung the rest near the creek where it would stay cool. The day was nearly spent by the time he pulled the cast-iron pan from the tent and sat before the fire. Skye watched as he cleaned and cut the tenderloin into one-inch thick steaks and seasoned them. "You're a regular mountain man, aren't you?" she said.

He grinned. "Sometimes."

"You found the elk, shot it, butchered it, hauled it, built the fire, and now you're about to cook your meat. Wow! Kind of like the Little Red Hen."

Colt laughed—not a polite, social kind of laugh, but a deep one that left him feeling lighter and happier than he had in years.

Once the logs had smoldered into hot coals, he put the pan over the heat. Hunched over the fire, he babysat the steaks, checking one then the other to monitor their progress. He didn't want them dried out—nothing worse than ruining a good steak by overcooking it. Every time he glanced up, Skye was watching him. He cut one steak in half and stuck his fork into it, then leaned back and blew on the steaming piece of meat. His mouth watered at the sight. Seared to perfection on the outside, still juicy red and bugling in the middle. When the hot food hit Colt's mouth, he sucked air to cool the meat as he chewed. Grinning in satisfaction, he pulled the pan from the coals and balanced it on the log. "Oh, Skye, this is so good. Come try a bite."

He forked the other half of the steak he'd cut and offered it to her. She plucked the meat off with her fingers and looked it over. Laughing, he cut into another steak and filled his mouth. Around the bite of food, he mumbled, "We forgot to say grace." He folded his arms, bowed his head, and offered a simple prayer before turning back to the food.

Seconds later, chewing another bite, he looked at Skye. She still held the piece of meat in her fingers. Colt chuckled and said, "I don't know why you're still looking at that. It should at least be in your mouth by now."

The last hint of daylight showed the disdain on her face. "I'm not sure I've ever eaten anything that's been killed before."

His chuckle erupted into another full-blown laugh.

Skye frowned. "Are you laughing at me?"

"No . . . maybe . . . I guess. But when was the last time you ate your chicken alive?"

She huffed and turned her back to him. "You know what I meant, Colt, and don't pretend you didn't."

He'd seen the hint of a smile before she looked away. Fighting to curb the next roll of laughter, he stuck another piece of steak in his mouth and forced himself to start chewing. "Skye . . . come on, you've got to admit that was funny. Please just try the steak. Trust me, you'll like it."

She turned around and finally nibbled at the steak. He waited a few seconds, then leaned forward and said, "So, tell me that isn't the best piece of meat you ever remember tasting."

She stopped chewing and tossed him a smirk, her head tilted and her eyebrows raised. "Are you making another joke now, about my loss of memory?"

He raised his hands in a show of innocence. "No, no. I didn't mean it like that. I'm being serious. Do you like it?"

"It tastes a lot like steak."

He speared another piece. "That's because it *is* steak."

"No it isn't. It's elk meat. I saw it for myself."

"It's the same thing, Skye. Steak . . . elk steak . . . beef steak. It's all steak."

Well, I do like it. As long as I don't think about where it came from."

Colt forked another piece and held it out to her. "That's good enough for me. Here, have another one. If you harvest the meat right, you can almost pass off elk tenderloin as filet mignon."

They finished the steak and shared an MRE. While they ate the last of the M&M's, Colt inventoried their food supply. Two MREs, a couple of packets of oatmeal, a few granola bars. *Good thing we're getting out of here tomorrow,* he thought. The amount of energy he'd expended on this hunt had left his stomach feeling like a bottomless pit. Tonight was no exception. The stack of elk steaks he'd eaten had barely satisfied his hunger, but he was too tired to cut and cook another batch. What he wouldn't give for an oversized bowl of cold cereal or a slice of his mama's apple pie heaped with vanilla ice cream. He dug into the bag of candies. Another handful of Peanut M&M's would have to suffice.

Utterly exhausted, Colt hit the sack with one thing in mind— sleep. But as soon as his head touched the sweatshirt he'd rolled into a pillow, Skye lifted his arm and ducked underneath it. Her hair brushed his cheek as she laid her head on his shoulder. "Hey, cowboy, I had fun today." Her fingernails swirled a pattern through the stubble on his chin. They ran down the side of his neck and onto his chest.

"So did I," Colt managed to say. Her touch had him completely mesmerized by the time she rolled onto her elbow and kissed him. Riding the wave of emotion, he let his hand circle the back of her head and pull her closer. Her fingernails tickled the hair at the nape of his neck.

Suddenly, he found himself on thin ice. He kissed her once more and then rolled onto his knees, detangling himself from her. He grabbed his boots. "I'd better leave."

"Colt," she whispered just before he left the tent.

Feeling jilted, Skye sat cross-legged with the sleeping bag tucked under her arms and waited. When Colt didn't come back, she began to wonder where he'd gone—if he had left her alone in the woods. In the dark. When she couldn't take it any longer, she slid her feet into her shoes and pulled back the tent flap. As still as a statue, he sat on a log, hunched over the dying embers of his fire. There wasn't much of a moon, and all she could see of him was a black silhouette.

He had to have heard the rustle of the tent, but he didn't move. What had she been thinking, taking liberties like that? If she had offended him, better to apologize now. Stalling would only prolong her misery. She walked forward and sat on the log, careful to keep a safe distance between them.

"Colt, I'm sorry. I just thought after this morning . . . it seemed like we had a connection, or something. You said yourself it had been a long time since the accident that took your fiancée. I thought you were over that, or I never—"

Finally, he looked at her. "This isn't about Janna."

Skye watched him drop a handful of sticks on the pile of embers. Sparks fluttered in the smoke and a flame erupted. He added bigger pieces of wood. She watched his face in the growing flame, but it was a mask of indifference as she waited for him to continue. When he didn't say more, she asked, "What is it then? You don't like me? I'm not your type?"

He turned, the hint of a smile softening his expression. "Try the opposite end of the spectrum. The problem is I like you way too much, and it scares me."

Furrowing her eyebrows, Skye folded her arms and turned to face him. "I don't see why that should be a problem."

Colt turned back to the fire, stirring the embers with a long stick. "I'm saving physical intimacy for marriage. You were a big temptation. I had to get out of there before I did something I shouldn't."

Embarrassed, she sat in stunned silence. *What was I thinking?* A shiver went through her shoulders as the wind picked up. "Colt, I'm sorry. I just got caught up in the moment, I guess. It won't happen again, I promise." She paused. "And by the way, I want to save myself for marriage, too."

He nodded. A sheepish look crossed his face, and one side of his mouth turned up. "For the record, I would like to kiss you again. Just not in my tent."

"I'd like that too." Skye looked down at her fingers—she was in sore need of a file. One of her nails had ripped, leaving a jagged edge.

When she shivered again, Colt said, "You'll get cold out here. Maybe you should go inside."

She hesitated before asking, "Are you coming?"

"In a while. I'll let the fire die out first."

Colt woke to the unwelcome beeping from the alarm on his watch. He quickly depressed the button to silence the annoyance—no need for Skye to wake up this early. At some point in the night she had snuggled next to him, her cheek pressed against his shoulder. Now, he turned his head and brushed his lips across her brow, then eased away and crawled toward his boots.

When they had first climbed under the sleeping bag the night before, he had laid out the plan for her. He would pack out the elk at dawn and load it in his trailer. Then he would return for her and take down camp. Hopefully, his brothers remembered to get his truck from the shop and drop it off at the trailer. If not, he'd have to come up with a Plan B.

Colt expected to get back to Skye midafternoon. He had showed her where he stowed the food and how to fix an MRE, plus he had filtered water and filled all the bottles for her. She should have everything she needed until he returned.

He saddled the horses in record time and loaded the meat. He draped the hindquarters over Duke's saddle, then loaded the front quarters in Charger's packsaddle. Next, Colt meticulously tied the elk's head and rack onto Charger's back. Before the first rays of the morning sun touched the valley, Colt led the animals out of camp. Snorting and shaking their heads, the horses seemed eager to go.

"Duke, old buddy, you ready to go home?" Colt said, patting the horse's furry neck. "You've got a warm barn and a pile of hay waiting. No more straining to nibble at blades of grass below the highline. It'll be a feast tonight, boys." Duke and Charger answered with nothing more than a slight toss of their heads as they followed him up the hillside.

Four hours later, Colt stepped onto the gravel road. The sight of his truck parked next to the trailer brought a smile to his face. *Thank you, Jared.* Colt dug the spare keys from his pocket and pressed the unlock button. He downed two water bottles and tossed the empty containers on the floor mat. His phone sat under a folded piece of paper, which he picked up and read.

Colt,

You forgot your phone. They had your truck done a day early, so Sam and I brought it up. Call me when you get off the mountain.

Jared

Colt dropped the note and powered on his phone. One bar. He dialed 411, intending to ask for the sheriff's office so he could give them a heads up about Skye. But the phone dropped the call before it connected. The display read "No service" when he tried the call again. Colt pocketed the phone, planning to try later. He might get a better signal on one of the ridges. A half-empty box of energy bars lay on the truck seat. He snatched them and slammed the door.

The urge to hurry back to Skye carried him like an incoming wave—he didn't like leaving her alone for so long. He threw a flake of hay next to the trailer for Duke and Charger and transferred the meat from the packs to the oversized coolers. With the trophy head safely locked in the tack compartment of the horse trailer, Colt pulled the reluctant horses away from their feed and turned back toward the mountains.

Skye didn't want to move. The only warm spot in the tent was beneath the unzipped sleeping bag they were using as a blanket. Colt must have left, but she'd dozed right through it. Her hand moved to the vacant place next to her. In a way, she dreaded the end of this day. The uncertainty of her future hung above her like a dark cloud. Where would she be tomorrow? Whom would she be with? If Colt took her to the authorities, what would happen to her? Would she be like her grandmother, not even knowing her own family? Skye pulled the sleeping bag over her head as fear gripped her heart. "Oh, why can't we just stay here forever?" she muttered.

Morning's call of nature finally forced her from her bed. She took her sweet time finding a suitable bathroom location and then wandered back to camp. No need to rush. She had hours' worth of time and only one chore: make breakfast. She heated the water with the Jet Boil like Colt had showed her and mixed the hot water with the packet of instant oatmeal. Minutes later she scraped the last of the oatmeal from the bottom of the bowl.

She stood and walked toward the creek. Make that two chores—eat breakfast and wash dishes. After scrubbing the oatmeal out of the bowl, she checked the pond for any sign of their neighbor, but the beaver was nowhere to be seen this morning. Skye shook the excess water from the bowl and spoon, walked back to camp, and set the dishes on top of the neat pile of supplies. *How sweet,* she thought, remembering the care with which Colt had filled all the water bottles and laid out the remaining food for her. *What did he take for himself?* she wondered. *Probably nothing but water.*

Wanting to help him, she went into the tent and rolled up the sleeping pads, then tied them with the bits of orange twine she found in the corner of the tent. Next, she stuffed the sleeping bag in its sack and pulled the drawstring tight. She left the tent to fold the tarp that had covered Colt's tack.

At the sight of a string of horses cresting the ridge above her, Skye froze. Anticipation at the thought of Colt returning was quickly replaced with fear. It wasn't Duke or Charger up there, but a dark bay horse followed by three sorrels and a gray. At least two of the horses had a rider. Strangers. And they were headed toward the camp.

Skye turned to run. But where? Colt had told her to not wander away from camp. The worry she remembered hearing in his voice convinced her not to leave. Still, she had no intention of talking to anyone if she could avoid it. Hoping the riders hadn't seen her, she darted into the tent and zipped the flap closed. She fought the urge to gasp for air as adrenaline raced through her veins. Hoof beats and the crackling of underbrush, along with a low murmur of deep voices, soon announced the strangers' arrival in camp.

Colt's bow, leaning against the pile of supplies, was the only weapon in sight. Small triangle razor blades covered the end of each arrow in the quiver. Skye reached for one, but a man's voice stopped her.

"Hello the camp."

A second man's voice said, "I could have sworn I saw somebody movin' about. Hey, anybody here?"

Skye closed her eyes. *Oh, where are you, Colt? Come back to me, please!*

Colt pushed Duke into a trot and crested the ridge, anxious to see Skye. Riding toward camp, he squinted against the bright sunlight. Everything looked in order from a distance, but when he entered camp, he saw a slew of hoof prints and a pile of fresh horse droppings in front of the tent, where he knew his horses had never walked. There was no sign of Skye.

He dismounted. "Skye!" he yelled, wondering if she had gone down to the beaver pond.

A noise drew his attention to the tent. He rushed to open the zipper and nearly cursed when it snagged. As he burst through the opening, a pale Skye exhaled in relief. She sat near his bow, holding one of his arrows in front of her with the razor-sharp broad head aimed at his chest.

Colt put out his hand. "What happened here?"

She lowered the arrow to the floor and dropped her head into her hands. He sank to his knees, then cupped her chin in his palm and raised her gaze to meet his. "Skye, what happened? Did someone hurt you? Who was here?"

She shook her head. "Nothing," she whispered. "It scared me, is all."

His heart aching, he pulled her into his arms and brushed her cheek with kisses. "I'm sorry, Skye. I'm so sorry I wasn't here for you. But tell me. Who came into camp?"

"Two men, I think, with five horses. I didn't want to talk to them, so I hid in the tent. They stayed here forever, it seemed, talking to each other."

"Were they hunters?"

"I don't know."

"Did they come into the tent?" Colt asked, wondering how close they'd been to her.

"No, they stayed out there."

"Good. Don't be afraid. They were probably hunters, packing in for the last week of the hunt. My guess is they only wanted to talk hunting—find out if we've seen anything."

Skye loosened her hold on him and slid her fingers down his arms. "Thank you for coming back."

He put his finger under her chin to tip her head up. Gazing into her bright-blue eyes made him forget everything else. He brushed his thumb over her lips and bent down to kiss her. One long moment later, he lifted his head. "You're welcome. Thank you for waiting for me."

She breathed out a sigh and then giggled. Colt raised his eyebrows and said, "What's so funny?"

"I distinctly remember you telling me we wouldn't be kissing in your tent."

"I— " Colt rocked back on his heels and propped his hands on his thighs. Then he shrugged. "That's right. But what can I say? I'm only a man, and you tempt me."

A pleasant blush colored Skye's cheeks as she glanced down. "Are you hungry?"

He picked up the arrow and returned it to the quiver. "Did you eat any lunch?"

"Not yet. I wanted to wait for you."

"Let me change my shirt, and then we'll eat the last of the food before we pack up."

"Didn't you change out of that shirt yesterday?"

Colt pulled the bloody T-shirt over his head. "Yeah, but I put it back on to haul out the meat this morning." He grabbed his last clean T-shirt from his bag and started to put it on.

"Wait! Let me think," Skye practically yelled.

Baffled, he looked at her. She sat staring at him in wonder.

"I've seen that shirt before, Colt."

He held up the shirt—white with "U of U Football" in red block letters. "This one? I haven't worn it before."

"My father wore a shirt like that," she said excitedly. "It's coming back to me. I remember him wearing it when he built a fire in our wood stove. When he finished, he left the door open a crack and pulled me onto his lap to watch the flames."

"That's good, Skye. What else?"

"I remember the house I grew up in. I remember playing with Breyer horses in our living room." The smile hadn't left her face, and her eyes had a faraway look as she shrugged her shoulders. "A few other random memories from when I was a kid—going to school, playing with my friends. But that's all I guess."

"It's a good start," Colt said. "Can I put my shirt on now?"

She waved her hand. "Of course."

He pulled the shirt over his head and loaded his arms with a water bottle, the Jet Boil, and the last two MREs. Outside, he boiled water and waited for the meals to rehydrate. When they were ready, he picked up the fork Skye had brought out. "Beef ravioli and meatloaf with gravy—that's all we've got left." He stabbed a ravioli and held it out to her. "Try this."

She opened her mouth and took a bite. "Mmm, it's good."

He scooped up a piece of meatloaf. "Now try this."

Again, she ate from the fork he held out. "That's good too."

"Which one do you want?" he asked.

"I don't care. Which one do you want?"

"Skye, I eat everything. You decide."

"Ravioli."

Colt dumped the ravioli onto the plate and handed her the fork. "There you go." Thinking of the cell phone in his pocket, he said, "I've got my phone now. We might be able to get a few bars up on the ridge, if you want to call anyone."

Skye shook her head. "No, that's okay. I don't know who I'd call."

"If you change your mind, or if you remember someone, let me know," Colt said. He grabbed the spoon and ate his meal from the bag, anxious to head to the truck.

Eight

While she finished eating, Skye watched Colt empty the tent and stack everything on the tarp she'd left half folded when the horsemen appeared. Then he collapsed the tent and began filling the packs on Charger's back. Colt appeared completely absorbed with his task, leaving ample opportunity for Skye to study him.

She wondered if she'd ever met a mountain man before— probably not. Colt's experienced hands buckled the leather straps and tied the sleeping bag and foam pads in place. He picked up his bow from where it lay against the trunk of a tree and shouldered the pack it was attached to. Bouncing on the balls of his feet, he adjusted the straps. He untied Charger's rope and led him over to Duke, then smiled and said, "Let's go, Skye. You ride in front."

She got up from the log and walked over to Duke. Colt now seemed as intent on observing her as he had been on packing up camp. She climbed onto the horse. Colt's muscular arm pressed against her waist as he grabbed the saddle horn to haul himself up behind her, but unlike the other times they'd ridden together, he left his arm wrapped around her.

"Where to?" she asked.

He raised his other hand, the one holding Charger's lead rope, and pointed. "That way. Over the ridge there's a trail heading west. We'll follow it for a while."

Two hours later, Colt lifted his hand and pulled back on the reins Skye held. "I think I'll walk," he told her. "My legs have had it." He dismounted and shook his limbs. Laying his hand over her knee he looked up into her face. "How are you doing?"

His touch opened the butterfly net inside her. Slow to find the words, she only nodded at first. Then she smiled. "I'm fine." Lifting her foot to look at her once-shiny black flats, she said, "I'm not wearing the best hiking shoes."

Colt stepped away and tugged on Charger's rope, pulling the horse into the lead. "Follow me, then."

Head bent to the ground, Colt trudged up the trail. They crossed open meadows, followed once-upon-a-time Jeep roads, forded streams, and climbed tree-covered mountainsides. The insides of Skye's legs ached, and soon she had firsthand knowledge of the definition of saddle sore. A plea to stop and rest hung on the tip of her tongue, but the sight of a graveled road below them made her forget the discomfort for a moment. "Colt, there's a road."

He turned to look at her. "Yup, that's where we're headed. My truck is parked a quarter of a mile away."

The setting sun threw long shadows across the trail, while the now familiar evening breeze swirled down the canyon. Every night the wind had blown, and Skye expected tonight would be no different.

Duke broke into a trot when his hooves hit the road, quickly coming astride Charger. Colt reached over and snatched the reins. "Whoa there, buddy. Walk," he said.

"He's in a hurry."

"Yeah, anxious to get to the trailer."

As they rounded the next bend in the road, she saw a white Dodge pickup parked in front of a horse trailer. While Colt made quick work of unloading the packs, she read the logo — a fancy red triangle with gray lettering — painted on the door of the truck. "J. M. & Sons Construction," she said. "That would be your father's company?"

"Yup. 'J. M.' is my dad, Jim Murdock."

"I see."

Colt dropped the saddles next to the trailer and let the horses eat hay off the road. He removed the elk head from the front of the trailer and arranged his gear there instead. Skye smiled at the care with which he placed the antlers in the bed of his truck next to two of the largest coolers she had ever seen.

"That's it," he said, pulling on Duke's rope. "We're ready to go." One at a time, both horses followed him into the trailer. The sound of their metal shoes echoed off the walls as they maneuvered into position. With a resounding bang, Colt closed and locked the door behind them.

He opened the passenger door of his truck and leaned in to move an empty water bottle off the seat. "Time to head home," he said to Skye.

She felt a rush of nervousness at the thought of her uncertain future. Once more, the idea of facing people who knew things about her — things she couldn't even recall — filled her with dread *How will I rely on someone I can't remember at all?*

Forcing a smile, she climbed into Colt's truck. He got in the driver's seat, started the ignition, and positioned the vehicle in front of the horse trailer, then climbed out to connect truck and trailer. Too soon, the diesel pickup rolled down the dirt road, taking Skye away from the only place, other than brief images of her childhood home, that she remembered.

The long horseback ride had offered hours of thinking time. Brick by brick, she had begun rebuilding the foundation of her memory. Glimpses of time spent with her father, and even occasionally her mother, had sprung to the forefront of her mind. Skye remembered a trip to the zoo, with both her parents excitedly pointing out the lions lying between massive gray boulders. Flashes came quickly. A birthday party with her parents singing to her. Sitting on her mother's lap for a bedtime story. Candles burning over a yellow butterfly cake. Riding atop her dad's shoulders in the park, her tiny fingers wrapped around his forehead. Revisiting those memories, while Colt maneuvered the truck down the steep terrain and through switchback turns, made her long to see her parents, to again feel their loving arms wrapped around her. But not one single memory gave her any clue as to their names or where she might find them now.

Skye's thoughts turned to her mysterious appearance on Colt's mountain. Something bad had happened, but what? Despite her insecurities, she would need to figure it out eventually. Yet she was reluctant to have her time with him end and decided to savor every last minute. It would be late by the time they got out of the mountains. She would start tackling real life tomorrow morning.

When the truck's tires hit the smooth asphalt of the highway, Colt slid his Bluetooth headset over his ear and punched numbers into his phone. "I should check my messages. See if I missed anything important." He clicked through them and listened to each one. When he finished, he asked Siri to call Mark Houston. "Hey, Mark," Colt said after several seconds. "It's me. I got your message about next Wednesday. I'll bring an extra set of the plans and meet you onsite in Highland first thing Monday morning, say around nine. I'm on my way out of the mountains now, and I've got a bull you're gonna want to see. Give me a call if there's anything else." After leaving his number, Colt hung up.

He pulled the Bluetooth off his ear and set it on the dash. Then, his excited voice interrupted Skye's brooding. "Hey, how about if I take you out to dinner when we get to Nephi? There's a little mom-and-pop diner there. They should still be open and the food's good."

Looking across the dimly lit interior of the cab, she smiled at Colt. "Sure. I'd like that."

"After over a week of MREs, my body is begging for a good, fresh-cooked meal," he said.

She switched on the radio and pushed the "Seek" button. "You've had it with eating out of a bag, have you?"

"A man can only take so much rehydrated food."

Skye turned her focus to the radio, searching for a suitable station. Her eyes shot to the side when Colt's hand covered hers and he said, "You've surfed the same channels at least ten times."

When she moved her hand back, he didn't relinquish his hold on it. She felt the warmth of his grasp as he gently pulled her hand toward him. "Isn't there anything besides country music around here?" she asked. "Are you sure there are only five channels?"

He smiled. "I was watching. Trust me, nothing but country out here. This is the land of big, wide-open country. Plus, I like this song." He turned her hand over and kissed it once before threading his fingers between hers.

Skye let out a sigh and listened with an open mind. She had to admit the song sounded all right. Not at all twangy like she expected country music to be. Colt swirled circles around the center of her palm with his thumb. The tension she'd felt at the thought of facing her future melted at his touch. She looked down at her fingers, nestled safely between his. Hopefully, he would be a part of her tomorrows. After what they had been through together, she couldn't imagine saying goodbye to him.

Colt clicked on his blinker and turned into the Chevron station. "I'll gas up the truck and get some ice. Then we'll go eat."

While his truck guzzled the diesel, he glanced at Skye's reflection in the side mirror. Once he began studying her perfect features, he couldn't pull his eyes away. So when she caught him staring, he could only plead guilty by winking at her. She raised her fingers and waved.

The nozzle clicked off, demanding Colt's attention. He replaced the gas cap and took his receipt, then darted inside and bought four bags of ice. The meat had cooled the night before, but the ice would be insurance—the colder the meat, the better. After stuffing two bags of ice into each cooler, he hurried around the front of the truck, wanting nothing more than to get Skye's hand back in his. Her dainty fingers fit perfectly between his, and he loved the feel of her polished fingernails beneath his rough skin.

He drove the short distance to the restaurant and parked the truck and trailer across several parking spots on the edge of the small lot. Skye unbuckled her seatbelt and slid next to him. He opened his door and they both climbed out. When they neared the entrance Skye slowed, pulling on his arm. Colt turned. "Are you okay?"

Her right hand shot to her hair and then touched her face. "I probably look awful. I haven't seen a mirror in days."

He grinned and pulled her forward. "It doesn't matter, Skye. To me you're beautiful. Plus, nobody's going to care. Look at me. The closest thing I've seen to a shower in over a week is that frigid creek, and I didn't even pack a razor. It doesn't get much worse than this."

She giggled as Colt held the door for her and followed her into the restaurant. While they waited to be seated, they looked at the chalkboard Welcome sign. "I think I'll get the grilled chicken with garlic mashed potatoes," Skye said, pointing at the handwritten description of the daily special.

"That does look good."

The hostess walked toward them with her head down. She picked up two menus and said, "Two for dinner?"

"Yes, please," Colt answered.

The hostess raised her eyes and froze, her face blanching. She stared at Skye for an uncomfortably long time, then sent a furtive glance in Colt's direction. "It will be just a minute. I'll be right back," the woman said before she hurried away.

Colt frowned. *Rude,* he thought, then looked at Skye. Her hurt expression left him wanting to give that hostess a piece of his mind. *Granted, Skye looks like she's taken a turn in the boxing ring, but still. That lady could have at least seated us and tried to keep her thoughts to herself. No need to flash them across her face like a billboard sign.*

Before he could say a thing to ease Skye's concern, she yanked her fingers out of his and declared, "I'm going to the bathroom." She nearly ran down the short hallway and into the women's restroom.

Colt leaned against the wall, wondering why he hadn't thought to offer to get some food to go. Maybe he had grown too accustomed to Skye's dark-purple bruises, one below her eye and another near her hairline on the opposite side of her face. The marks just begged to be stared at. He shook his head and scratched his scruffy beard as he saw it all through the eyes of the young hostess. She probably saw him as a rough-and-tough jerk who beat his wife. No wonder the girl had turned tail and run.

He looked across the nearly vacant restaurant. Two TVs droned out the nightly news. He listened. The weather would be on following the commercial break. The hostess stood conferring with a waitress and another woman. A moment later the other woman, whom Colt figured managed the place, walked over with the menus. She flashed a smile so wide it couldn't be genuine. "Right this way, sir. Sorry for the delay."

"I'm with someone, so I'll wait to be seated," Colt said, reading her name badge and confirming her title of manager. She looked down the hall toward the bathrooms while he talked to her. "But both of us would like the daily special—grilled chicken with garlic mashed potatoes—if you don't mind putting in the order. After a week in the mountains, I'm starving."

She met his gaze with that big, fake grin. "Are you sure? We have a table ready," she said, again glancing in the direction of the bathrooms.

"I'm sure. Two daily specials, and we'll sit down in a minute."

"Certainly." The manager pulled a pad of paper from her apron pocket and wrote down the order.

"Thanks. I appreciate that," Colt said.

"When you're ready, you can take a seat in any of the booths along the wall," the manager told him, then spun on her heel and walked toward the kitchen. She paused to say something to the waitress, who immediately set down the coffee pot she was holding and headed Colt's way. As she passed, she smiled at him and said hello.

Colt nodded and mumbled a greeting, then watched her make a beeline for the bathroom. He turned in the direction of the TVs again. Now the hostess, the manager, and a man from the kitchen were huddled together, deep in conversation. The hostess pointed a finger at Colt, then quickly dropped it as if realizing he'd seen her. The man from the kitchen looked at Colt, then dropped his eyes and wiped his hands on his white apron.

What on earth is going on? Colt thought with a frown.

Nine

Skye took a deep breath and dabbed the tissue under her eyes. She had to get these tears under control. Nothing could have prepared her for what bombarded her mind when the hostess had looked at her—stared was more like it. Yet it wasn't the staring but the pained expression in the girl's eyes that had triggered the memory. Like she had something important to say but was afraid to say it.

Strange, the stories written in one's eyes, Skye thought. Her mother's blue eyes held a story once—a long time ago, when Skye was eleven. She came home from school that day and found her mother sitting at the kitchen table. Skye had chattered incessantly while she scavenged through the cupboards, looking for a snack. When she asked her mother a question and received no response, Skye stopped what she was doing and truly saw her mother for the first time since walking in the door. Her mother's eyes brimmed with tears as she looked with pity on her daughter. Reading the agony in that gaze, Skye had dashed into her mother's open arms and asked what was wrong.

It had taken awhile before her mother could speak. But when she did, her words broke Skye's heart as well. Her mother had just returned from the doctor's office. He had diagnosed her with terminal ovarian cancer.

Within two short years, Skye witnessed the same look in her grandmother's eyes. Pity and sadness, mixed with a fear of saying what needed to be said. Skye knew her mother had passed into the next life. Her father had been at the hospital with her mother all night. He had called with the news moments before. Skye had heard the phone ring, but had thought nothing of it at the time.

Those memories from her mother's final years flooded her mind, most of them bittersweet and heavy with sadness, like branches sagging under the weight of winter snow. The deluge of emotions had sent her scurrying to the bathroom in search of privacy. This wasn't the kind of thing she wanted to process in front of a nosy waitress.

She'd locked herself in a bathroom stall and cried, again living through the agony of losing her mother, as the memory of it moved back home and settled into its rightful place in her mind. So many things from her past still lay hidden, but slowly they were revealing themselves. She only wished the memories weren't painful.

When Skye had cried her eyes dry, she left the stall and splashed water over her face. She pulled two paper towels from the stack and covered her wet cheeks. But one look in the mirror triggered a fresh round of tears. Eyes the same brilliant blue as her mother's stared back at her. The dainty nose and blond hair that had made her mother so beautiful now graced Skye's face. She smiled through the tears, remembering how as a child she had admired her mother. At the funeral, countless well-wishers commented on her remarkable likeness to her mother.

Now, Skye straightened her back and took another deep breath, fanning her flushed cheeks with her fingers. If she didn't pull herself together, Colt would be wondering what had happened.

The door to the bathroom opened. One glance and Skye knew it wasn't Colt looking for her. She dropped her gaze and tossed the paper towels in the trash. A waitress stood behind her, waiting and watching. "Excuse me," Skye said, reaching for the door.

"What's your name? Are you all right?" asked the woman.

Skye kept her eyes averted. "Yes, but someone's waiting for me. I've got to go."

"Aren't you the—"

Skye didn't hear what the waitress had been about to say. The bathroom door slammed closed as Skye hurried to where Colt stood scowling, with his hands in his pockets. He wrapped an arm around her shoulders and said gently, "Were you crying? I'm sorry they were staring. I should have thought of that before bringing you in here."

She shook her head. "It's not that. I remembered something . . . something sad. I'll tell you about it when we're alone."

He slid his hand down her arm and led her to the corner booth. "I ordered you the daily special. I hope that's okay. We could try to get our food to go if that would make you more comfortable."

Skye smiled up at him, hoping to ease the lines of worry creasing his forehead. "Thank you, Colt. But I'll be fine, really."

In the restaurant booth, Colt pulled Skye closer and wrapped his arm around her. He wanted nothing more than to protect her from everyone and everything. He didn't like seeing her upset, and it frustrated him that there wasn't more he could do. She leaned her face against his chest. What memory had surfaced to cause her such anguish, leaving tear-streaked cheeks and swollen eyelids in its wake?

The store manager suddenly appeared, interrupting Colt's thoughts with her overly cheerful voice. "I can get you something to drink, if you'd like. Your meals should be ready shortly."

Skye scooted away from Colt a bit and said, "I'll just have water, please."

"Me too. Thanks," Colt added.

He followed Skye's gaze. The man in the chef's apron had returned to the kitchen doorway and stood watching them. The manager's gaze lingered on Skye before she turned and left. The waitress who'd followed Skye into the bathroom gawked as she walked by. Colt narrowed his eyes at her, finally succeeding in turning away her stare. The hostess had disappeared into the kitchen and had yet to show her face again.

Skye tilted her head up and brushed her lips across Colt's ear to whisper, "Is it me, or does it seem like everyone is giving us funny looks? I mean, we don't look that bad, do we? From the stares we're getting, you'd think we showed up in dirty clothes at the prom, not a small rural diner."

When she giggled, Colt relaxed, thankful she could find humor in such an awkward situation. "You're right. They're definitely staring. I didn't think my beard made me look that bad. Do I have blood and dirt smeared across my face or something? A little elk fur dangling from my hat?"

Skye smiled and shook her head. "No, I like your beard. You do have a smudge of something right there, though." She licked her thumb and rubbed it across his cheek. "Ah, much better."

The manager deposited two glasses of ice water on the table, smiling all the while. When she left, Colt said, "I'll bet that guy from the kitchen looks out here at least three more times before they bring us our food."

Skye looked across the restaurant at the man. "You're being paranoid. How much do you want to bet?"

He smiled back her. "I'll bet you a kiss."

"All right, it's a bet."

Soon Skye and Colt were exchanging knowing glances each time one of the employees glared in their direction. When the manager finally emerged from the kitchen with their food, the late-dinner crowd had thinned substantially. Around the doorframe peered the chef. Colt shook his head, feeling smug.

"That makes three. I'm sure looking forward to a little privacy so I can collect that kiss."

Skye looked over at him. "Are you sure he came out three times? Did you actually count?"

"Of course I'm sure. With stakes this high, you think I'd forget to count?"

She laughed. "At least I didn't bet you money. I'd have a hard time paying up."

The manager set a steaming plate in front of each of them. "There you go. Is there anything else I can get you?"

Her artificial smile grated on Colt's nerves. He couldn't wait to get the heck out of there. "No thank you, just the check." He picked up his fork.

"Enjoy your meal."

An oversized bite of Parmesan toast soon followed a forkful of chicken and potatoes into his mouth. He chewed then swallowed. "Mmm, this sure hits the spot. How does—"

Before he could finish his question, the sound of running feet pulled his attention away from Skye. She let out a startled scream, and Colt turned to see a group of police officers, guns drawn, descending on them.

"Hands up, hands up! Move away from each other," yelled one of the officers.

What the heck? Colt dropped his fork and turned, keeping his body between Skye and their guns. He could feel the tension in the air, like static electricity pinging between the officers and him. He raised his hands and slid to the end of the bench as Skye looked from the cops to him in confusion.

Colt faced the officers. "What's the problem? There must be some mistake."

An officer snapped a pair of handcuffs onto Colt's right wrist and moved his arm behind his back. Then he pulled Colt's left hand down and clicked the cuff into place. He yanked him to his feet and away from the booth. Another officer, who began searching

Colt for weapons, said, "We're taking you down to the station for questioning." The cop's hands continued roving. Down one leg and then the other. The hunting knife was pulled off Colt's belt, and his wallet and keys were removed from his pockets.

With four pistols trained on his chest and no indication that the officers would change their minds, Colt started to worry. "Why? What's going on? I haven't done anything wrong."

Now the cop who had taken Colt's keys and wallet piped up. "Then you've got nothing to worry about. But you just showed up in town with the missing victim, and you match the description of the suspect, so for now—" The officer paused, looking through the wallet. "Mr. Murdock, you're under arrest for the armed robbery of the One National Bank, assault with a deadly weapon, aggravated kidnapping of Lily Vanasche, and the attempted first-degree murder of a bank employee."

"Are you serious? I didn't do that. I found her in the—"

"You have the right to remain silent," continued the officer as if Colt hadn't spoken. "Anything you say, can and will be used against you in a court of law. You have the right to have an attorney present during questioning. If you can't afford an attorney, one will be appointed for you. Do you understand these rights?"

Colt felt as if he'd taken a bad fall off Duke, with his horse landing on top of him. "I didn't do any of that. I found her in the mountains. She had amnesia. I barely even know her. She—"

From behind him, Skye asked in an agonized tone, "Why are you arresting him? He is the one who helped me!"

Colt turned his head and found her face beyond the crowd of officers hovering around him. His heart ached for her. After everything she'd been through, and all the uncertainty she faced with the amnesia, he hated that she had to watch this. He'd seen the fear in her eyes the first day he found her. Over the time he had known her, she had shed that fear. But now it was back. She glanced between Colt's face and the officer holding his arm. She tried to step closer to him, but a cop put his hand out to stop her.

As they moved Colt toward the door, the only female officer in the group asked, "Aren't you Lily Vanasche?"

When Skye didn't answer right away, Colt leaned back and craned his neck to the side, trying to see her face. Her eyes, wide with shock, met his. *Lily Vanasche—could that be her real name?* he thought. After several seconds, she moved her gaze to the officer. "Yes, I am Lily Vanasche."

A shove on the back sent Colt stumbling forward. He wasn't certain, but Skye didn't look particularly happy about discovering her identity. Again, he stopped and turned. Smiling, the female officer stepped toward Skye. "That's good, Miss Vanasche. Everyone has been worried. Your fiancé is going to be happy to hear from you. Why don't you come with me?"

The officer reached for Skye, but she resisted. "What about Colt?"

"He's being taken in for questioning," said the female officer.

Colt's mind was busy processing one thing, one word—*fiancé*. Of all the bad luck, he had gone and fallen for a girl who was already engaged. And now the police had arrested him in a case of mistaken identity. Here he'd thought things were finally looking up for him—a big bull and Skye—or Lily—all in the same week. *Guess it was all too good to be true.*

The bellowing voice at Colt's ear demanded his attention. "Sir, do you understand your rights?"

"Yeah, but I haven't done anything. There must be a mistake. You've got the wrong guy."

Having ventured from the kitchen, the man in the chef's apron sneered as he called out from behind the officers, "After what you put that girl through, you've got the nerve to deny it?"

Panicked, Colt looked from the chef to the officers. "I swear, I was only trying to help her. She was lost and didn't remember—"

Another officer joined the ranks of the one forcing Colt toward the exit. "Save it for the detective. He's the one who'll want to hear your story."

They led Colt to a patrol vehicle and opened the door. With one hand on Colt's head, the arresting officer lowered him into the backseat. The door closed.

Colt looked over his shoulder, hoping to catch a glimpse of Skye — *Lily, actually,* he corrected himself. Two cops ushered her toward another patrol car, and she didn't look thrilled about it. Talking animatedly, she pointed at the car Colt sat in. He hoped she could say something to help him . . . and that they would listen.

The cops must have won out, because they got her into the car. *Oh, Skye, what happened to you?* Colt thought, squeezing his eyes shut. *Bank robbery. Kidnapping. What kind of nightmare did you go through to get on that mountain?*

The thud of Duke's hoof against the wall of the trailer brought Colt back to his own problems. Of the remaining officers, two stood next to his truck, talking with each other. Another two climbed into the front seat of the vehicle Colt sat in, and two others left in their squad car.

From the passenger seat, the older of the two officers turned his dark gaze toward Colt. The man's salt-and-pepper hair and mustache were both trimmed to perfection. As casually as if asking who won the football game, he said, "I'm Lieutenant Decker. I hope you have a tag for that bull in your truck."

"I do. It's on the antlers," Colt said, hoping he'd punched the right date and that the tag was still intact and in place.

Decker strapped on his seatbelt and nodded to his partner, who turned the key in the ignition. "Good. That'll save me from writing you up for poaching."

Duke pounded the inside of the trailer, loud enough to be heard over the sound of the car's engine. Colt leaned forward. "What about my horses? How long is this going to take? They need water and feed."

Without looking away from the road, the older officer said, "They'll have to be patient, and so will you, Mr. Murdock."

"Who can I talk to? Because I haven't done anything wrong. I've been gone hunting for over a week. I found that girl injured on the side of the mountain and brought her out. I had no idea she was involved with a bank robbery."

The officer clicked on the dome light above his head and turned to look at Colt. "The FBI and the local police department have been notified. You'll need to talk with the detectives assigned to your case."

My case? When did this become my *case?* "What do I need to do to convince you I'm not the guy you're after? I swear, I found her unconscious on an old Jeep road up near Fish Creek. I've been stuck in the mountains for the past nine days."

The cop driving the car spoke into the radio on his shoulder, answering a question from the dispatcher. Lieutenant Decker leaned forward to type on the police cruiser's computer. Neither officer appeared to be listening to Colt. He wanted to rub his eyes and readjust the camo baseball cap sitting at an awkward angle on top of his head. Even knowing he was handcuffed didn't stop his body from trying to answer the urge. His arm jerked as his wrist met the metal restraint. Frustrated, he rolled his head against the back of the seat and closed his eyes.

Moments later the cruiser's blinker came on. Colt lifted his head to see the county jail looming ahead. Lieutenant Decker and his partner ushered Colt through the doors and into a room, where they handed him off to the jail guards. One of the guards set a pile of orange clothing in front of Colt and undid his restraints. The other guard opened a paper sack and set it on the table. "We'll put your clothes in this bag."

Colt raised his eyebrows. "You want me to take my clothes off?"

The guard spread his feet and clasped his hands behind his back. "Yes, sir."

No one cracked a smile, leaving Colt with no doubt they were completely serious. With a frown he looked at the orange clothes and then started with his hat, handing it over to the guard who wore latex gloves.

This is definitely a first, Colt thought.

He unlaced his boots and stepped out of them before stripping off his sweaty socks. He dropped his jeans to his ankles and pulled his sweatshirt and T-shirt over his head. Then, he reached for the pile of orange jail-issue clothing.

"Sir, we need you to take off everything," the guard announced.

Colt glanced down at his underwear. "Everything?"

"Yes, sir."

Talk about humiliating. However, he was in no condition to argue. He kept going until he stood in front of them in the same outfit he'd worn coming into this world. The latex-gloved guard gathered up Colt's belongings, which filled two large paper sacks. Holding both hands protectively in front of him, Colt nodded toward the jail-issue clothing. They didn't look so bad, now that he was standing here naked. "Should I put those on?" he asked.

"Go ahead."

Colt picked up a pair of men's briefs—orange. Then he stepped into the jumpsuit, also orange. A pair of orange crocs completed the ensemble. *Put a green hat on my head and I'd be a pumpkin.*

The guard replaced the handcuffs and said, "This way."

Harsh fluorescent lights spaced at even intervals reflected off the heavy metal bars. An oppressive feeling closed in on Colt. The guards stopped in front of a cell and held open the door. Colt's heart thudded in his chest as fear raced through him. In a moment, they'd leave him alone for who knew how long. The guards pushed him through the doorway. Time was running out. Colt wanted answers to some questions, and fast. "Where are my horses?"

The older guard, with a shiny bald head and a generous paunch, replied, "Son, you'd better worry about yourself. You're in a lot of trouble. Those horses will be fine."

The door to his cell began closing. "Wait! They won't be fine. And when can I talk to somebody? I didn't do any of that stuff you think I did."

"When the detectives arrive, someone will come get you."

Normally, Colt couldn't have eaten at a time like this, but his metabolism must've gone into overdrive. He had expended so much energy during the last few days of the hunt that he felt ill from the lack of food. "Any chance I can get something to eat?"

"You missed dinner, and breakfast isn't served until five in the morning." With that, the door slammed closed.

Alone in a holding cell, Colt turned to survey his new quarters.

Ten

Lily looked over her shoulder as the patrol vehicle, with lights flashing, sped Colt away from the diner. She wanted to scream at them to stop, but a whirlwind of thoughts left her speechless. Seeing the officers had flung open the floodgates to her past, and the rush of memories felt like a rush of cold water in her face. Suddenly in her mind, she knelt over her father's body, which lay limp on the asphalt. She heard the sirens of emergency vehicles, but help seemed to take forever to arrive.

The accident had happened the fall of her senior year in high school. After her mother passed, Lily's father had not remarried, and he and Lily developed a close relationship. During her junior year, the two of them got bicycles for Christmas. Together they'd taken up cycling. Lily had loved it—both the cycling and the time spent with her father. On that particular evening, everything that could possibly go wrong had done so.

Her father had come home from work late. The last of the sun's rays had shot across the valley from the western horizon as they peddled their bikes down the suburban streets toward the foothills. "Lily, how was your day?" her father had asked.

Lily smiled. She had been waiting for the question. "It was great, Dad. No, it was better than great. It was fabulous. You'll never guess what happened."

He had glanced at her over his shoulder. "Well, tell me. What made your day so fabulous?"

"Remember Matt?"

They had kept peddling, her father in the lead with Lily following a bike length behind.

"Hmm . . . I don't remember a Matt."

"Dad! The guy on the football team. I told you about him last week. He's in my English class. Don't you remember?"

"Ahh, now I remember. What about him?"

The road had crested a hill, so Lily quit pedaling, grateful for the opportunity to coast. "He asked me to the homecoming dance. Can you believe it? For once the guy I dreamed of going out with actually asked me."

Her father's bike had pulled farther ahead. He responded, but the wind pirated his words away.

"What did you say?" Lily yelled.

Her father turned to shout over his shoulder. "I said I'm—"

"Dad!" she screamed. An SUV had run a stop sign and now barreled into the intersection and her father. In that instant, Lily fell from cloud nine into the depths of despair. The SUV tossed her father onto its hood. Then, as squealing tires skidded across asphalt, the vehicle threw him onto the road. Lily squeezed her brakes too hard and nearly lost control of her own bike.

A blur of hysterics had followed—Lily's mixed with those of the young mother driving the vehicle. Distracted by her crying infant in the back seat, she had turned to offer the baby his bottle. When she faced the road again, the glare of the setting sun had blinded her. The woman never saw the stop sign. One moment was all it took to take a life . . . and inalterably change another.

Time slowed, punctuated by the events that followed. Flashing lights filled the street. An ambulance, police cars, and even a fire truck lined the usually quiet suburban neighborhood. People stepped onto their porches to watch the drama unfold. Lily held her father's hand, begging him to wake up. Gasps for air were his only response.

Her father had worn a helmet but secured it too loosely. The doctors later told her he had died of severe brain trauma and a broken neck.

"Miss Vanasche? Excuse me, Miss Vanasche?"

Lily jerked her head up. "I'm sorry. What?"

"I'm Officer Simmons," explained the female officer. "We'll have a doctor take a look at you first, and when the detectives arrive, they will ask you some questions."

Lily leaned forward, propping her hands on the back of the seat in front of her. "The guy I was with. Why was he arrested?"

Officer Simmons looked surprised. "He is being questioned as a suspect in the bank robbery and your kidnapping."

"He would never do something like that! Colt found me in the woods. He rescued me."

"If he isn't responsible, what happened to your kidnapper— the guy who robbed the bank?" asked Officer Simmons. "Could you ID him if you saw him again?"

Lily shook her head slowly. *Bank robbery?* Though she had tried, she still couldn't recall how she had ended up on Colt's mountain. "No. I believe I've had amnesia. I don't remember all that much prior to waking up in the woods. What exactly happened to me?"

Officer Simmons exchanged a skeptical glance with her partner behind the wheel. "An armed man, whose height and build match that of Mr. Murdock, entered the bank where you work. When he took you hostage, the bank manager tried to intervene. In the confusion, the manager was shot. The robber took you and the money and fled. He used a stolen vehicle as the getaway car. Miss Vanasche, if you can't remember who robbed the bank and kidnapped you, couldn't our suspect be the man responsible?"

Lily shook her head. "No, it can't be Colt."

"Well, the FBI, along with the police detectives, will have to make that determination."

A knock sounded on the door of Lily's hospital room. White tissue paper crinkled beneath her when she sat up. The smell of hospital antiseptic tickled her nose, and she raised her hand to cover her yawn. Would this night ever end?

The door opened, and a nurse bustled into the room. "You can dress now. The doctor has everything he needs," she said, and Lily smiled at the distinctive British accent. "You should have your primary care physician take a look at your head in two weeks," the nurse went on. "Sooner if you experience any unusual symptoms—nausea, headaches, or additional memory loss. It's all jotted down for you." The woman handed Lily a clipboard. "Sign here, dear. I dare say, you'll need to go on holiday after the ordeal you've endured."

Lily signed the discharge papers, then accepted her copy and folded it twice. "A vacation would be nice. Were they able to get a hold of my fiancé?"

"Oh, yes, I believe so. What a lucky girl you are to catch someone like Nick Borino—so good-looking and charismatic. I prefer his news station to any other. Why if I were twenty years younger . . . Did you know he offered a reward for you? So romantic. On nearly every commercial break for days, the station ran the clip Nick put together. I believe his plea had every person in all of Utah out looking for you. Now, dear, I'll give you some privacy so you can dress. Someone will come get you when your fiancé arrives."

The nurse closed the door behind her, leaving Lily alone. She shed the hospital gown and retrieved her pile of clothes. Once she was dressed, she opened the door. The two officers stood talking in the hallway outside her room, as if she were a prisoner instead of someone who had been rescued. Lily sat down to wait, watching the constant stream of activity surrounding the nurses' station. She pressed Colt's jacket to her chest.

It smells like him.

Anxious to leave, she stood and paced. After going over every square inch of her body, the doctor had drilled her with an endless list of questions. By the time he had finished, Lily's head spun and she was blushing with embarrassment.

Dr. Spalding had said that although most short-term memory loss due to head trauma resolves itself with time, Lily might never recall the details of the events surrounding her injury. Evidently, that was one of the brain's mechanisms for dealing with traumatic events.

An officer with a name she couldn't remember filled the doorway. "Miss Vanasche, Detective Hansen and FBI Agent Dawson are here to speak with you."

Two men in street clothes entered the room. One of them closed the door before they shook Lily's hand and introduced themselves. Agent Dawson pulled the doctor's stool across the tiled floor, sat in front of Lily, and said, "Tell me what happened, Miss Vanasche."

Lily recounted the events of the past few days, explaining that she had no memory of the bank robbery or how she came to be in the mountains. As she answered "I'm sorry, I don't remember that" for the tenth time during the officers' list of questions, she sensed that they thought she had somehow helped the bank robber. *What really happened that day?* Lily needed to remember, and soon. She was so tired the fluorescent lights seemed to be pulsating.

Finally, the men stood and handed her their business cards. "We'll call you early next week to set up a time to finish," Detective Hansen said. "If you have any questions before then, or if anything else comes to mind, please give one of us a call."

Lily glanced down at the cards. "I will. What's going to happen to Colt?"

"We'll be talking with him next," replied Agent Dawson.

After the two men stepped out of the room, Officer Simmons returned and said, "Nick Borino is here to drive you home. I'll take you to him when you're ready."

Nick, the news broadcaster. Who is he? Could I really be in love with him? I don't even remember him. "Thank you," Lily said, then slid off the exam table. She slipped her arms into the coat and pulled it tight across her chest. Guilt prodded her conscience as she walked to meet her fiancé. At the moment her thoughts preferred to linger on a particular hunter. Where was Colt now? She missed him. How long would it take law enforcement to clear his name and release him? Or would they still suspect he was part of this mess, even after they talked with him?

The officer held open the door to the lobby while Lily stepped through. She scanned the crowd of weary faces, searching for a familiar one. She knew him the moment her eyes picked him out of the crowd. Nick Borino stood and crossed the room in a few confident strides. His Italian ancestors had generously bequeathed him a head of dark hair, matching eyes, and a naturally tan complexion. A warm smile lit his face as he wrapped his arms around her. She leaned against his solid chest, his warm embrace bringing random memories of their time together. He breathed a sigh of relief. "Lily, thank goodness you're safe."

With the next sentence, Nick took on the familiar role of news reporter. "Officer, can you tell me where Miss Vanasche was found?"

Officer Simmons shifted her weight and clasped her hands behind her back. "She was recognized at a restaurant."

"Has the suspect been apprehended?"

"A person of interest is being held for questioning, but since it is part of an ongoing investigation, I can't say more than that." The officer nodded once to Lily and left.

Nick steered Lily toward the door, away from the prying eyes and ears of those in the hospital lobby. "How are you, Lily, really?" His thumb gently caressed the bruise on her cheek.

"I'm fine. Just tired. Take me home, please."

"I will, sweetheart, but first we need to shoot a little clip for the morning news. Everyone's been so worried. You have no idea."

Through the double sliding-glass doors, Lily caught a glimpse of the news van. Her jaw dropped. "You brought your camera crew?"

"They won't be here long. I promise. Just a quick interview, and then I'll send them back to the station."

Lily shook her head and took a step back. "Nick, no. I don't want to talk in front of the camera. Not now."

He grasped her arm and smiled. "Don't worry. I'll do all the talking. Just tell me what happened."

After speaking with the detectives, Lily had pieced together the events preceding her appearance on Colt's mountain. It all started on Tuesday morning, when the bank where she worked as a loan officer was robbed. The first customer had asked for more than a typical withdrawal. Brandishing a gun and hiding beneath a camouflage ski mask, he held Lily hostage and demanded money. A bank employee filled the robber's bag with bills from the till. Then the thief, now known as the Camo Bandit, shot the manager and fled the scene, taking the money and Lily with him. What happened after that was still as much a mystery to Lily as it was to law enforcement.

"You know about the bank robbery, right?" she asked Nick.

A look of impatience crossed his face. "Yes, of course. We've run the security film over the air for days. What everyone wants to know is how you escaped and where you have been for the last four days."

She pulled her hair aside to show him the scabbed-over cut and what was left of her goose egg. "I must've gotten away, because when I woke up in the mountains, I was alone. I injured my head and I've had amnesia. I don't remember anything about the bank robbery, Nick. A hunter found me in the woods. He rescued me."

"Rescued you? You said you woke up alone. Were you lost?"

Lily shrugged her shoulders, not wanting to say anything about Colt that Nick might sensationalize. "Of course. I was in the middle of nowhere."

"When did the hunter find you? What day?"

"Tuesday night."

Nick took her by the hand and shook his head. "Why didn't you call me?"

"We didn't have a phone and the location was quite remote. It took hours on horseback to even get to the nearest road, and that was only a dirt road."

"I can't believe he didn't have a phone. Why didn't you ride out of there on Wednesday?"

"Nick, I told you. I had amnesia. I didn't even remember my own name, let alone anything about you or being abducted in a bank robbery. You have no idea how frustrating it is to remember nothing."

Wearing a stiff smile, Nick squeezed her hand. "Never mind. We'll talk about it later. Right now what's important is that you're safe. Come on. The camera crew needs to get back to the station."

The crew rushed forward the moment Nick and Lily stepped out the door. The crew members' faces were hidden behind their bulky cameras and equipment. "Here you go Nick," one of them said, passing him a microphone.

Bright light flooded the sidewalk as the eye of the camera focused on Lily. Hating the attention, she lowered her gaze. She had never understood why Nick liked this.

He straightened the collar on his shirt and squared up his shoulders before glancing at her. "Lily, what are you wearing?"

"It's a camouflage jacket."

"I'll have one of the guys get something from the van that you can put on."

Lily folded her arms, bothered by his expression of disdain. "I'm comfortable just as I am. Don't make me wish they had called Angela to come pick me up."

Nick threw his hand up. "Sorry. I didn't want you to have to wear some redneck hunter's jacket when I could get you something nicer."

Lily rolled her eyes. *Typical Nick. Always concerned with appearances.* He turned his face to the camera and gave the signal for the crew to begin filming.

"This is Nick Borino, with my fiancée Lily Vanasche, reporting from outside the county hospital. Earlier this evening one of our viewers recognized Lily from our broadcasts and notified the authorities, leading to her safe recovery. Miss Vanasche spent the past four and a half days in a wilderness area, where a hunter found her. According to a statement by a county deputy, a man has been taken into custody who is a person of interest in this case. We'll keep you posted as additional information is released. For now this is Nick Borino, Channel 2 News, saying thank you to all of our faithful viewers who helped in the search for Lily Vanasche, my fiancée." Nick gave the camera his winning smile.

He returned the microphone, then settled his gaze on Lily as the cameraman lowered his equipment. The lights and cameras were turned off, and the men shook hands. "Glad you're back, Lily. This guy was a mess without you," said Joe, a cameraman she recognized from last year's company Christmas party.

"Thank you," she said.

Joe turned to load his equipment into the van. "See you back at the station, Nick."

Leading Lily toward the parking lot, Nick raised his hand in farewell. "Thanks, guys." He smiled at her. "That wasn't so bad, now was it?"

She smiled through her annoyance, ready for this night to be over. "No."

Nick opened the passenger door of his top-of-the-line BMW. Between student loans and the rent on his downtown condominium, this was probably a luxury he couldn't afford.

With Colt, Lily hadn't sensed any façade. You got what you saw with him. There was no pretense, no acting cool. He seemed comfortable in his own skin. He sat as confident with his messy hair and dirty T-shirt on his sweaty horse, as if he wore a leather jacket and drove a sports car.

In addition, Colt savored an elk steak cooked over the fire and seasoned with salt and pepper with more gusto than Nick had ever enjoyed a meal at any of Salt Lake's finest restaurants. Would the simple pleasures of life ever be enough to satisfy Nick? Or would he always be hot on the heels of the next trend? Lily didn't know, but those questions needed to be addressed later, when she wasn't so tired.

She lowered herself onto the black leather seat of his car and closed her eyes. She must have dozed off during the drive to her townhouse, because the next thing she knew, Nick reached over to pull a single key from his glove compartment. "Home sweet home, Lily," she said.

When her father had died, Lily lived with her grandma until she went away for school. During Lily's senior year of college, her grandmother had moved into a care facility and her house had been sold. After Lily paid for college, there was a little money left in the trust fund her father had set up for her. It was enough for a down payment. The townhouse, located within a mile of the bank, seemed like the perfect starter house.

For the first time, she thought of her cats, Romeo and Juliet. She put her hand on Nick's arm. "Did anyone feed my cats?"

"Of course," he replied. "Angela and I took turns. They missed you, but they're fine." Angela had been Lily's best friend for years. They had roomed together in college, and then Angela had rented the extra bedroom in Lily's townhouse. After Damian proposed to Angela, she had moved back home with her parents to save money for the wedding. Thankfully for Lily's cats' sake, Angela still had her key. And Lily had given one to Nick when she had taken a girls' trip to Las Vegas over the Fourth of July weekend.

He pulled the handle on the door, and the light came on. Lily offered him a grateful smile, then watched him walk around the car to open her door. She set her hand in his and stepped out. In the pale glow of the porch light, he lifted her left hand to his lips. "Where's your ring?"

With those three simple words, Lily flashed back to last Friday night and Nick dropping to one knee after a romantic candlelight dinner. Of course he'd had an accomplice who caught the moment on film, with the whole restaurant for an audience. The proposal wasn't entirely unexpected, but she had hoped for a little more time to figure out what she wanted. She was only twenty-four and felt no rush to marry. Nick had presented her with a sparkling diamond ring. It fit loosely, so the jeweler promised to resize it by Monday. But Monday had come and gone, as Lily was swamped with work. The lunch break she had expected to use for running errands never happened. And Tuesday . . . well, that was front-page news.

She tipped her head to meet Nick's gaze. "It's still at the jewelers. With everything that happened, it obviously didn't get picked up on Tuesday like I'd planned."

He turned and walked up the sidewalk. "We'll stop by and get it tomorrow." He released her hand and worked the key into the lock of her front door. "Should I stay? I've got to work in the morning, but I'm happy to stay with you for a few hours if you'd like."

Lily shook her head. "No. Thank you, though."

Nick wrapped her in a hug and kissed her. "I'm glad you're safe. I was so worried. I'll call you as soon as I'm off work and we'll do something. Sound good?"

She nodded, forcing a smile. The conflicting emotions at war within her left her unsure of what she wanted. Hopefully, a solid night of sleep and a little meditation would help clear up the confusion. She pulled away from Nick and stepped over the threshold. "I'll talk to you tomorrow. Good night."

Lily locked her door and leaned against it. Hot tears threatened to escape her clamped eyelids. The patter of tiny paws on tile floor announced her two cats — one calico, one black with white socks. The felines rubbed their faces on her ankles and arched their backs, begging for attention. Juliet, the vocal one, started a chorus of meowing. Lily bent and scooped them into her arms. Romeo's rough tongue flicked out of his black-and-white face and licked her neck. Juliet rubbed her pink nose across Lily's cheek. "I missed my sweet kittens." She giggled as Romeo licked behind her ear. "Or at least I would have, if my brain had been working properly."

All but one of her wayward memories seemed to have taken their places. The only missing piece to the puzzle of her past was her abduction during the bank robbery. Hand in hand with the factual memories came the emotions. Sorting through those feelings might take a while.

Experiencing amnesia had made Lily realize something. At seventeen the sadness and despair over being left an orphan had triggered her metamorphosis into someone filled with bitterness. At once, she had doubted everything she'd ever believed. Her childlike trust in both God and her earthly father had disappeared. Her dad had promised he'd never leave her, but he did. She knew it was foolish to blame him, but he had no right making a promise he didn't have the power to keep.

Lily remembered the moment she'd laid the blame at God's feet. A distant relative she had never met before had made an offending remark at the funeral. Something about what a good man her father was and how he must have been needed in the next life. How he was in a better place and with her mother again. The man had commented that Lily's mother must be happy. Thinking back on it now, Lily could see he only meant well, but at that time she had needed her father. And she knew her mother would not have wanted her father to leave their only daughter to face the world alone. Lily couldn't believe her mother would be at all happy about the circumstances Lily had been left in.

How could God, if he truly loved her, allow her father to die? Hadn't she lost enough when her mother died of cancer? The unfairness of it had eaten at Lily like a cankerous sore. On that day she had turned her back on God and religion, ignoring the repeated efforts of friends, her pastor, and even her grandma. Lily wanted nothing to do with their preaching on forgiveness and the happiness that comes through the gospel of Jesus Christ. Religion hadn't worked for Lily anyway. Turning to God had only made her sorrow more painful. She'd prayed for her mother to get well and what happened? She'd died. Lily had prayed, no—pleaded—for her father's life on skinned knees that fall evening in the middle of an intersection. But what had her sliver of hope gained her? What fruits had her young faith yielded? Nothing but a broken heart and an unwanted move into her grandmother's house. Lily's belief in God's power had only given her false hope, magnifying her loss. Since God wasn't there to answer her prayers in her time of need, Lily had vowed to go it alone from then on.

Now, she kissed Juliet and lowered the cats to the floor, then wiped the tears from her eyes and pushed herself away from the door. Time to get on with living. With the flip of a switch, light flooded the small kitchen. The cats' water bowl was full, but Lily topped off the food bowl. An open box of cereal and a stack of unopened mail lay on the counter. She peered into the fridge and perused the shelves, settling on a yogurt. Then she dropped two slices of wheat bread into the toaster. She knew it was almost straight carbs, but she was too tired to cook anything. As she sank into the soft cushion of her couch, the log next to Colt's campfire came to mind. Lily let out a long sigh. When she finished eating, she added her plate and utensils to the sink and went to her room, Romeo and Juliet hot on her heels.

Trying to wash away the awful day, she stood in the shower until the water ran cold. How could something that started out so promising end so badly? Lily felt more miserable now than she had in the midst of full-blown amnesia. No wonder she'd forgotten everything. There wasn't much in her past worth remembering.

With her hair wrapped in a towel, she gathered up her dirty clothes. She dangled the cashmere sweater over the wastebasket, then drew it back. Maybe she would give the dry cleaners a chance at resurrecting the sweater before she tossed it. After all, it was one of her favorite items of clothing.

Everything else except the camouflage jacket fell in a heap in the clothes hamper. Lily brought the coat to her face and breathed in the smell of campfire smoke, horses, and Colt. Her parting glance of him haunted her. With handcuffs binding his wrists, he had craned his neck to look at her as armed men dragged him from the restaurant. The expression on his face seemed to morph from shock to hurt when the officers mentioned Lily's fiancé.

Unless she had lost her touch in reading people, Colt had feelings for her. Had her mind been doing its job the last few days, she never would have allowed herself to become so familiar with him when she was engaged to Nick. But the fact of the matter was, she hadn't remembered her commitment and most definitely had allowed herself to develop feelings for Colt. In fact, she'd openly flirted with him.

Angry with herself, she threw down the jacket. She would do what she could to ensure that Detective Hansen and Agent Dawson cleared Colt's name, and then she would forget about him. After all, she loved Nick.

Eleven

"Did one of the officers read you your Miranda rights?" the detective asked.

Colt lifted his handcuffed arms to scratch his forehead. "Yeah." After being pulled from his cell and left to sit alone for what felt like an hour in a small interrogation room, he was now talking to Detective Hansen of the local police department, and Agent Dawson of the FBI. Hansen was a tall, lanky guy with a goatee and receding hairline, and Dawson, the younger of the two, sported buzz-cut black hair. Dawson perched on the edge of the table, eyeing Colt suspiciously.

The officers asked him a bunch of questions they would've known the answers to if they had bothered to look at his driver's license. Dawson looked at the open laptop in front of him on the table. "Your prints didn't come up when we ran them through AFIS — Automated Fingerprint Identification System. One speeding ticket in Utah County last year, but prior to this arrest, you had a squeaky-clean record."

"Has the analysis come in on that partial yet?" Detective Hansen asked Dawson.

"Not yet."

Hansen glanced at Colt. "When did you meet Miss Vanasche?"

"I found her on Tuesday evening, unconscious, near an old Jeep road."

The detective raised his eyebrows. "Tuesday, you say?"

"Yeah."

"That was four days ago. Why didn't we hear about this on Tuesday?"

Colt's conscience yelled, *I told you so*. Right now his excuses for not notifying the authorities seemed pretty lame. He sat up a little straighter on the hard metal chair. "I was going to call, but I didn't have my cell phone, and even if I did, where I found her was a long way from any cell service. I would have considered coming down out of the mountains on Wednesday, but my truck transmission went out right before the hunt, and I knew I wouldn't have a vehicle waiting for me until the weekend when my brother could bring it up to the trailhead. It wasn't a life-or-death situation, and I was so far back in the mountains that it wasn't feasible to come out sooner when I didn't have a vehicle. Plus, Lily asked if she could stay in the mountains with me. Practically begged me not to take her down."

The FBI agent stood and circled the room while he said, "Let me make sure I understand what happened. So, you find a woman with obvious head trauma, and against your better judgment, you follow her advice. In the process, you deny her medical attention by keeping her in the mountains for days. Do you have any idea how many man hours and resources have been expended in the last four days searching for her?"

Colt swallowed hard, trying to keep down the bile that rose in his throat. "I'm sorry. I didn't think about that. She was very persuasive." He'd made a mistake — a critical lapse in judgment — and now he was paying for it. He should have put more than a halfhearted effort into finding a phone to call the cops when he first found her. He could have located the sheepherder. Searched for other hunters. Spent a long day and ridden Duke down to the main highway to flag down a motorist. But at the time Colt had no idea she'd been involved in something so serious—so criminal. Or maybe he just hadn't thought it through hard enough because he wanted to spend time with her.

"Where exactly is this Jeep road where you found Miss Vanasche? Could you point it out on a map?"

Colt nodded. "Of course."

Dawson looked at Hansen. "Can you grab a map of the area?"

The detective left, and Agent Dawson fired off another question. "Were you hunting with anyone?"

"My brother pulled the horse trailer up to the trailhead and dropped me off. Since he and my dad didn't draw tags, I hunted alone."

"In the past week, were you with anyone, other than Miss Vanasche, who can vouch for your whereabouts?" Dawson asked.

Colt's heart rate picked up a notch as he realized he had no alibi for the day of the bank robbery. He shook his head. "Other than the sheepherder I talked to on opening day, no."

The agent didn't respond immediately, because the door clicked and Hansen walked in. He spread a topographical map across the table. Colt leaned forward and studied the map. The chains rattled as he moved both hands over the intricate lines representing the familiar ridges and draws. He pointed as he explained, "I was here when I first saw her with my binos. I rode down this hillside, crossed this creek, and found her near this section of road. It isn't much of a road—you'd need an ATV or sturdy Jeep to get there."

The detective marked the location and typed something on his laptop.

Agent Dawson pinned his steely gaze on Colt. "Did you see any sign of a vehicle near where you found her?"

"Nothing. No tracks, either, but there were heavy rains earlier that day."

"Did you look around? Try to figure out where she came from?" Dawson said with a smirk.

"I glassed the entire valley with the binoculars but didn't see anything. No car. No one but her. There was no time to investigate. A bad storm was moving in—lightning, thunder, heavy rains. For both of our safety, I needed to get us to shelter."

While Dawson peppered Colt with questions, Hansen had been snooping through Colt's personal effects. He waved Dawson over to show him something on the camera. The detective lifted his head to stare at Colt. "So you'd never met Miss Vanasche before you found her on Tuesday, correct?"

"That's right."

Hansen lifted the camera and turned it toward Colt. "For complete strangers, the two of you are sure cozied up here. Maybe you can explain this picture to me."

The picture of Colt kissing Skye, posing between the massive elk antlers, seemed to laugh at him from his camera. Thinking about things from law enforcement's point of view, he realized his story seemed full of holes. He had made plenty of mischief as a kid, and more than once he'd been blamed for something his brother or one of their friends had done. But the closest Colt had come to real trouble was a one-day suspension for a prank gone bad during his sophomore year. How on earth had he managed to land himself in the county jail, restrained by cuffs on his hands and ankles, with a bunch of cops thinking he'd robbed a bank?

Colt's frustration flared at being accused of something he didn't do—this time in an epic way. "What does it look like? I'm kissing her."

The detective scowled. "I can see that. But this isn't the kind of picture strangers usually take of themselves. I'm starting to think you've known Miss Vanasche for quite some time."

"What? No! I told you I found her Tuesday evening. Maybe y'all didn't notice, but she is very pretty. And it didn't really matter to me that she was a stranger." Colt let out a disgusted grunt, knowing he'd given a flippant answer. The fatigue of the last few days had caught up to him.

The detective clicked off the camera and slid it into an evidence bag, along with Colt's wallet, cell phone, and keys. "I'm inclined to think you and Miss Vanasche staged that little kidnapping. Wouldn't you agree that robbing a bank would be a lot easier with a bank employee in your back pocket?"

Colt took a deep breath. "I wouldn't know. I've never robbed a bank."

"Where's the money, Mr. Murdock? It hasn't turned up in our search of your truck or trailer. Did you hide it in the woods?"

"I don't have the money," he said tightly. "I didn't rob any bank. I found Miss Vanasche on Tuesday night, and my story is never going to change, because I'm telling you the truth."

The detective removed a file from his briefcase and dropped it onto the table. "The surveillance cameras outside the bank caught the little scuffle between you and Miss Vanasche. She pulled the ski mask off your face so we have your picture. Colt, we know you were there. Maybe you were a pawn in Miss Vanasche's plan. Maybe it wasn't even your idea to rob the bank, or shoot anyone. Like you said, she's very persuasive. We'd like you to tell us what happened. Did things get a little out of hand? The man you shot didn't die, so you're lucky. Was it an accident?"

Colt looked from one interrogator to the other. "I have never shot anyone or robbed a bank. I don't know who you have pictures of, but it isn't me."

Detective Hansen pulled out a series of photos and slid them in front of Colt. He recognized Lily in her black dress pants and blue sweater. She appeared to be struggling as her abductor pushed her toward a white Ford Ranger. The man they thought was Colt wore a camouflage jacket and ski mask. In the second picture, the ski mask was on the ground. With the distance and graininess of the photo, Colt had to admit the guy did look like he could be his long-lost twin. He studied the picture looking for something they might have missed. "That's not me. Look! The guy has longer hair. And I've never owned a ski mask like that."

Undeterred, Dawson declared, "You'll need to give me something more convincing than that. Hair can be cut. Clothes can be borrowed, or used once and thrown away."

Colt let out a deep breath. "But if we were in this together, like you say, why would Lily pull off the ski mask? She's obviously struggling to get away from the guy. She's the victim here."

"Why don't *you* tell *us* why she tried to pull the mask off. Did you two have a little lover's spat when things didn't go like you planned in the bank?" said Dawson.

"I don't know! How many times do I have to tell you that I wasn't there? You have the wrong guy—end of story."

As if he was Colt's new best friend, Hansen said softly, "If you tell us where the money is and give us the details of Miss Vanasche's involvement in the robbery, we can put in a good word for you with the prosecutor and probably get you a reduced sentence. The courts will be much more lenient if they know you cooperated with us."

Colt raised his voice a notch. "I've been in the mountains for over a week. I had nothing to do with any bank robbery. If Lily Vanasche was involved, you'll have to ask her about it. I found her Tuesday evening, lying next to a patch of scrub oak with a goose egg as big as Texas, and blood dripping down her face. And yes, I kissed her three days later. But the last time I checked, kissing a woman wasn't a crime. You know what? I'm done talkin' to y'all. I'm going with that right to remain silent option until I can hire an attorney."

"Are you sure? We can speak to the prosecutor on your behalf. If you help us out a little, things will go a lot better for you."

Colt scowled back at them as he stood, turned his back, and shuffled toward the exit, the chain anchoring his wrists to his ankles rattling with each step. Agent Dawson walked ahead of him and signaled to the guards. The lock released and the door opened. "You let me know if you change your mind," Hansen said. "Prison is a hard place. I'd hate to see you get a longer sentence because you were unwilling to work with us."

Colt ignored the detective, and the guards escorted him back to his cell. In the stillness, the door clanged shut behind him.

A guard had delivered breakfast around five that morning. Colt had devoured everything on the tray, but that was three hours ago and it hadn't come close to filling him. Now, after the interrogation, if someone were to spread a feast in front of him, he doubted he could eat even a bite of it.

None of this would be happening if only Colt had listened to his conscience. When he had found Lily, he knew he should contact law enforcement as soon as possible. Instead, he had focused on his dream of taking a big bull elk with his bow. Lily's request to stay on the mountain for a few more days had conveniently gone along with that dream.

Twelve

Lily awoke briefly and peered at the surrounding darkness before trying to escape into sleep once more. She'd dreamed of riding Duke, her arms wrapped around Colt's waist. Her sleep-befuddled brain noticed the tent wasn't flapping in the wind, and for once her nose didn't feel cold. Half awake, she reached for Colt. Instead, her fingers slid across silky Egyptian cotton sheets.

With that Lily shot awake and turned on the bedside lamp. Of course there would be no Colt. He'd been ripped out of her arms. Frustrated, she threw off the down comforter and scooted to the edge of her bed. She needed to talk to that detective again. They must have spoken with Colt by now and realized he was not to blame for the robbery and kidnapping. He didn't deserve to be accused of those crimes, when he had been nothing but kind and helpful. Once she knew he was free of the mess she'd dragged him into, Lily could put his memory to rest. She glanced at the clock. Five in the morning was too early to do anything.

After tossing and turning for another two hours, she donned her silk robe and went in search of the detective's phone number. She found his business card in the pocket of Colt's jacket, only to realize she still didn't have her phone. She changed into yoga pants, a lightweight jacket, and Nikes. Looking at the row of high-heeled shoes across the bottom of her closet, she realized how lucky she had been to wear flats on the day she was kidnapped. Hiking mountains in dress flats was one thing, but hiking in heels would have been impossible.

Lily's purse was locked in her desk at the bank, so she dug a handful of twenties out of the emergency cash envelope in her nightstand drawer. She stuffed the bills, along with Detective Hansen's business card, into her jacket pocket. On her way out of her condo, she grabbed her extra set of keys and locked the door.

The wind whipping around the Point of the Mountain blew Lily's hair across her face as she jogged down the street. When she turned east toward the convenience store, the sun nearly blinded her.

"Thank you," she said to the man who held open the door for her. The girl behind the counter popped a bubble with her gum and didn't even look up from her magazine when Lily asked, "Do you have any of those disposable cell phones?"

The clerk pointed. "Third aisle on the right side."

Lily bought a phone and a small bottle of orange juice. Walking back toward her townhouse, she ripped open the packaging, clicked the phone on, and dialed the number on Detective Hansen's business card. After several rings, the call went to voicemail. Lily waited for the beep and then said, "Hi, Detective Hansen. This is Lily Vanasche. We spoke last night at the hospital about the robbery at the One National Bank. I wondered if you'd had a chance to talk with Colt Murdock and if he'd been released yet. Also, I wanted to make sure you knew he had no part in the robbery or my abduction."

She paused, then added, "If you could give me a call at this number, I'd appreciate it. Thank you." She disconnected the call and put the card and phone in her pocket.

Back at her house, Lily poured a glass of orange juice and sat at the table, staring at the phone and the business card. How

long would she have to wait for word on Colt? Was he sitting in a jail cell somewhere, or had the police come to their senses and released him?

She grabbed a notepad and pencil. She'd listened to him leave his phone number in a message to someone. If she could piece together the number, she could call him herself. Like many other Utah phone numbers, it had the familiar 801 area code. The next three numbers were 471, the same as her friend Angela's phone number. The last four digits were . . . what? Lily stuck the pencil in her teeth while she thought. After straining to recall the number Colt had spoken, she scribbled four different options on the paper, eventually scratching out two of them. With a hopeful smile she tried the first number combination.

The phone rang twice before a woman's voice answered. Beginning to cross out the number, Lily said, "I'm looking for Colt Murdock. By chance, is this his cell phone?"

"No. You must have the wrong number."

"Oh, I'm sorry," Lily said. She hung up the phone. If she recalled correctly, the second combination of numbers should be Colt's. Then again, her memory hadn't been her most reliable asset as of late. She dialed and waited. Five rings later, voicemail picked up. "This is Colt. Y'all leave your name and number and I'll call you back."

Relieved at getting the number right, Lily smiled at his subtle Southern drawl. Then an unexpected nervousness hit her with the force of a windstorm. *Considering what he's been through, I'm probably the last person on earth he wants to hear from.*

She disconnected the call, put her elbows on the table, and dropped her head to her hands. After five minutes, she sat up and redialed the number. Regardless of how Colt felt about her, she had to know what happened. She waited for the beep and said, "Colt, it's me, Lily . . . or I guess it's Skye to you. Look, I'm so sorry about last night. Call me, please. I hope you're all right. Bye." Disappointed, she hung up the phone and settled in to wait.

Thirteen

Sandwiched between two police officers, Colt scratched his bearded chin and scowled at the back of a third officer, who led him toward the exit of the county jail. Colt was long overdue for a shower, a shave, and a decent meal. This little detour had been a pain in the rear.

About an hour after Colt's return to his cell that morning, the door had swung open and Agent Dawson had stepped in. "I called in a favor with a friend at the crime lab. He said your fingerprints don't match the partial from the suspect," Dawson announced. "You're welcome to go as long as you don't leave the state. I expect to be able to get a hold of you if I have any more questions."

"Yes, sir."

Now, Colt's thoughts turned to Lily. Detective Hansen's comments during the interrogation still bothered him. Had Lily been involved in that bank robbery, or was she an innocent victim? If she was involved and it had gone awry, maybe her partner-in-crime had taken his fist to her face and abandoned her in the wilderness. Lily could have been playing Colt all along—could have made up the whole amnesia story. Had she used him? At the time, he'd found it strange that she hadn't been anxious to return to civilization. But if she was guilty, what better place to hide out for a few days, than with an unsuspecting hunter who had no access to the news?

The guards returned Colt's clothes and personal effects, and he found himself a free man once again. He rounded the corner and spied his truck and trailer sitting in the lot behind the jail, his horses tied next to the trailer. When the officers stepped aside, Colt made a beeline for the truck. He shielded his eyes against the glare of the morning sunlight. They'd given him the zip-top bag containing his personal effects, so he pulled out his keys and unlocked his door. Duke lifted his head and let out a shrill, ear-piercing whinny at the sight of him. "You and me both, buddy," Colt said. "Let's get the heck outta here."

He loaded his horses and tossed the water buckets into the truck bed. With the jail behind him, he checked his voicemail messages. His mother had called twice, Jared once. There were two missed calls and a voicemail from a number Colt didn't recognize.

He listened to his mama's voicemails. Sounding worried, she asked him to call her as soon as possible. His family knew he had planned to ride out on Saturday, and his first stop would be his parents' place to drop off the horses and the trailer.

Jared's voicemail message was about the same, but he added, "I guess I'll hike in and start looking for you if I don't hear anything by this afternoon."

Knowing Jared might change his mind and start searching sooner, Colt pushed the call-back option on the voicemail screen. After one ring, his brother said hello.

"Hey, Jared. I'm in Nephi. On my way to Mom and Dad's."

"Is everything okay? We got worried when you didn't answer your phone last night."

"I'm good," Colt said, not wanting to go into all the details over the phone. "Will you be at Sunday dinner?"

"Planning on it," his brother replied.

"We'll talk then. I've got a monster bull to show you, too."

"Ahh, I can't wait. See you later," Jared said and hung up.

Next, Colt left a message for his mama—no doubt his parents were still at Sunday church services.

He glanced at the last new voice message on his phone, from someone who wasn't in his contacts list. *Probably for work*, Colt thought, deciding it could wait until Monday. He tossed his phone onto the seat of the truck.

Forty minutes later, he turned down the road to his parents' ten-acre lot, which backed up to the foothills of Springville. During the years since they'd bought the place, the suburban neighborhood had crept closer, until only a few acreage properties remained.

Colt turned his horses out to pasture, unhooked the trailer, and parked his pickup in front of the shop. His family had always raised a beef cow or two, and years ago his dad had built a small meat locker. Now, Colt turned it on and checked the temperature gauge before hauling in both coolers and the trophy head. After giving the locker a few hours to cool down, he would hang the elk quarters.

He heard the crunch of footfalls on the gravel, followed by his dad's voice. "Colt, that you?"

He closed the door to the locker and turned. "Yeah, it's me."

His father, dressed in his Sunday best, stepped into the shop, followed by Colt's youngest brother, Sam. "Hey, Colt, did you get anything?" Sam asked.

Colt smiled as he tilted his head toward the door of the meat locker. "Do bears poop in the forest?"

Sam darted for the locker, a big grin on his face. His dad placed a hand on Colt's shoulder as he began unpacking his gear. "Your mother was worried last night. We expected you back before the Sabbath."

Colt shrugged. "Just took me longer than I expected to get out of the mountains and back home." Guilt lanced his conscience for not being completely forthright. *Later.* He would tell his father everything later, when the wound wasn't so raw and Colt wasn't so tired and hungry.

"Would you look at this!" Sam stood in the doorway, holding the elk head by the antlers. "What do you think this will score?"

Colt watched as his dad and brother admired the rack. They even pulled out the tape measure, a pencil, and a scrap of paper so they could write down the details. Ten minutes later, Sam looked up from the calculator app on his phone. "Colt, you got yourself a whopper—379 and 3/4. Round up and you've got a 380 bull!"

Colt smiled as his dad walked by him and slapped his shoulder. "Way to go, Son. Your mother's making lunch, so hurry on up to the house when you're finished here."

Sam stayed at his big brother's side, helping him unload the gear and spread out the tent and tarps to dry. "Help me get the trash out of the cab, and then we'll go eat," Colt said.

The sun was high in the sky, and here in the valley it felt more like the peak of summer than the beginning of fall. Sam lifted an old soda can from the floor mat in Colt's truck and then held up the zip-top bag that had held Colt's personal effects during his brief incarceration. Sam read the slip of paper itemizing the bag's contents and said, "You were in jail?"

"Give it here." Colt leaned across the seat to grab it.

Chuckling, Sam moved the bag out of reach. "Is that where you were?"

Colt raised his eyes to meet his brother's. "Give me that."

"What did you do anyway? Get caught poaching that monster bull?" Sam took a step back and slammed the passenger door.

Colt headed around the front of the truck. "No. Besides, you know they would have confiscated the elk if I'd poached it."

"Come on, Colt, what happened? I won't tell nobody."

His seventeen-year-old brother was a head shorter than him, so relieving him of the evidence by brute force was easy. Colt grabbed the kid and yanked the bag from his hand, then stuffed it under the driver seat and locked both doors. Ignoring his pesky brother, he put his phone in his pocket and gathered an armful of empty water bottles to carry to the house.

Sam took a running step to keep up with him as he marched across the gravel. "You were in jail, weren't you?"

Colt doubted he would give up now that his curiosity had been piqued, and the last thing he wanted was Sam asking questions in front of their parents before Colt could even shower and get a bite to eat. Slowing his pace as he neared the back door, he nodded.

"For how long?" Sam asked.

"Overnight."

"What did you do?"

"Nothing."

"Come on. Guys don't spend a night in jail over nothing."

"They thought I was someone else," Colt said, thinking this was the last story he wanted to be telling right now. "I promise I'll fill you in later, but until then keep it quiet."

Sam opened the back door to the house. "Fine, I'll wait."

After downing two of their mom's turkey sandwiches and a bowl of ice cream, Colt showered and stretched out to take a nap. The guest bedroom in the basement was at least ten degrees cooler than the rest of the house, perfect for a Sunday afternoon siesta. At some point during his dream about hauling out elk quarters while policemen chased him down the mountain, he heard his ringtone. He rolled over and picked up the phone. The call looked like it had come from the same unknown number that had left a message while he'd been in jail. He closed his eyes until the phone pinged to let him know he had a new voicemail.

Pans rattled in the kitchen and floorboards squeaked overhead—it must be nearly time to eat. Family dinner was a Sunday tradition at the Murdock household. Mama cooked the traditional fried chicken and mashed potatoes. All the children, even those married with kids, were invited. Following dinner, everyone sat around the living room and visited. Before Colt left tonight, maybe he could pull his dad aside and talk to him about what had happened.

Colt got up and stuffed his phone in his pocket as he headed upstairs. Jared sat on the couch with his wife, Danielle. The source of the noise became apparent as Sam, pretending to be a bear, chased Jared and Danielle's three kids across the living room and down the hall. Colt moved out of the way to let the giggling children race past. Jared jumped to his feet and smiled. "Brother, where's that monster bull? I've been waiting for hours for you to wake up."

Colt grinned. "Yeah, right. You just got here."

Jared grabbed him by the shoulders and squeezed. "Come on, let's see it. Is it out in the shop?" Colt nodded, and both brothers turned for the door.

In the meat locker, Jared took one look at the elk head and gave a low whistle. "Whoa, that there is a dandy. Where did you find him?"

Jared and Colt each had a hand wrapped around the elk's rack as they faced each other. "In the timber just below the meadow to the east of where I camped," Colt said, then launched into the play-by-play account of the moments leading up to the shot. Of all his siblings, he shared the closest bond of brotherhood and friendship with Jared. Growing up, the two of them had been inseparable.

Nearing the end of his story, Colt said, "After the bull went down, I realized I'd left my headlamp in my saddlebag. The sun had set, and where he lay in the heavy timber it would be too dark to field dress him without it. Plus, I wanted to hurry back and check on this lady I found a couple of days earlier, so I—"

Jared's eyebrows shot up. "Say what?"

Conjuring up the image of Lily smiling at him, Colt shook his head. "It's a long story." Sam yelled from the back porch to say dinner was ready, and Colt jumped at the excuse, stepping away from the elk head and toward the door. "Come on—you know how Mama gets when anybody's late to dinner."

Jared followed him out of the shop and gave him a playful jab. "Wait a minute. You can't mention a girl and then leave me hanging. What do you mean you *found* her? Or are you just pulling my leg?"

"It's no big deal. I'll tell you more about it later." Normally Colt would have enjoyed telling the story of finding Lily, just as he enjoyed telling hunting tales, but after being arrested and interrogated, the experience had left a bad taste in his mouth. If Colt lucked out, his brother would assume it was nothing more than an exaggerated hunting story from a proverbial bachelor, and he'd stop asking for details. At that moment, Colt would just as soon forget he ever met Lily Vanasche. But that was proving to be more difficult than he'd imagined. The frequency with which the "lady with no name" popped into his mind kept mocking his efforts to banish her from his memories. The taste of her lips, and the way her fingers fit perfectly between his—it was all too good to be real. He had to let it go. She was nothing but trouble anyway. And for Pete's sake, on top of everything else, she was engaged.

"You okay?" Jared asked.

Colt glanced to the side and realized he must have been scowling, because Jared was watching him with a furrowed brow. Colt forced his lips to turn up in a smile and said, "Yeah, just tired is all. You know how much work it is getting a bull out of the mountains."

His brother nodded. "Yeah, that's true. But did you really run into a girl up there? Was she hunting?"

"Boys, hurry up!" yelled their mother from the porch. "Food's gettin' cold waitin' for y'all."

Relieved, Colt said to Jared, "I'll tell you the whole story after dinner."

The family gathered around the long table, with the younger kids sitting on barstools at the kitchen counter. A feast, second only to what Colt's mother served on Thanksgiving and Christmas, lay spread across the table. Steam rose from the mashed potatoes and chicken. Colt's father said grace and then everyone loaded their plates. But as the first bite hit Colt's tongue, his brother Sam declared, "All right, Colt, let's hear the story."

The front door opened, and Colt's younger brother Bo walked in. "Sorry I'm late."

Their mother, with a mix of gray and strawberry-blond hair, waved Bo toward the table. "Come sit down, honey, we just said grace." Then she narrowed her eyes at her youngest son. "Now Sam, let Colt eat. I'm sure he's hungry. There'll be plenty of time for hunting stories later."

"I don't care about the huntin' story," Sam said. "I just wanna hear why he spent a night in jail."

If Colt could have shot daggers with a glare, he would have silenced Sam for good. Jared's kids were the only ones still eating. Everyone else sat motionless, gawking at Colt.

Fourteen

Lily huffed in frustration. Twice she'd called Colt's number and left messages, but he hadn't called back. According to one of the detectives, he had been released from jail hours ago. Lily phoned Agent Dawson, who refused to tell her what had happened with Colt. Dawson informed her that the FBI wanted to speak with her again and would be in touch in the next few days.

His statement left her with an uneasy feeling that law enforcement didn't believe everything she had told them the night before. Lily hadn't given their questions much thought but had simply answered them off the top of her head. After all, she was the injured victim, so wasn't it obvious? Thinking back now, she recalled the skeptical glances between the detectives, the lift of Agent Dawson's eyebrows whenever her answer was "I don't remember" or "I don't know," and the way Detective Hanson murmured "Uh-huh" after Lily said something. Were these signs of the officers' doubt? What had Colt told them? They had discouraged her from contacting him, but she didn't care. She needed to talk with him.

The doorbell rang, followed by the click of the lock. Lily listened. "Lil, it's me," Nick yelled up the stairs.

She exhaled and picked up her lipstick. "Almost ready." She applied the color, rubbed her lips together once, and then tilted her head to the side, leaning closer to the mirror. Her foundation, applied liberally to the bruise on her cheek, pretty much hid the ugly yellow-purple hue of her skin. Hopefully the blemish would fade away soon. The cut on her palm still hurt, so she covered it with antibiotic ointment and stuck a small bandage over it.

Nick stood waiting at the bottom of the stairs, one hand in the pocket of his jeans, the other resting on the railing. She had known him for years. He had been one of her best friends in college, and she could always count on him. Like he had done probably a hundred times, he smiled at her and said, "You look great. What do you feel like eating tonight?"

Lily reached the last step, careful not to trip over her cats. They had been underfoot all day. Nick pulled her into his arms and pressed his lips to hers in a quick kiss. He inhaled, one side of his mouth quirking up. "You *smell* nice, too," he said. "A lot better than last night when you were wearing that redneck jacket."

She pulled back. "What's that supposed to mean?"

Nick smiled, his hands finding her waist. "Nothing, except I missed you."

He moved toward her, and she stepped back until the wall halted her retreat. "It sounded like you were slamming the coat that kept me from freezing to death while I was stranded in the mountains." Her tart reply surprised her. She had known what Nick meant, but that hadn't stopped her reaction.

He gave her a sultry smile. "No never. I'm only trying to pay you a compliment on how delicious you smell right now. Maybe we should dine in."

Lily mentally cursed the image that popped into her mind. She'd seen that same hungry expression in Colt's eyes the last time he had kissed her. Never a fan of love triangles, she felt annoyed that her memory seemed bent on making this date a threesome. She forced a giggle, then glanced at the door. "I feel like Italian. What about that little place we found last summer?"

Nick chuckled, then slid his fingers over her wrist and took her hand in his. "Italian it is, my love. Nana Stella must be rubbing off on you."

At the mention of Nick's grandmother, with her curly gray hair and vibrant personality, Lily said, "Your nana does have a knack for getting people to see things her way." The older woman reminded Lily so much of her own grandmother, before Alzheimer's got hold of her.

The high-backed booth and the Italian bistro's dim lighting gave Lily a welcomed sense of anonymity. She had flipped on the television that afternoon, and a partial clip of what Nick had filmed the night before was the teaser for the evening news. His face was already well known throughout the state, and his efforts to rescue Lily had flooded the media with her photo and story. She feared the two of them together would stand out like a beacon. Already, wherever they went, people would stop to chat with her fiancé, or simply ask out of curiosity if he was Nick Borino, the news guy, so Lily imagined it would only be worse now. According to Angela, he had garnered the sympathies of just about everyone in Utah when he had pleaded for the public's help in locating his kidnapped future wife.

Lily took a deep breath and gazed at her handsome fiancé. "It is so nice to feel normal again. The sensation of not knowing yourself is awful. Terrifying, actually."

Nick reached across the table and took her hand in his. "I can't imagine. I'm sorry I wasn't there for you."

"I managed, and I was lucky that hunter found me when he did, or it could have turned out much worse."

"Tell me about him. Was he some old-timer living out in the boonies?"

Flashing back to the image of Colt loading his elk quarters onto his horses, his muscles bulging under the strain, Lily couldn't help but smile. "No, not exactly. He's probably closer to your age."

Nick's eyes narrowed. "Was there anyone else with him?"

"Just his horses—Duke and Charger."

"Where did you sleep? Was there a cabin or something?"

Lily shook her head, thinking of the endless expanse of mountains dotted with meadows, pines, aspens, and wild flowers, like an intricate patchwork quilt. "No, there was nothing like that. He had a tent."

"You slept in his tent for four nights?" Nick demanded to know.

"Where else was I supposed to sleep? It poured rain that first night." This was not the dinner conversation Lily had hoped for.

Nick leaned back and huffed. "I still don't get it. Why didn't he bring you out of the mountains the next day? Why did you stay with him for so long?"

"I didn't remember anything—not you, not Angela, nothing about my job or my life. At the time, he was the only person I knew, so it seemed like a good idea to sit tight until some of my memories came back . . . until I at least had a vague notion of who I was. All things considered, I did the best I could."

The waitress brought the food, and Nick and Lily watched as she set the steaming plates on the table. "Can I get you anything else?" the girl asked. "More bread?"

Lily shook her head. Nick smiled at the waitress and said, "No thanks. This looks great."

She walked away, heading for another booth.

"Lily, I'm sorry," Nick offered. "Just don't ever do that to me again. I was worried sick about you."

She knew he meant to apologize, but why couldn't he sympathize with her a bit? It wasn't her fault she had been kidnapped, beaten, and dumped off in the mountains for dead— and on top of it all, had lost her memory. Instead of showing empathy and concern for her, Nick was making it all about himself. However, since the last thing Lily wanted right now was an argument, she replied, "It's okay. If I get my way, I'll never again be held hostage during a bank robbery, then kidnapped and abandoned in the mountains."After cutting off a piece of chicken and spinning some fettuccini noodles around her fork, she held the bite over her plate and watched a line of steam dissipate into the air. How could she change the subject? Finally, she said, "Anything exciting happen in the news while I was gone?"

Nick swallowed the bait and launched into a summary of the nation's top news stories for the week, while Lily savored the flavor of her food.

As they left the restaurant, an older couple stopped them at the door. The women said, "Nick Borino?"

Nick smiled. "Yes?"

"Is this your lovely bride-to-be?"

Lily pasted a grin on her face.

The woman grabbed her husband's arm. "Look, Henry, this is the cute couple I was telling you about. She got kidnapped in that bank robbery, and if it weren't for such a dedicated fiancé, she might not have been recognized. Can you imagine? The poor thing had amnesia." She turned back to Lily and Nick. "Are you feeling better, dear? You look well."

"I'm doing much better. Thank you," Lily said as Nick reached out to shake the woman's hand. She looked like she might have blushed when he held her wrinkled hand between both of his.

"Thank you for watching our news broadcast. It's because of faithful viewers like you that I found my sweetheart."

The gray-haired woman adjusted her glasses and laughed, obviously enchanted by Nick's charm. "Oh, you're welcome. I wouldn't watch anyone else."

Fifteen

Jared leaned back in his chair, smiling. "Jail, little brother? How long were you going to keep that one a secret? Please tell me you didn't do something stupid like forget to tag your bull."

Colt met his brother's amused grin with a glare. "I tagged the bull." He turned to Sam. "You agreed not to say anything. You really let me down, you know that?"

His dad cleared his throat, and when Colt looked into his eyes, it was like facing a double-barreled shotgun. "Colton, what do you have to say for yourself?"

He lowered his fork to his plate and squared up his shoulders, feeling eight years old instead of twenty-eight. "I didn't do anything wrong, Dad. I spent the night in jail because the police thought I was some guy who robbed a bank and kidnapped a lady named Lily Vanasche. After fingerprinting and interrogating me, they let me go."

Colt's little sister, Lizzy, jumped into the conversation. "The Camo Bandit? They thought *you* were the Camo Bandit! Why would they think that?"

"Whoa! You were the hunter who found Lily Vanasche?"

Colt nodded in response to Jared's question. Lizzy leaned forward and said excitedly, "Her picture was all over the news this week, and so was the surveillance video of the kidnapping. It was crazy how it happened. She's so pretty, and did you know she's engaged to Nick Borino from Channel 2 News? Last year, he was voted one of the state's most eligible bachelors. Anyway, you've got to tell us what happened, Colt!"

He frowned. "She's engaged to the guy on the news?"

"Of course," Lizzy said. "His channel ran the clip about her kidnapping almost every commercial break for days. It was so romantic—the way Nick begged everyone to look for her. I hope I fall in love with someone as devoted as that."

Colt's mama put a hand on his arm. "Y'all be quiet now and let him tell us what happened."

He looked at his sister first. "Lizzy, after dinner I want you to show me that news clip with the surveillance video."

"Okay, but tell us how you found her."

Colt relayed the events of the past four days, careful to leave out the romantic kisses, the laughs, and the personal stories Lily had drawn out of him. Even though he recited the story more like a travel log than a novel, his family seemed to hang on every word.

When he finished, Lizzy jumped up from the table and darted down the hall.

"Sounds to me like the Lord had a hand in putting you on that particular ridge at that precise moment," Colt's father declared. "I wouldn't have wanted my daughter spending a night alone in the high country, especially during a thunderstorm. I don't understand why you didn't ride her out of the mountains that next day, but all's well that ends well, I suppose."

"In hindsight that would have been the smart thing to do," Colt said, looking at his now-cold plate of food.

Jared chuckled. "I don't know what it is about you, Brother, but you're a magnet for trouble."

Danielle gasped and smacked her husband's arm. "Jared, that isn't nice."

"Well, it's true," he insisted. "Ever since we were kids, Colt's been in the thick of things."

Colt slid his knife through his piece of chicken, then skewered the bite with his fork. "That's because I always had your back, big brother." He raised the knife toward Jared for emphasis. "I saved your skin more times than you can count. I never once ratted you out to the principal — or Dad, either — and don't you forget it."

"No arguing at the table, boys," their mama said.

Bo, who had always been the studious and serious brother, put in, "I'm glad you're back safe and everything turned out okay, Colt. She sounds like the one who's a magnet for trouble. Good thing she's someone else's problem now."

All afternoon Colt had told himself the same thing. So why did Bo's words, which were probably true, make him feel like he'd taken a load of buckshot in the gut?

Lizzy returned and set the laptop on the edge of the table next to Colt. "Watch this."

The Channel 2 News logo filled the screen, and their theme song blasted out of the computer's small speaker. Colt couldn't help but feel a strong dislike for the handsome Nick Borino, who stood in front of a bank, giving a brief summary of the facts relating to the recent robbery there. "The FBI said the suspect walked into One National Bank and fired two rounds, disabling two surveillance cameras. He approached the teller's desk with an army-style duffle bag and demanded money. The man took one bank employee hostage, then shot and injured the bank's manager before getting away with an undisclosed amount of cash. The suspect is described as a white man in his late 30s or early 40s, between 5'10" and 6'2", and weighing 180 to 200 pounds, with light hair and a beard. He was wearing a ski mask, camouflage shirt, and blue jeans. The FBI is investigating in partnership with the police department." The screen showed a quote from the bank president, and the voice changed to a recording. "A reward of up to $10,000 is being offered for information leading to the arrest and conviction of the suspect and any accomplices. One National Bank is committed to the welfare and safety of its employees and customers."

While Nick Borino spoke, the video feed switched to a brief clip from the surveillance tape. Wearing a camouflage jacket and ski mask, a man entered the bank with a raised handgun. He wore a glove on his left hand, which held the duffle bag, but the hand holding the gun was bare. Methodically, he shot out two camera lenses, leaving nothing but gray static, before the feed switched to a different camera.

The outside cameras captured the man leaving the bank and dragging Lily toward an older white Ford Ranger with a shell that was missing the back hatch. She fought her captor all the way and yanked the ski mask off his head as he opened the passenger door. Colt felt his fists clench when the man brought the butt of his gun down on her head. The robber shoved her crumpled body into the passenger side of the truck, slammed the door, and then picked up the ski mask before running around to the driver's side. On the way, he tossed the duffle bag through the broken back hatch and into the truck bed.

The screen showed Lily's picture. Her blue eyes sparkled. Her blond hair fell as straight and smooth as corn silk down to her shoulders, and pink lipstick outlined her perfect lips. Reporter Nick Borino informed the public that the woman taken in the bank robbery was Lily Vanasche, his fiancée, and pleaded for help in finding her. The screen switched to a still shot of the robber just before he bent to pick up the ski mask—it was one of the pictures Colt had seen during his interrogation. A picture of the Ford Ranger, with the blurred face of a different man standing next to it and the license plate number enlarged in the lower left corner, came up on the screen next. "The vehicle used in the robbery," Nick Borino said, "was stolen from the Timpooneke Trailhead parking lot at the base of Mount Timpanogos in American Fork

Canyon. If you have any information that can help the police find this vehicle or identify the man in the surveillance video, also known as the Camo Bandit, please call one of these numbers." FBI and local police department phone numbers followed.

When the clip ended, Lizzy closed the laptop and looked at Colt. "With your beard, you do look like that picture of the Camo Bandit."

"Thanks! But I'm definitely not him. I can tell you that for sure," Colt said, then resumed eating his dinner.

His little sister smiled. "Don't you think they're the cutest couple ever? He's like her knight in shining armor—"

Colt almost gagged on the piece of broccoli in his mouth. "Knight in shining armor? The guy probably couldn't mount a horse to save his life."

"Whatever," Lizzy said. "Nowadays, knights in shining armor don't ride ponies. They use technology."

"Nick Borino and all his fancy technology did nothing to rescue Lily. It was Duke that got her out of the mountains."

"Maybe so, but it was someone who watched the news clip who saw her and called 9-1-1," Lizzy argued. She liked to argue everything. "That's how she ultimately got back to Nick."

Thinking that his sister would make a great lawyer someday, Colt said, "Lily was doing just fine with me, and I spent a night in jail because of that guy's stupid news clip."

Lizzy tossed her hair over her shoulder and set the computer on the counter. "You disagree with everything? I'll bet you think she's pretty, though, right?"

Colt raised his eyebrows. "Oh, I know she's pretty."

His sister's mouth fell open. "I totally thought you'd blow me off and say something like 'Not really,' or 'She's okay.'"

He stood and picked up his plate. At the kitchen sink, he paused to scrape the last bite of food into his mouth. Lizzy followed him with her dishes. "Do you like her, Colt?" When he didn't answer, she said, "Come on, tell me."

"Liz, I don't even know her," he said, raising his voice in agitation. "She wouldn't tell me anything . . . kept saying she didn't remember. I figured out her name at the same time the cops slapped the handcuffs on me."

"Lizzy, drop it!" their mama interrupted. "Come help me dish up the peach cobbler. Sam and Bo, finish clearing off the table. And y'all let Colt be. He's had a rough week, and the last thing he needs is a bunch of pestering from his family."

Later that evening, as Colt loaded the last of his things into his truck, his mama said, "Honey, this is the week your dad and I will be in Tennessee, remember? I want you to stop by and check on Sam and Lizzy while we're gone. Maybe spend the night. They should be fine, but I'd feel better if I knew someone was with them."

He hugged her then closed the tailgate. "Sure thing, Mama. Thanks for dinner."

Colt's dad wrapped his arm around his wife and asked, "You have everything you need for the meeting tomorrow, Colt?"

"Yeah, I worked up all the contract details before I left. I'll let you know how it goes after I talk with Mark."

"Sounds good. I'll be in Spanish Fork with Jared in the morning for inspections, and then I'm taking your mother to the airport." Colt's father smiled at her before looking at his son once more. "Call me if anything comes up."

Colt climbed into his truck and put on his seatbelt. "Okay, have fun. Hey, Dad, I already mentioned this to Jared, but you two might get a call from the FBI."

His dad's face grew serious. "All right."

"Good night, Dad."

As Colt drove down the long driveway, he worked his phone out of his pocket. He might as well check the voicemails from those missed calls, in case it was someone from the Alpine School District, wanting to reschedule the meeting. He touched "Play" and switched his phone to speaker mode. The feminine voice gave him a jolt of adrenaline. "Colt, it's me, Lily . . . or I guess it's Skye to you. Look, I'm so sorry about what happened last night. Call me, please. I hope you're all right. Bye."

He tossed his phone onto the passenger seat and switched on the radio. After the mess she'd gotten him in, she was the last person he should be talking to. He surfed through his preset favorites, trying to find a song he liked. But instead of distracting him, he conjured up the memory of taking Lily's hand in his own while she had pressed the same buttons on his radio a day earlier. Colt flipped the power off and ran his fingers through his hair.

In spite of his best efforts, he thought of nothing but the pretty blond during the twenty-minute drive to his apartment in Orem. Arms loaded with gear, he climbed the flight of stairs and piled everything on the welcome mat his mother had given him for Christmas. Inside the apartment, the air felt warm and stuffy. Colt dropped his gear by the couch, cracked open a couple of windows, and went back to the truck for his bow, cowboy hat, and phone. He clicked the lock button on the keyless remote and heard his truck honk once in response.

With the kitchen light on, he unrolled the set of blueprints and began reviewing his construction notes regarding the contract proposal for the new elementary school in Alpine School District. After ten minutes of staring at the black lines and measurements without really seeing them, he left the table.

The fridge was bare except for a can of root beer, some cheese, half a loaf of bread, and condiments. Colt popped the top on the soda can and took a swig. His phone sat on the counter, begging him to call Lily back. But maybe it wouldn't be smart, in case the detectives decided to snoop around in his personal life. They had discouraged him from having contact with anyone involved in the case. Plus, Colt had no right to be thinking about her like he was—she had her fancy fiancé to take care of her now. Why would the girl even care what happened to Colt anyway? He'd be better off forgetting he ever laid eyes on her.

Sixteen

Standing in the pale porch light, Lily tucked her hair behind her ear and kissed Nick goodnight. "Thank you for dinner. Hopefully, I'll have my car, purse, and phone back tomorrow."

He smiled. "You will. I'll call you after my shift and we can get together. Sleep tight, sweetheart."

"You too, Nick."

She stepped inside and closed the door behind her. Insistent meows pierced the air. "Come on you two. Time for bed." Romeo and Juliet followed her up the stairs, watched as she brushed her teeth, and then climbed into bed with her.

Lily let out a long sigh. The day had bordered on miserable, especially when compared to the time she'd spent in the mountains. Just as she began to analyze the odd direction of her thoughts, her disposable cell phone rang. She jumped up and ran to grab it from the counter, then connected the call and said hello.

"Hey, Lil, are you still out with Mr. Hot Stuff?"

Normally, Angela's spunky voice triggered a smile, but tonight Lily bit back a negative comment and said, "No, Nick just dropped me off. How are you?"

"I'm great. I know I already talked your ear off this morning, but remember that bridesmaid dress I showed you last week?"

Thinking, Lily ran her fingers through her hair, and when she didn't answer immediately, Angela said, "Oh, I almost forgot about the amnesia thing. It's okay if you don't remember. I found the perfect bridesmaid dress online last week, and today I was in this bridal shop and they had the exact dress in stock. I need you to come with me and try it on. My sister loves it, but I want you to tell me what you think, since you've got to wear it too."

Lily got back in bed and propped a few pillows behind her. "Sure, but tomorrow will probably be crazy at work, and I might be doing something with Nick in the evening. Could we try for Tuesday or Wednesday?"

"On Tuesday, Damian and I meet with the photographer. Let's do Wednesday. Did your hunter guy call you back yet?"

Lily sighed. "No. I've called twice and I'm still waiting. Do you think he's ignoring me?"

"I doubt it. Maybe he had a ton of messages and he hasn't gotten to yours yet. It's not like he would recognize your number. Or maybe he's just swamped after being on vacation. You did say he'd been in the mountains for a week or something, right?"

That made sense to Lily. "I'm sure he has a million things to do and calling the crazy lady who interrupted his hunt is probably the last thing on his list."

"From what you told me," Angela said, "it's more like the hot chick who spiced up his hunt. The guy would be nuts not to dial your number the second he hears that message."

"I hope you're—"

"Oh, Damian's calling me. Can I call you back in a minute?"

Lily smiled. Angela would win the prize in a most-smitten-bride contest. "Go! Talk to Damian," Lily said. "Don't worry about calling me tonight if it's late. I'm dead tired anyway."

"Thanks, you're the best. See you at work."

Angela's excitement had been bubbling over the top since the night she said yes to Damian. Lily wondered what was wrong with her that she had barely enjoyed her date with her own fiancé after being away from him for days.

Romeo climbed into her lap, and the moment Lily's hand touched his neck he purred like an engine. "Why can't I be as happy as Angela? Huh, Romeo? Do you have any words of wisdom for me?" After a long pause, she said, "Probably not, considering who you're named after."

As expected, the feline didn't offer more than a curious stare from his gray-green eyes. Lily leaned her head back, concentrating on the tickle of his whiskers against her arm and the soft purr in his throat instead of her problems. She jumped when her phone rang and fumbled between the folds of the covers to find it. "Hey, Angela, that was quick."

A deep male voice chuckled, then said, "Sorry to disappoint you, but it's not Angela."

Lily leaned forward and held the phone with both hands. "Colt?"

"Yeah, it's me. I got your messages."

"Are you okay? I was so worried about you."

"I'm fine," he said, the laughter gone from his voice.

"Tell me what happened. Please." He didn't say anything, so Lily added, "I feel so bad you got dragged into this. I would have done a hundred things differently if I'd remembered what was going on in my life. This whole thing is a nightmare. I'm so confused right now. All day I've been wondering if maybe the police didn't believe me last night. The FBI wants to talk to me again, and I don't know what else to tell them. I honestly don't remember the bank robbery, or being kidnapped, or . . ."

"I'm sure it'll be all right," Colt assured her. "Everything usually works out in the end, you'll see. Just have a little faith."

Lily couldn't repress a huff. "I'm not even sure I know what faith is."

"You need to hold to your belief that they will find whoever is responsible and don't lose hope. My uncle is a criminal-defense lawyer, and he says that given enough time, the truth always comes out."

Lily had been fighting to keep her emotions in check ever since she heard Colt's voice. All she felt like doing was crying on his shoulder. She pressed her fingers to her eyes and took a deep breath. "Okay. Thank you for the pep talk."

"You're welcome."

"So what did you do today?"

Colt chuckled. "Let's see. My day started at five AM with a tray of breakfast at the county jail—three pancakes that tasted like wet cardboard, two links of grisly sausage, and a cup of mushy fruit that must have been canned over twenty years ago. Then I got to experience the pleasure of walking in hand-and-ankle cuffs to the interrogation room. That was fun. Then I sat through a brutal interview with two detectives who asked me stupid questions and didn't bother listening to any of my answers, while they tried every angle possible to pin your kidnapping and that robbery on me. If not for the fact that my fingerprints didn't match with the partial print they had from the real criminal, I'd probably still be sitting in that jail cell."

"Oh my gosh, Colt. I'm so sorry," Lily said. "What happened with your horses?"

"They stood tied to the trailer all night. But give them a couple of days out to pasture and they'll be as good as new."

"I'm glad it worked out okay."

"Me too," he said.

"We should get together soon. I'm still trying to piece together what happened, and maybe it would help to hear about what they told you."

"That's probably not such a good idea, Lily."

Her heart raced. The thought of never seeing him again nearly made her sick. She spied his fleece jacket in a crumpled pile next to the wall. "Well, I've at least got to get your jacket back to you, so what if we meet after work tomorrow?"

"You can keep that one. I've got two others just like it."

"I am absolutely not taking your jacket. Where will you be at 5:30 PM?"

"It's no big deal, really—"

She raised her voice, cutting him off. "Colt, I won't take no for an answer. Where can we meet?"

"I can stop by the bank. Will you be there at 5:30?"

"Yes. Do you know where it is?"

"I saw the news clips your fiancé did."

"Oh." Lily remembered the video segments she'd watched on the Internet earlier that morning. Nick stood in front of One National Bank, talking about the robbery and listing the cross streets. The anguish and worry in his face caused her to consider the situation from his perspective. Poor Nick had been through a harrowing experience as well. The Sunday morning news had featured him summarizing the details of Lily's rescue and mentioning her amnesia and injuries. While grateful for his unrelenting efforts on her behalf, by the time she'd watched every clip the station had posted, she was tired of hearing about her ordeal.

After a moment of silence, Colt asked, "Are you doing okay? How's your head feeling?"

"I'm good. The doctor says I may never remember all the events surrounding my injury, but at least my goose egg is almost gone, and with a little makeup, you can hardly tell I've got a bruise on my cheek."

"I'm glad to hear it," he said. "Look, I'd better get to bed. I've got work early tomorrow. You have a good night."

"You have a good night too." Hearing his slight Southern twang made her smile. She could listen to that for a hundred years and never grow tired of it.

Colt tossed his phone back on the couch and took another swig of soda. One minute he had been listing off all the reasons he should be grateful Lily Vanasche was out of his life, and the next his thumb was pressing the "call back" button. That voice of hers, so soft and inviting, had drawn him into a full-blown conversation. He didn't think he'd ever met a more persuasive female. So much for avoiding anyone involved in the case. Before he knew what had hit him, Colt had committed to meeting her the next day.

He checked the clock, then picked up the TV remote and muttered, "Let's see what that idiot fiancé of hers has to say tonight." After a deodorant commercial, the Channel 2 News logo flashed across the screen. "I'm Shelley Contreras," said a female news anchor. "And I'm Nick Borino with your nightly news," said the guy Colt suddenly disliked very much. Colt leaned forward to get a good look at him. Dark hair gelled and styled to perfection, blue dress shirt, no doubt professionally starched by the dry cleaners. Tailored suit that looked finer than Colt's Sunday best. Teeth that seemed a little too white. *Lily's in love some high-class city slicker who probably hasn't done a day's worth of real work his entire life.*

The third story featured a picture of Lily. Nick expressed his gratitude to the viewers who had helped look for his fiancée and then commented on her head trauma, which had caused the amnesia that contributed to her being lost in the mountains for so long. Shelley Contreras mentioned that a hunter had found Lily and that police were interviewing a person of interest in the case. "Because of Miss Vanasche's injuries," the reporter said, "she has been unable to identify her kidnapper." Now the surveillance video and a photo of the stolen getaway vehicle appeared on a split screen as Contreras explained that a reward had been offered for information leading to the arrest and conviction of the bank robber and kidnapper. The reporter encouraged anyone who might have seen the vehicle or who could identify the so-called Camo Bandit to notify the FBI or local police immediately.

Having seen about all he could take of Nick Borino, Colt stood and crushed the pop can with his hand. If he wanted any hope of thinking clearly when he saw Lily, he'd better get some shuteye.

The next morning, Colt showered and shaved, then hauled the blueprints and his laptop out to his truck. He and Jared, along with most of their subcontractors, preferred to use the electronic version of the plans, but their father was old school and insisted on a paper set of plans for every project. Colt hit a drive-through for a couple of breakfast sandwiches and some orange juice.

By the time five o'clock rolled around, he felt more like a UPS driver than a part-owner in a construction company. He had been up and down the Wasatch Front checking on projects in process, dropping off plans and bids, and meeting prospective clients to look at their sites. For the third time that day, he took a northbound on-ramp to I-15. Minutes later he exited the freeway, and One National Bank came into view. This was a newer part of town. Colt recognized the cultured stone pillars and arched entryway from the news clips. Thankfully, good old Nick wasn't standing next to the left column like he had during his broadcast.

His phone rang. "Hey, Jared," he said, "what's up?"

"I spent the last thirty minutes on the phone with your buddy Agent Dawson."

A wave of frustration washed over Colt. "What did he say?"

"He was checking your story. Don't worry, I had your back. Sounds like he believes you."

"Good. Thanks, Brother. I gotta run into this next appointment. Talk to you tomorrow."

Colt stepped out of his truck and, using his hand to shield his eyes from the sun, looked across the street at the strip mall his company had built five years ago. Then he let out a long exhale. *Might as well get this over with.* He walked over to the bank and stepped into the building, then paused to let his vision adjust to the dimmer light.

Seventeen

At the chime of the bell over the bank's front door, Lily glanced up and felt her heart jump into her throat. The glare of the sun outlined a familiar, broad-shouldered frame. She stood and walked across the open space.

Colt moved toward her. "Good to see you again, Lily."

She smiled, and without thinking, reached up to touch his face. *So good-looking.* With the beard he'd worn on the hunt, she hadn't noticed his square jawline. She pulled her hand away, letting her fingertips slide across his chin. "You shaved. It looks nice." Aware of the blush creeping up her cheeks, she glanced down for a moment at the marble tiles on the floor.

He tucked his thumbs in the pockets of his jeans, the keys in his right hand jingling as he moved. "Thanks. You look real pretty yourself. Although I think those old sweats you were wearing in elk camp might have been more flattering."

Wondering if something was amiss, Lily looked down at her pinstriped brown slacks, fitted black silk shirt, and high-heeled pumps. But as she met Colt's blue-green gaze again, he said, "I'm just kidding. Your head feeling better?"

She pulled her hair aside to show him. "Yes, it's good."

He leaned closer, peering at the wound, but didn't reach out to examine it like he had every time he'd checked it on the mountain. Finally smiling at her, he took a step back. "I should get my coat and head to the grocery store. After being gone so long, I discovered my cupboards are bare. The best things I've got in my fridge are cheese and ketchup."

"Let me grab my purse." Lily moved to her desk, unlocked a drawer and pulled out her purse and phone, and stowed all the papers from her desk in the locking drawer. Romeo's blue eyes watched her from a framed photo, and next to that a picture of her with Juliet curled around her neck. Lily walked back to where Colt stood, his gaze traveling from one end of the bank lobby to the other. "After we talked last night," she said, "I realized I should wash your jacket before giving it back to you. The problem is, I fell asleep without moving it to the dryer. So, we need to swing by my place. I don't live far from here."

As Colt reached to open the door for her, Lily heard the rhythmic click of high heels behind them. "Lily, you aren't going to sneak out of here without introducing me to your handsome cowboy are you?" Angela's loud voice rang through the bank.

If Lily thought she was blushing earlier, she knew without a doubt that comment had reddened her face to a downright mortifying shade. Before she could make a proper introduction, Colt turned and stuck out his hand. "I'm Colt Murdock. You must be one of Lily's friends." The skin around his eyes crinkled as he flashed Angela a flirtatious smile that, surprisingly, made Lily feel a touch of jealousy.

In the time she had dated Nick, plenty of women had tried to pry his attention away from her, but Lily had simply ignored their attempts. So why would Colt flirting with Angela even bother her? Angela was no threat. She was so smitten with her fiancé, Damian, that she'd never give Colt a second glance. Of course, he didn't know that.

As Angela shook Colt's hand, she said, "Yes, I'm the *best* friend, Angela."

"We were friends in high school, roomed together in college, and then shared a house for a couple of years," added Lily.

Colt smiled again. "It's a pleasure to meet you."

Angela turned to Lily. "This is the guy, right?"

"Yes, Colt is the hunter who found me in the mountains."

"Awesome. Thanks for taking care of my girl." Angela reached out to give Lily a one-armed squeeze. "Hey, you two have fun tonight."

Before Lily could clarify that she and Colt weren't doing anything together, her friend spun around and walked back to her desk.

Colt pulled open the door and held out his hand. "After you."

Frowning a little at his amused expression, Lily stepped outside, digging through her purse for her sunglasses and keys. She clicked the remote to unlock her Prius, and Colt leaned in front of her to open the car door. "I'll follow you," he said.

Admiring his every movement, she watched him walk to his Dodge pickup with the red logo on the door. She shook her head. *Get your mind off him and back on the task at hand—driving home.* The last thing she needed was to get in a car accident because she was looking in the review mirror at the sexy guy following her. She would grab the coat out of the dryer, give it to Colt, and say goodbye. In theory, it should be simple.

She pulled into her driveway and used her remote to open the garage door. Slowly, she maneuvered her vehicle into the narrow space. The rumble of Colt's diesel truck filled the air as she climbed out of her car. He parked behind her and turned off his engine. Before Lily stepped into the house, she waved for him to follow her. She dropped her purse and keys on the counter, then dodged her two meowing cats as she hurried upstairs to the laundry closet. She pulled the fleece jacket out of the dryer and pressed it to her face, inhaling. Gone was the woodsy, campfire smell, mixed with horses, and Colt's distinctly masculine scent. She'd always loved the smell of freshly laundered clothes, but with this particular article of clothing it wasn't an improvement.

Lily folded the jacket as she walked down the stairs. Colt sat on his haunches, petting both of her cats. Their soft purring, and the occasional meow that ensued if his hand fell away from one of them, brought a smile to her face. "They like you," she said, holding the jacket to her chest.

He glanced up. "What are their names?"

"You'll probably laugh if I tell you."

"No, I won't. I promise—cross my heart, hope to die." Colt brought a finger to his heart and made an *X*.

Trying not to laugh, Lily said, "Only if you pinky-swear promise, too."

Colt stuck out his pinky finger and stretched his hand toward her. "I pinky swear, or whatever that means."

Lily wrapped her pinky around his. "Their names are Romeo and Juliet."

Colt smiled, then put his hand over his heart and tilted his head back as he dropped to one knee. With a dramatic shake of his head, he raised the pitch of his voice and quoted, "'Oh Romeo, Romeo! Wherefore art thou, Romeo? Deny thy father and refuse thy name. Or if thou wilt not, be but sworn my love, and I shall no longer be a Capulet.'"

Lily giggled as Colt stood. "Well, keep going. Quoting Shakespeare—that's quite a talent you have there."

"Sorry. Those are the only lines I remember," he replied. "My sister was Juliet in the school play a couple of years ago. I lost the coin toss with my brothers and had to help her practice."

"What kind of pinky-swear promise was that, anyway? You promised no laughing."

Colt raised his eyebrows. "I didn't laugh. That was you doing the laughing."

"But you made me laugh."

"Little lady, I can't be held accountable for your actions. Next time you'd better make your own pinky promise."

Still laughing, Lily pushed on his shoulder, making him take a step back. "Knock it off. You're nothing but a bunch of trouble, you know that?"

"Of course I know that. Growing up, I heard it at least a thousand times from my mama." Colt's gaze roamed across the kitchen and the living room. "You've got a nice place."

Lily took a deep breath. "I like it, although it has been pretty quiet since Angela moved out and went to her parents' house. She's engaged, so she wanted to save money and be there to plan the wedding with her mother and sisters."

Colt put out a hand. "I guess I should get going. Thanks for washing that for me."

Lily glanced down and realized she was clutching the jacket to her chest as if it was a lifeline. She quickly pushed it toward him. He tucked the jacket under his arm and took a step away.

Feeling like part of her life was about to walk out the garage door and disappear, she followed him and said, "Wait. Are you hungry? I haven't had any dinner yet, and . . . well, buying you dinner is the least I can do to thank you for feeding me all those MREs and letting me ride Duke out of the mountains."

Colt grimaced and shook his head slightly. "I don't know, Lily. That's probably not a good idea."

"Please, it's just dinner." When he didn't say no right away, she grabbed her purse and forged ahead. "Come on, I know a great Chinese place that's close by." Colt still seemed to be thinking it over, but she grabbed his hand and pulled him out the door. "Oh, I forgot you're parked behind—"

"I'll drive," Colt interrupted.

Lily sighed at the realization that she wouldn't need to say goodbye to him quite yet. Later, when she had time alone to think, she would try to figure what that meant. She punched in the numbers on her garage door keypad and listened to the door close as she followed Colt to his truck. He opened the passenger door, stowed a laptop under the seat, and tossed a roll of blueprints into the back. Lily placed her foot on the chrome step bar and climbed in.

"Where to?" he asked.

Eighteen

Colt handed his menu to the waitress and settled his gaze on the beautiful woman sitting across from him. This was the last place he thought he would be tonight. *What's going on?* he asked himself. Lily had used the lame excuse about washing the jacket to get him to her house, and then she'd sprung dinner on him. If he hadn't been starving, he might have summoned the willpower to turn her down. It didn't seem like a good idea for them to spend time together, with her being engaged to someone else. Still, if Colt could get her talking, he just might find some answers.

He made a big show of looking over his shoulder and said, "I'm having déjà vu. I keep wondering when the police are going to bust in here and arrest me."

Lily smiled. "Don't say that. You might jinx us." That smile of hers was Colt's Achilles heel—so much for getting his jacket and getting out of there.

On the television screen hanging on the wall, Lily and Colt watched a news reporter explaining the latest on the case of the Camo Bandit. The police were asking for any information that might lead to the recovery of the stolen Ford Ranger or the arrest of the man responsible for Lily's kidnapping and the robbery.

When the news broadcast went to a commercial break, Colt said, "So, where's Nick Borino tonight?"

Lily's smile faded. "Why do you ask?"

"He is your fiancé, right?"

"Of course."

"Shouldn't he be sitting here in my place right now?"

She shrugged her shoulders. "If he didn't have an emergency at work—some exclusive interview with a guy in Ogden for this story he's working on—then I guess he would."

"Do these emergencies happen very often?"

"It's not too bad. He's working really hard right now, trying to make a name for himself. Eventually, he wants to land a job with one of the national news shows back in New York or D.C."

Colt nodded. "I see. So tell me a little more about him—his hobbies, and what you two like to do together."

"Why do you want to know so much about Nick?"

"Just curious."

"Well, he likes reading, mostly nonfiction and the news. He gets three different newspapers and probably reads every article. On the weekends, we go to the movies and out to dinner, or socialize with people in the community. He has a large circle of friends and an even bigger social network, so there is always some party or civic function we're attending. Nick works out at the gym at least three times a week, but I don't think he really enjoys it. He just can't afford not to look his best when he's in front of the camera all the time."

"Any other hobbies? Anything outdoors?"

"He's not really an outdoors kind of guy. Sometimes he'll play video games, but he's more of a workaholic, mixed with social butterfly."

Colt chuckled, then glanced up when the waitress stopped at their table and put small bowls of egg-drop soup in front of them.

"Thank you," he said. He took a spoonful of the steaming liquid and blew on it. "So, now that you've got your memory back, what do you like to do?" he asked Lily.

"I love running, and exercising at the gym is how I release all the tension from the workday. I like reading, too, but I'm an all-fiction kind of girl. I want to escape reality and be entertained when I read. I also love hiking. Angela and I pick three or four mountains each summer and hike them together. We always take our cameras. You should see some of the pictures we've gotten."

"I'd like that," Colt said. "What else do you like?"

"In the winter, Angela and I do a little snowboarding. I'm not any good, but I still love it and can at least make it down most of the runs. When I was a teenager, I took horseback riding lessons every summer. I actually love riding, but other than Duke, I haven't ridden a horse in years."

Colt decided his soup had cooled enough to try a bite. The liquid warmed a trail down his throat. Between bites he said, "You're welcome to ride Duke any time you'd like. He could use a little exercise between the hunts. By August he's usually as fat as a pig and totally out of shape. Sometimes he huffs and puffs so hard hiking into elk camp that I wonder if he's even going to make it."

"Are you serious? Would you really let me come ride him some weekend?" Lily asked excitedly.

"Sure, of course I would."

Their plates of food arrived, and Colt tucked into his with gusto. When he'd cleared half his plate, he glanced up at Lily, who was watching him.

"You must be pretty hungry," she said.

He scooped another bite into his mouth and chewed. "Starving. Thanks for dinner, Lily."

"You're welcome."

He pointed his fork in the direction of her left hand. "Why didn't that fancy fiancé of yours give you a ring?"

Lily's eyes darted to her hand. "Oh, he did. We got engaged a couple of days before the bank robbery, and the ring was in getting sized when I got taken. I just picked it up from the jeweler today." She paused as she leaned to the side and rummaged through her purse, coming up with a black velvet ring box. Inside was a white-gold ring, loaded with diamonds.

Colt let out a low whistle. "Whew, that's some ring."

"I know. Could he have picked anything bigger?"

Laughing at the sarcasm in her voice, Colt plucked the ring from the box. It had a wide band and a large, square-cut diamond in the center, surrounded by numerous smaller diamonds. "Well, let's see what it looks like on you." Lily held out her hand, and Colt wiggled the band over the knuckle of her left-hand ring finger.

She turned her hand and gazed down at the ring. "I would have picked something more delicate and elegant, not so boxy."

"Nick didn't ask you what kind of ring you wanted?"

"I didn't even realize he planned to ask me to marry him. We had dated for about a year, and known each other back in college, but I didn't think we were at that point yet. The whole thing caught me off guard. He proposed in a crowded restaurant in front of some of his friends, and he even had a hidden camera crew catch the event on tape. It feels as if I got caught in a tidal wave and now here I am. Don't get me wrong. I love Nick. I just don't handle change very well. I think that's all it is."

Colt's brow furrowed as his mind raced in a hundred different directions. Before he could say anything else, the waitress brought the check. Lily pulled the ring off her finger and stuck it back in the box. "We pay up front," she said as she grabbed the check and slid out of the booth.

He followed her out the door, deep in thought. "How about dessert?" she said, smiling as she pointed across the wide parking lot. "See that new ice cream place? I'm dying to try it, but Nick is a total health-food nut. He'll never go with me."

Colt shoved his hands in his pockets and sucked in the cool evening air. "I'm no health-food nut, that's for sure."

Lily stepped next to him, wrapped her arm around his elbow, and pulled him toward the curb. "Then come on."

"I'll only go if you let me buy. My mama would tan my hide if she knew I let you pay for my dinner. I can't even count how many times I've heard the lecture on Southern hospitality and chivalry. 'A gentleman always buys,' she says."

Lily squeezed his arm. "It's a deal. I can't wait to sample that Southern chivalry, along with my ice cream."

A faint glow in the western horizon signaled the arrival of twilight—Colt's favorite time of the day. The streetlights began winking on, polka-dotting the parking lot with a yellow glow. He chuckled. "Lily, you're something else, you know that?"

"What is that supposed to mean?" she asked.

He shrugged his shoulders but said nothing as they walked between cars in the parking lot. For being engaged, Lily sure seemed set on spending the entire evening with another guy— him. Either she was an insufferable flirt, or Nick Borino didn't know how to show a lady a good time.

They shared a banana split at one of the rickety metal tables set up on the sidewalk in front of the ice cream shop. Then Colt spent the next hour talking and laughing with the girl who'd captured his heart on the elk hunt. When his back started aching from sitting so long in the uncomfortable chair, he stood. "It's getting late," he said. "I'd better get you home."

Lily yawned and stretched her hands over her head. "You're right. I think it's my bedtime."

She tucked a strand of golden hair behind her ear and looked up into his eyes. Colt offered her his hand, and she paused only briefly before sliding her hand into his. He pulled her to her feet and, just to see what would happen, entwined his fingers with hers as they walked toward the Dodge. He opened the passenger door, but as Lily tried to pull her left hand out of his, he raised it to his lips. "I like your hand a lot better without the ring."

Her jaw dropped and she stared at him as he let go of her hand and walked to the driver's side. She didn't climb into the truck until he closed his door behind him. Before he turned the key in the ignition, he smiled at her. "Thank you, Lily. I had a real nice time tonight."

"Me too, Colt."

Silence filled the cab during the short drive to her townhouse. Her porch light came on when the truck turned into the driveway. She jumped out before Colt could walk around and open her door, but he followed her to the front door. If she hadn't been engaged, he definitely would have kissed her good night. But he'd already crossed the line by holding her hand — and kissing it. Heck, dinner, dessert . . . the whole thing had been a date in disguise, as far as he was concerned.

Lily dug her keys from her purse and sprung the lock. Then she turned. "Colt, thank you, for everything."

"You bet. Have a good night." He stepped off the porch and heard the door close behind her and the deadbolt click into place. The yellow glow lighting the sidewalk at his feet became a notch brighter. She must have turned on the light fixture in her entryway. At the same moment, a bone-chilling scream came from the house.

Nineteen

Colt spun around and ran back. He slammed his fist against the door, rattling the frame on impact. "Lily, open up!"

"Oh, my gosh! I can't believe this. Help me." Muffled by the door between them, her voice sounded shrill and hysterical. It seemed to take her forever to unlock the door. When it swung open, she launched herself into Colt's arms, crying as she buried her head in his chest.

The sickening, metallic smell of death filled his nostrils. "Did you see anyone inside?"

"No, but look at my cat."

Keeping Lily at his side, Colt crossed the threshold and pushed the door closed with his boot heel. Written in blood on the tile floor leading into her kitchen were the words "I WANT MY MONEY!" Beyond that lay Romeo in a pool of red. Next to the cat was an envelope with Lily's name in bold block letters.

As they got closer to the dead animal, Lily put her hand over her mouth, then jerked away and ran to the kitchen sink. The sound of her throwing up followed a moment later. Colt sank into a crouch. Dull, lifeless eyes met his. Someone had slit the cat's throat. The envelope wasn't sealed, and beneath it sat a padlock with a key in the keyhole. Colt pulled a folded piece of paper from the envelope and read:

What a clever girl you are, playing the amnesia card. I didn't think you'd have it in you, but obviously I was wrong. While I'm willing to buy your silence by splitting the cash with you, I won't walk away with nothing. After we crashed, I know you took the money and ran. Where did you hide it? I'm not a patient man. You have until tomorrow night to return my half, if you ever want to see your other cat alive. Before the Deseret Recreation Center closes at 9:00 PM, put the money in this duffle bag and lock it in a locker in one of the family changing rooms near the pool. Use this padlock and keep the key. You'll need it to get your cat the next morning when the center opens at 8:00. I'll be watching. If I even smell a cop, your cat is dead and then I'm coming for you.

Colt closed the shutters in the living room. The water at the kitchen faucet turned on. He scanned the house as he walked toward Lily. The guy had trashed the place. Every drawer looked like it had been searched, the contents spilled onto the floor. Some of them had been yanked from the cupboards and dropped on top of the pile of shattered glassware, cutlery, and cookware. The couch had been sliced open and the cushions and pillows tossed to the side. Colt imagined the garage and the second floor would look the same. He shut the blinds in the kitchen.

Lily stepped over a pile of hot pads, zip-top bags, and aluminum foil, to grab a paper towel and dry her mouth. Her face had taken on a deathly pallor, especially next to the black of her blouse. Big tears, dark with mascara, ran down her face. "Where's Juliet? Is she dead too?"

Colt held out the ransom note. "Not yet. Tell me the truth. That first day in the mountains—did you hide the stolen money before I found you?"

"What? No, of course not!" Lily yanked the note from his hand and stepped back. "I may not remember exactly what happened, but I know I'm not a thief." She shut her eyes and shook her head slowly before meeting Colt's gaze again. "First the police, and now you. I can't believe you'd trust a crook's note over me." She looked down at the paper, then wiped her tears and stared at it again. Another sob tore through her chest, and she covered her face with her hands. "Now I'm crying so hard I can't even read the stupid thing."

Colt crossed the space between them and wrapped his arms around her. "I'm sorry, Lily. I want to believe you."

"Then please do, because I know I'm innocent."

Several seconds ticked by as he weighed the facts against what his heart told him. Finally, he replied, "I will believe you."

"What does the note say?" Lily asked tremulously.

"He wants half of the money delivered to a locker by tomorrow night, or he says he'll kill Juliet and then come for you." The only response Colt got was a gasp, followed by more crying. "Lily, why do you think the police don't believe you?"

"Just all the questions they keep asking. Today they called and wanted me to come to the station so they could interview me again, but I refused. I've already told them everything I can remember."

Colt thought back to the day he found Lily. It had rained hard several hours earlier. The claylike dirt on the Jeep road where she passed out would have turned as slick as ice shortly after the downpour began. If her kidnapper was still driving the Ford Ranger from the bank robbery, he could've easily lost control of the vehicle and gone off a steep embankment. That would explain the crash mentioned in the ransom note. Plus, the duffle bag had been tossed into the truck bed, and the back door of the shell was missing. If the vehicle rolled a few times, the bag containing the money could have tumbled out. With the dense foliage and the remoteness of the area, it was possible no one had located either the money or the truck yet.

Colt glanced over his shoulder. "Let's get out of here. For all we know, whoever did this is watching us, or could have bugged the place."

Lily moved out of his arms. "What about calling the police?"

"Read the last line. We'll talk about that later."

She looked at the paper, covering her mouth with her hand and shaking her head. "What am I going to do?"

Colt led her to the stairs and they started up. "Get a change of clothes and whatever else you need so you don't have to come back here for at least twenty-four hours." They reached the top of the stairs, and he put out his arm to keep Lily behind him. The first room was bare, except for a bed, now ruined by the intruder's blade. The next had a computer desk and some bookshelves. Again, everything had been torn apart. Lily's room was in the same state of disarray. Colt checked the closets and the bathrooms, making sure whoever had broken in was gone.

Once he nodded to Lily that all was clear, she started picking through the clothes on the floor of her bedroom. She tossed jeans, a T-shirt, a sweatshirt, and a pair of socks into a backpack, then moved out of sight into the bathroom.

Colt's next thought left him feeling sick. What if Lily hadn't invited him to dinner? Or what if he had said no, like he'd almost done? She would have been here alone when the guy broke in. Instead of the cat, would Lily be lying on the kitchen floor with her throat slit?

"Colt, are you okay? I said I'm ready."

She stood in front of him. He shook his head, trying to clear the disturbing images from his mind. He pulled the backpack from her hand and slung it over his shoulder. "I'm fine. You should get a coat and comfortable shoes—hiking boots if you have them."

She darted into her closet again and came back carrying both items. He hurried down the stairs, with Lily following. Then Colt crossed to the front door. After picking up the padlock, he asked, "Where's the note?"

Lily pointed to the bag he held. "In there."

Colt pulled the zipper aside and dropped the lock on top of the note. He moved to the door and stooped to grab her purse and keys. With his hand poised over the light switch, he said, "Anything else?"

She shook her head and then looked behind her. "I feel bad leaving Romeo like that."

Colt felt bad leaving the cat too, but getting Lily out of that house and to safety was his first priority. The cat would have to wait. "We'll come back later, and I'll help you bury him. For now, we need to go."

The night air seemed colder, making him wonder if the temperature had actually dropped that quickly or if the dread hanging over him had left him chilled.

When Colt got to his truck, it wasn't locked. On a night like this, that bothered him. He stuck his hand under the passenger seat—his laptop was still there, and nothing looked out of place.

Earlier, he didn't have any intention of setting foot inside Lily's house, no matter what she might have said to persuade him. But for some reason, things had a way of not going as expected when she was around. Colt took the hiking boots from her and set them, along with her bag, in the back.

At the sound of voices, he jerked his head to the side. A Hispanic man walking a pit bull passed by on the sidewalk, talking on his phone and barely glancing at Lily and Colt. Nothing about the guy seemed suspicious. Colt exhaled in relief.

Lily stood shivering as she clutched her coat to her chest rather than putting it on. When she didn't move to get in the truck, Colt started to wonder if she was in shock. "Come on, let's get you in here." He grabbed her elbow and guided her into the truck, going so far as to pull the seatbelt down in front of her and put it in her hand. He shut her door and jogged around to his.

Once he closed the driver's side door, he clicked the lock button and hurried to get his key in the ignition. His imagination conjured up an imminent confrontation with the gun-wielding Camo Bandit as they backed out of the driveway. When Colt shifted from reverse into drive, he noticed that neither he nor Lily had bothered to turn off the light in her bedroom.

Twenty

Lily watched the streetlights pass as Colt pressed the accelerator and they left her neighborhood behind. He turned the vehicle's heater on high. "Give it a second and it should be toasty in here."

Her hands and feet felt like ice, her fingers numb and tingly. She sucked in a lungful of air and exhaled, trying to stop her heart from beating into her throat.

Colt glanced at the rearview mirror, then back at the road, his expression unreadable. She wondered what he was thinking. It crossed her mind to ask, but her head was pounding. Plus, she feared that if she spoke, she would start crying again. Instead she stretched her hands toward the vents and focused on the warm air rushing past her trembling fingers.

The truck sped past billboards lining the freeway, and Lily tried to read each one, hoping to give herself something to think about beside the horrific image of her sweet cat, slaughtered for revenge for something Lily didn't even do. But in spite of her best efforts, the words blurred before her eyes.

Soon, Colt slowed the truck and exited the freeway. Large warehouses and businesses lined the streets of the industrial area.

At this late hour, the place was nearly vacant. He turned into a parking lot and positioned his truck so it faced the road. Then he shut off the engine and killed the headlights.

The fluorescent glow from the streetlamps lit the side of his face. The muscle in his jaw twitched as he stared in the direction they had driven a moment before. Following his gaze, Lily asked, "What are we doing?"

"Checking to see if we're being followed. Maybe I'm paranoid, but I'd rather be safe than sorry."

Two cars drove past—an electrician's van and a red Prius—but neither driver seemed to pay any particular attention to the white Dodge pickup.

Lily's phone rang, startling her. Colt looked down at her purse and she yanked on the zipper, all the while trying to keep her fingers from shaking. She pulled her phone out. "It's Nick. What should I tell him?"

Colt took the phone from her hand and declined the call. "Nothing." He handed the phone back.

"You hung up on him?"

"I don't think you should say anything to anyone until we figure this out."

Lily looked down at the phone, tempted to call Nick back. But what would she say? If he knew about the vandalism at her house, he would call the police. And Colt was right. They needed answers, not long, drawn-out discussions with Detective Hansen and Agent What's-his-face.

She dropped her phone back into her purse. "What are we going to do, Colt?"

He glanced her way. "One option is we go back to the mountain and retrace your steps. If he didn't take the money off the mountain, it could still be there. I told the detectives where I found you, but maybe they never located the crash site. The news report tonight sure made it sound like they didn't. The way I see it, if we can find the stolen vehicle and the money, then call

Hansen and Dawson, we can clear your name. They can watch the drop site and hopefully catch the guy. With four-wheelers we can take a look and be off the mountain by midday. If we don't find anything, there'll still be time to bring in the police before that deadline this jerk gave you."

"What's the other option?" Lily wanted to know.

"Call 9-1-1 and do what the police tell us to do."

The tick in Colt's jaw was still twitching, and maybe it was the poor lighting, but his expression looked dark. "Are you angry?" Lily asked softly.

He watched as a Jeep drove slowly down the road in front of them and disappeared around the corner at the next intersection. "What makes you ask that?" he said.

"You look mad."

He turned his face away from her and grunted. A crooked half-smile softened his expression when he looked back at her. "Of course I'm mad. Some crazy guy trashed your place and killed your cat, and I'm not sure what to do about it. One minute I think we should dial 9-1-1 and go back to your house, then the next I wonder if that will only anger the guy—make you more of a target." Colt ran his fingers through his hair, leaving it sticking out at weird angles. His voice dropped a notch when he said, "The fact that this psycho is out to get you makes me want to give him a taste of his own medicine and . . ." Colt fell silent, not finishing his thought.

"You're right about one thing," Lily said, reassured by his concern.

"What's that?"

"Calling in the police will upset this guy. After Romeo, I don't doubt he'd do the same or worse to me. I want answers— the same ones the police keep asking me for. But if I don't remember anything about the day of the robbery, how can I defend myself?"

Colt stared over the dash, the muscle in his jaw his only

detectable movement. Realizing he was probably still weighing their options, Lily waited a bit before asking, "What do you think we should do?"

"I honestly don't know," Colt admitted. "There are pros and cons with every option, but I keep coming back to something that occurred to me when I was sitting in jail. I read once that the first person to report an incident is more likely to be considered the victim."

That made sense, but Romeo's lifeless form hung at the forefront of her memory. Her cats were her family. Her eyes stung, filling with tears. "I want Juliet back." Her voice cracked under the surge of emotion.

Eyeing her, Colt nodded. "If he's watching, a 9-1-1 call tonight might not be wise. But I am calling Agent Dawson."

"I hope he doesn't send patrol cars to my house," Lily said.

Colt reached into the glove compartment and pulled out a business card. He dialed the number and waited. It must have gone to voicemail, because he said, "This is Colt Murdock. Lily is with me, and I've got some new information on that case. The Camo Bandit left her a threatening note tonight. Give me a call as soon as you can."

He put the key back in the ignition and started the engine. "Unless Agent Dawson advises us differently, we're taking a quick trip to the mountain, to see if we can find your answers."

They drove across town and parked at an apartment complex. Lily placed her hand on Colt's arm to stop him as he reached for the door handle. "I'm sorry, Colt. After everything you did for me last week, here you are stuck with me again. I feel like such a burden."

A genuine smile lit his face. "Trust me. Being stuck with you is anything but a burden."

He jumped out and walked to the passenger side as she pushed the door open. "Come inside with me," he said. "I have to get a few things and then we'll go to my parents' house."

He unlocked the door to an apartment on the second floor, turned on a light, and ushered Lily in ahead of him. "Sorry about the mess. Make yourself comfortable while I change clothes."

He walked down the short hallway toward the bedroom. Lily watched him reach behind his neck and tug on his collar, then pull the polo shirt over his head as he entered his room. The muscles in his shoulder bunched when he flicked the door with his fingers. It swung closed behind him.

A worn leather sofa sat next to the wall. Against the opposite wall stood an oak TV stand, complete with a flat-screen TV. In the center of the room, a coffee table was littered with dishes, an empty soda can, and a pile of magazines— *Outdoor Life* and *Field & Stream*. Clothes and jackets Lily recognized from his elk hunt were heaped next to the laundry closet.

She took a deep breath and slowly exhaled. Every sinew in her body felt tense. She gathered up the dirty dishes and dumped them into the sink. Since the dishwasher was empty, she rinsed the plates, bowls, and glasses and loaded them. As Lily bent to gather up the forks and spoons, a pair of hands gently grasped her shoulders. "You're doing my dishes?" Colt's strong fingers massaged the knots of tension running the length of her neck.

"I needed to do something to keep busy, and cleaning is one of those mindless jobs I find therapeutic." Lily sighed, relaxing at his touch. "Mmm . . . that feels nice."

Colt chuckled. "I should have taken a longer shower so you'd have time to clean the whole apartment."

Lily flicked her wet fingers over her shoulder, splashing him in the face. The next instant his arms wrapped around hers and pinned them to her side. "Okay, young lady, that's it. You're done with the water." Colt lifted her off her feet and moved her to the side, then grabbed a handful of utensils.

"I'm almost through. Let me finish." Lily tried to elbow her way in front of him.

"Nope." Colt held his ground. "Did my phone ring?"

"No. With how late it is, Agent Dawson might not get your message until tomorrow."

"But at least he'll know I tried to tell him what happened."

She dried her hands and folded her arms, then watched Colt load the soap in the dispenser and start the dishwasher. He had traded his polo and nice jeans for a plaid flannel shirt over a white tee and an older pair of well-worn Carhartts. A baseball cap in hunter orange covered his damp hair. He looked every bit the redneck that Nick had accused him of being, but it didn't bother Lily. In fact, she found herself smiling back at Colt when he moved so close that his chest nearly touched her arm as he reached behind her to grab a towel. He winked, causing her to drop her gaze and move away.

"This is a nice apartment complex," she said. "It looks new."

A pile of gear sat next to the couch, with Colt's bow on top. "They built these units probably two years ago," he said as he moved his bow and dug through his stuff. He pulled out the binoculars, a map, a saw, and a flashlight, then stood, arms full. "Let's go."

A half an hour later, he turned his truck down a tree-lined driveway onto a property nestled at the base of the foothills, next to an upscale neighborhood. "This is my parents' place," he explained. "But you won't meet them, since they flew out to Tennessee earlier this evening to visit my mama's sister."

Under the light of the full moon, two cows and a group of horses, one she recognized as Duke by his distinctive Appaloosa markings, grazed on sparse tufts of dried grass. A large metal building stood to the left and behind the one-story brick rambler. Mature fruit trees circled the patch of grass surrounding the buildings. The house was dark except for the porch light, which glowed a soft yellow, and one basement window. Towering cottonwoods stood like sentinels along the fence line, probably acting as a windbreak. "This is beautiful," Lily said.

Colt backed his truck next to the oversized garage door on

the building behind the house. "Yeah, they've got ten acres, much to the chagrin of all the residential developers in this area." He turned off the engine and opened his door. "I'm going to load the four-wheeler, and then we'll go up to the house."

Lily got her coat on and jumped out of the cab. "We're not riding the horses?"

Colt pulled the door up and shoved it above his head, the wheels squeaking against the metal track. "No, the four-wheeler will be a lot faster. We'll take the Jeep road to the area where I found you and start looking from there."

A string of fluorescent lights lit the room. He walked to the back of the large shop and returned with a ramp, which he propped on the open tailgate of his truck. After gathering a coil of rope and some tools, which he packed in the compartment on the back of the four-wheeler, he straddled the machine and turned the key. The engine sputtered to life. Colt drove the ATV up the ramp and parked it in the truck bed. He pulled red tie-downs from a Rubbermaid bin near the door and secured his cargo. When he finished, he folded the ramp and placed it next to the four-wheeler. He strapped a red five-gallon gas can near the front of the truck bed, then lifted the tailgate into place with a resounding bang.

The chill of fall was in the wind whistling out of the mouth of the canyon, and Lily shivered as she watched him. Colt tossed his baseball cap onto the dash and passed the hiking boots to her, then pulled out the backpack with her things and his maps. "Let's get you inside," he said, wrapping an arm around her.

Two terracotta pots, each growing a rose bush, framed the front door. Colt tipped the left one up and grabbed a key from beneath it. After unlocking the door, he returned the key to the hiding place. He held the door for Lily, and she stepped into the dark house. Then he flipped a light switch and said, "This way. Follow me."

He walked across the room, flipped off the light, and then started down a dimly lit stairwell, the faint light coming from a room downstairs. "You can stay in the guest bedroom," he said.

"We'll get an early start, so we've only got a few hours to sleep." Before they reached the basement, Colt asked loudly, "Hey, Sam, you dressed?"

"Yeah. What're you doing here?" A teenaged boy stepped into the hall directly in front of them, wearing only boxer shorts.

Colt put his palm on Sam's forehead and pushed him back into the room. "Checking in on my kid brother. You call that dressed? Get back in there and shut the door. We've got company."

As Lily walked by the bathroom, she said hi to the boy.

Grinning as he kept walking, Colt glanced over his shoulder at her. "That's Sam."

The boy called out from the bathroom doorway. "Hey, are you the girl Colt found in the mountains? The one who was kidnapped in that bank robbery?"

She faced him. "That's me."

"Why are you hanging out with my brother? I thought you were marrying that guy on the news."

Colt frowned as he put his hand on her back. "Don't listen to him. He puts his foot in his mouth daily." He gave Lily a gentle nudge, moving her into the bedroom.

"Aw, Colt, I'm just askin' a simple question."

"Nothing about your questions is ever simple. Good night, Sam," Colt said with finality as he closed the door.

Giggling, Lily raised her hand to her mouth. Colt dropped her backpack on the bed and asked, "What's so funny?"

"You. Your brother. It must have been fun growing up in a big family."

"It was fun until that one came along. The things he says can make a man hotter than a snake in a wagon rut in Nevada. Last night at family dinner he blurts out, 'I want to hear why Colt spent a night in jail.'"

Lily laughed wholeheartedly. It felt amazing. *Whoever said laughter was good for you must be right*, she thought.

"Earlier that afternoon, I'd asked Sam to keep it on the

lowdown," Colt continued. "I could have wrung his skinny little neck, I was so mad."

Lily sighed. "Oh, I'm sorry. How awful for you."

"Aw, it's fine. I was going to tell them eventually." He paused, rerolling the maps he held into a tighter tube. "Well, we should get some rest. I'll kick Sam out of the bathroom, so it'll be all yours. If you need me, I'll be on the couch in the family room."

He opened the door and started to leave. Lily reached out and touched his sleeve. "Thank you."

Twenty-One

Colt ushered his little brother out of the bathroom, telling him to keep it free for their visitor. After a bit of persuasion, Sam let him borrow a pair of basketball shorts to sleep in. Colt pulled a pillow and blankets from the closet, tossed them on the couch, and spread out his maps. He found the red dots he'd used to mark possible campsite locations before the hunt, then followed the contour lines to the place he had actually set up his camp. From there he traced the path he had taken a week ago—the day he'd found Lily Vanasche. He touched the blue ballpoint pen to the map, making an *X*. If he had remembered correctly, that marked the spot they should begin their search for the stolen Ford Ranger and the bag of money. Colt couldn't help but smile—there was nothing like a treasure hunt to bring out the kid in a guy.

He followed the Jeep road on his map, plotting the quickest route and making notes in the margin. When he knew where he'd be taking Lily the next morning, he rolled up the maps and dropped them next to his hiking boots, pants, and flannel shirt. He checked his cell phone for missed calls and set the alarm, planning to be on the mountain before first light. He'd try Agent

Dawson again in the morning. Colt switched off the lamp next to the couch and lay down.

The door to the bathroom opened before the hallway went dark. It had been a long day, and he was still trying to get caught up on sleep. His mind drifted to Lily, staying in the next room. Lying on his stomach—one arm hanging off the couch, his fingertips brushing the carpet—he started to drift off.

Suddenly he sensed someone watching him. He opened his eyes to see bare feet with painted toenails, standing in a small patch of moonlight. Colt rolled to his side and looked up, following the silky pajama pants to a baggy T-shirt, and then Lily's face. "Lily?" He rubbed his hand across the kink in his neck.

"I couldn't sleep. I close my eyes and all I see is my apartment, and the blood, and Romeo. I'm sorry for waking you. I just . . . I don't want to be alone."

She turned, but Colt caught her hand in his before she could leave. He pulled her closer as he sat up. "It's okay." Her hand felt cold in his. He stood up and lifted the blanket. "Take my spot. I'm going to use the bathroom. I'll be right back."

She lay down on the couch and he covered her with the quilt. "Thank you," she said, tucking it under her chin.

Colt returned with the pillow and blanket from the guest bed. He swiveled the other couch so they were facing each other, a foot of space between them. After he lay down, he said, "Is that better?"

Looking more like a little girl than a grown woman, Lily asked, "Can I hold your hand?" Colt reached across to her couch, and she quickly pulled his hand between both of hers. "Yes, that's better," she mumbled, then closed her eyes.

Colt watched the anxiousness leave her face and heard her breathing deepen. She was beautiful. How unfortunate that Nick Borino had already staked his claim to her. Then again, engagements could be broken. Colt's dad had always said anything worth having is worth fighting for. Maybe this girl was worth fighting for. And just maybe, with a little bit of luck, Colt had a chance at coming out on top if he went head to head with Nick Borino.

At 4:00 AM, Colt woke to the chime of his phone alarm. Lily had his hand clutched next to her, the smooth skin of her neck against his knuckles. She stretched her arm over her head and yawned. "Good morning, beautiful," he said.

She smiled as she released his hand and sat up. "Good morning, cowboy." She reached for his phone and turned off the alarm. "Is it really time to get up?"

Colt turned on the lamp. She looked half asleep. He climbed to his feet and pushed the couch back where it belonged. "Yeah, let's go. While you get changed, I'll make us a lunch. Come upstairs when you're ready."

Lily folded her blanket and set it on top of the pillow before heading to the bathroom. Colt gathered his phone, maps, and clothes and went to the kitchen. After making a stack of sandwiches, he raided his mother's pantry, commandeering granola bars, apples, pop cans and water bottles. When the small cooler was packed, he set out bowls, spoons, and cold cereal.

Lily stepped into the kitchen wearing jeans and a sweatshirt, her hair pulled back in a ponytail. She walked to the table and set her backpack on the floor. Colt caught himself staring and looked back at the refrigerator door that stood open in front of him, remembering he needed the milk.

They ate a quick bowl of cereal and left. Colt locked up quietly, relieved he'd escaped without having to deal with his nosey little sister. Thankfully, she was a deep sleeper.

Lily hadn't said much all morning, but she'd probably yawned twenty times. Now she closed her eyes and sat with her head in her hand, her elbow pressed against the window. Colt wondered if she'd gotten more than an hour or two of sleep last night. A pair of gloves and his jacket lay on the seat between them, so he tossed them in the back. "Lily, if you're tired you can lie down and put your head on my leg."

She opened her eyes and looked from his face to where his hand rested on his thigh. "Thank you. I can't stop yawning." She covered her mouth as another yawn hit. She loosened her seatbelt, tucked her feet up next to the door, and rested her head on his leg. When she shifted positions, her shoulder rubbed against him, and he forced himself to focus on the freeway. Colt glanced down a few minutes later and smiled to see her sleeping.

Two hours later they drove through the little town of Fairview and turned toward the canyon. Before he lost cell service he called Agent Dawson. Again Colt got Dawson's voicemail and left a detailed message.

Soon, the paved roads ended and the truck rumbled over the rough gravel. Lily sat up, rubbing her eyes, and looked around. "Can you hand me the map?" Colt motioned over his shoulder.

She reached behind him and grabbed the map, then handed it to him. "Here you go."

Colt slowed the truck and glanced at his notes. The faint glow of the upcoming sunrise lit the eastern horizon, painting the mountaintop with a pale hue. A few miles later, he turned down the Forest Service road that would take him to the Jeep road where he'd found Lily a week ago.

When they had gone as far as they could in the truck, Colt found a place to turn around and park. He unloaded the four-wheeler and packed their lunch in one of the smaller compartments at the rear of the vehicle. Then he straddled the ATV, standing on the footrests, and put his hand out. "Come on, Lily. Let's go for a ride."

She took his hand and stepped up behind him. He locked the truck and zipped the keys into the pocket of his jacket. The air rushed past Colt's face as the four-wheeler accelerated, and he felt Lily press against his back, her arms wrapped tight around his waist.

Roughly five miles from where he had found her, he eased off the gas and slowed. In places, the terrain dropped off steeply on one side or the other. Thickets of trees and brush lined the roadside, surrounded by mature forests of pines and aspens, or open meadows dotted with the last of the summer wildflowers. Colt scanned both sides of the road. Only a small amount of dust clung to the leaves and plants bordering the road, so it must not have seen much traffic recently.

"I know we're looking for the stolen truck," Lily said, "but how do you think we'll find it? The trees are so thick in places you can hardly see anything."

"If the vehicle slid off the road, I'm hoping to find slide marks, or broken branches—something to give us a clue."

"Oh, I see."

The road made an S-curve, but before Colt rounded the final turn he stopped the ATV. A large aspen lay in front of him. The leaves were still intact, although browning under the sun. He guessed the tree hadn't been down long; the thunderstorm from the night he found Lily was probably to blame. As he hunted during the days following the storm, Colt had noted several fresh trees down. Now, he threw the transmission into park and cut the engine. With both sides of the narrow road heavily timbered, he didn't see a way around the downed tree.

"What should we do?" Lily asked.

Colt grinned at her worried expression. "We'll move it out of the way." He dug his saw and ax out of the largest compartment at the back of the four-wheeler. Then, pushing aside some branches and breaking off smaller ones, he made his way to the tree trunk.

When his saw blade was three inches deep in the wood, he ripped off his sweatshirt and tossed it to Lily. Already, sweat covered his brow and ran between his shoulder blades. The sun had crested the mountain peak, and morning sunlight streamed through the trees, warming the air. The dew from the night before evaporated before Colt's eyes. When he pulled back on the saw, he couldn't resist flexing his bicep, just in case Lily was looking.

As the tree bent, the last bit of the trunk splintered off. Colt glanced at Lily. Her eyes were still focused on him. She seemed to be deep in thought as he walked back to get the cable from the winch. He looped it around the trunk and dragged the tree's top section to the side of the road.

Colt took his sweatshirt from Lily and stowed it with the saw and ax. "Scoot forward, please," he told her, so she did. He settled himself behind her and said, "You can drive us for a bit."

She leaned forward and swiveled her head to see him. Her eyebrows arched up. "I can?"

Colt raised a water bottle to his mouth, winking at her. "Yup, your turn."

Lily reached for the handlebars, glancing left then right. "What do I do?"

He crushed the empty water bottle, reducing it to the size of a baseball, and dropped it into one of the compartments behind him. He slid forward until his chest pressed against Lily's back, and then he wrapped his hands around hers. "Left hand is the brake. Right hand is the gas—press with your thumb here. But first, squeeze the brake, then shift the machine into high." Leaning over her shoulder, Colt smiled at the way she held herself so still as he picked up her right hand and moved it to the gearshift lever. He pushed it forward, watching the digital letters on the display: P-R-N-L-H. He sat a little straighter, imagining she might be able to concentrate better without him hovering. "Give it a little gas."

The ATV shot forward with a lurch. Colt's head snapped back, and Lily bumped against his chest as if he were a backrest. He laughed as the machine rolled to a stop. Starting to stand, Lily said, "If you're going to laugh, you can drive."

He pulled her down next to him, thinking how much he'd like to leave his hands on her waist. Instead, he rested his hands on his thighs. "You'll get the hang of it. Try again." This time she gave it gas so slowly they inched forward like a caterpillar.

With a chuckle Colt said, "A little more gas, please. We don't have all day."

Lily glared at him over her shoulder. "Like I already said, you're welcome to drive, Mr. Hotshot."

Colt leaned back and propped his elbows against the storage compartment behind him. "You got this one. I'm going to relax and enjoy the scenery."

"Oh, are you now?" she said sarcastically.

"Just tell me when we get to the crash site, sweetheart."

Lily shook her head and finally broke into a smile. "Yes, sir."

Twenty-Two

Lily's heartbeat had finally settled back into a normal rhythm. What was wrong with her? One flirtatious touch from Colt had sent her pulse racing and turned her brain to mush.

She turned her full attention to the roadside, looking for the stolen Ford Ranger. Suddenly, Colt wrapped his arms around hers and took over the controls, stopping the four-wheeler on the downward slope just as the road made a hairpin turn. He said, "I thought I saw something," and moved the gearshift into park.

To the right, the rocky terrain rose steeply above Lily. Grass lined the road, and beyond the outcropping of rock stood a thick stand of evergreens. On the left, the ground dropped away, with tall evergreens again dominating the landscape. Nowhere could she see anything remotely resembling a vehicle. "I don't see it," she said as she followed Colt off the ATV.

He bent to inspect the ground, then pointed to a bush that was bent over at the base, the trunk splintered, next to a tiny tree that lay sideways. He climbed down the embankment, past the bush. "Look at the ground," he said excitedly. "And see how this sapling and the elderberry bush have been pushed over?"

Lily picked her way down the slope as Colt scrambled ahead of her. Three trees lay on their sides, as if some kind of domino effect had recently been in motion with two of them crossing trunks like an *X*. The downed trees made a formidable wall of branches and wilting pine needles, blocking the view to what lay below. Colt stepped onto one of the mature trees and climbed up. He turned and smiled back at Lily. "The *X* marks the spot."

She gasped. "You found something?"

He jumped off the trunk. "You bet. Come and see."

Lily took the hand he offered and let him help her through the tangled mess of branches and over the barricade of trees. Smaller trees, some bent or broken, filled the space between where she stood and the smashed remains of the white Ford Ranger. Pieces of red and clear plastic—shattered headlights and taillights—polka-dotted the ground, along with a tent, sleeping bag, and several cans of food. The truck lay wedged against a large Douglas fir, like an opossum playing dead, its four wheels in the air.

A chunk of the fiberglass shell had cracked off. Colt flipped it over, then rushed down the steep incline, his feet nearly sliding out from underneath him. As she followed him, Lily steadied herself by holding onto tree trunks and branches. Colt searched the dented cab and the truck bed, kicking out another piece of the truck's shell and tossing camping gear onto the hillside.

"It's not in the truck," he said, looking at Lily.

"Could it be underneath?"

Colt circled the truck again and looked closer. He came up shaking his head. "The way it's leaning against the tree, you can see there isn't anything there."

Lily reached the truck and looked at the damaged passenger doorframe. A flashback of climbing out that door to freedom went through her mind. The terror she felt at the time, fearing the man's large hands would grab her ankles before she could escape, came to the forefront of her memory. She looked at the jagged piece of metal sticking out from the doorframe, and then at the tender pink spot on her palm where it had sliced open her skin.

Colt pressed his hand against her back. "You okay?"

The memories faded as she looked into his face. "I was trying to remember what happened."

He nodded, then caught his hat brim between two of his fingers and yanked it off, before running the rest of them through his hair. She smiled as his eyes narrowed and he readjusted the baseball cap at least three times before saying, "The bag isn't in the truck, so if he didn't take it and you didn't take it, it has to be somewhere between the road and here."

"Unless someone else found it."

Colt seemed to think for a moment. "It's possible, but I'd bet in the last six days no one has been here. These three trees and the one across the road that I cut away probably came down in that storm the night I found you."

She looked at the tangled collection of bushes — most of them resembling the one Colt had called an elderberry — the ferns and grass, and the fir trees of every shape and size. The bag could be in any one of a hundred different places beneath all that greenery. "Let's widen our search radius," Lily suggested.

She and Colt searched every bush, peered under each fern, and combed the grass until both of them panted from the exertion of maneuvering the steep hillside. Colt climbed atop the downed trees. "It has got to be under here." He paused and shook his head. "If it isn't, I don't know what we'll tell those detectives."

Lily walked closer. "You can't even see the ground under all those branches."

"We'll thin them out a little then."

Colt jumped to the uphill side and returned with the saw he had used on the other tree, and an ax with a leather case covering the blade. He handed Lily the saw. "Ever limbed a tree before?"

She looked from the saw to the trees. "Uh no, I haven't."

"This is a long shot, I know, but let's clear out enough to make sure that money bag isn't here. We've looked everywhere else."

He hacked off branches and threw them behind him as he worked his way up one side of the tree and then down the other. Lily used the saw to take off several tree limbs. When the branches piled up underfoot, she cleared away the foliage and began to feel around beneath the pine needles for any sign of the duffle bag. She found a cast-iron pan and the broken remains of a camping lantern. She pried a piece of glass from her skin. The pinesap stuck to her fingers like superglue.

Colt was midway through the second tree when he paused to wipe the sweat off his brow. "Halfway done."

Lily pulled back on another branch and dragged it to the pile she had accumulated. When she dropped to her knees a few feet away from where Colt was working, she felt between the tangle of twigs and pine needles. Her fingertips brushed across something soft yet decidedly manmade. Canvas. "Colt! I found something." She grabbed a handful of the material.

He leaned the ax against the trunk and knelt beside her. Using both hands, he yanked and pulled from side to side, eventually freeing the olive-green duffle bag. He held it out so Lily could see as he opened the top. They peered inside. Wadded bills of mixed denomination—what had probably come from the bank teller's till—were tucked between several bundles of cash. Lily fingered the money, smiling to see that most of the bundles were of one- and five-dollar bills. The robber had escaped with only a few twenty-dollar bundles. Karen, the assistant manager who had filled the bag, had done a good job of minimizing the bank's losses.

Suddenly, images from that day flashed through Lily's mind. After the Camo Bandit had thrown the canvas duffle bag to Karen, he'd crossed the lobby and grabbed Lily. He had pressed the gun to her temple and threatened to kill her if Karen didn't move fast enough. When Scott, the manager, had tried to reason with the guy on Lily's behalf, the robber shot him.

Lily gasped and covered her mouth.

"What's wrong?" Colt asked.

"I remember . . . what I saw during the robbery."

"Isn't that good?"

"I guess. But he had a gun. To my head." She paused, biting her lip hard. "I saw him shoot my boss!"

Colt reached for her hand. "It's over, Lily. You're safe now. And your boss is going to be just fine."

"Yeah, I talked with him yesterday. But it just makes me sick to realize how close he came to dying." After a long pause, Lily added, "Let's go find Agent Dawson."

Colt stood and collected his ax. He pulled up the bottom of his T-shirt and wiped the moisture from his face.

He pulled up the bottom of his T-shirt and wiped the moisture from his face. "I didn't expect to get a workout this morning." With the hem of his shirt at his neckline, he grinned at her. "But then again, if treasure hunting was easy, everyone would be doing it."

Lily eyed his perfect abs before his shirt dropped back into place around his middle. She giggled. "I don't know. It does have its rewards."

Colt pointed to the road above them. "Should we go eat something before we head back to the truck? I don't know about you, but I'm starving."

Once they had gathered their things, he stuffed her coat and the saw into the duffle bag, then slung it over his shoulder. Then he pulled his phone out of his pocket and held it up for several seconds. "No service. Thought it was worth checking." He moved the ATV a couple hundred feet to where he could pull off the road onto a relatively flat piece of ground, covered in grass and shaded from the sun. Lily shifted her weight on the four-wheeler seat and forced her eyes to take in the scenery. During the entire time they ate peanut butter sandwiches and apples, she couldn't focus on anything but Colt. His easy smile and perfect physique were hard to look away from. He sat on a boulder next to the ATV, with his attention focused on her.

No, she thought, forcing her gaze to sweep the ridge top across the valley. *We'll turn in the money and tell law enforcement where the vehicle is. They should be able to arrest this creep before he follows through on his threat to Juliet. And my name will be cleared.* Lily and Colt had a plan, and when this was over, they would both return to their own lives. Plus, she needed to get back to civilization and call Nick. He would be worried if he didn't hear from her soon.

Colt yawned. "We should get moving."

Standing, Lily tried in vain to stifle a yawn. She pointed up the road to a stand of trees. "I'll go use the restroom and then I'm ready to go get this whole thing resolved with the police."

Twenty-Three

Though Colt fought the fatigue as he waited by the ATV, his eyes must have slipped closed. Maybe he even dozed off for a minute. But the distant whine of an engine brought him to his feet, his heart racing. Farther down the valley, a red Jeep rumbled along the dirt road, a trail of dust swirling in its wake. Nerves tense, Colt fired up the four-wheeler and moved it into the trees and out of sight. With a duffle bag full of stolen money in his possession, he'd rather not talk to anyone right now.

He walked to where Lily had disappeared into the forest. She hadn't gone off and got herself lost had she? "Lily!" he yelled.

Colt heard the snap of a twig and walked toward it. As soon as he saw her, she asked, "Is something wrong?"

"Somebody's coming."

The Jeep stopped and idled for a moment before the driver cut the engine. Colt looked behind him, but whoever had stopped was beyond his line of sight, and from the sound of things probably parked on the hairpin turn. Before Colt had driven away from the crash site, he'd looked back. From the road not much seemed out of place. But if someone stopped to peer over the edge, they would see two of the downed trees nearly limbed and an impressive pile of branches stacked on the downhill side.

Colt walked quickly to Lily, grabbed her hand, and put his finger to his mouth. "Shh," he whispered. "Let's see who's here."

He hurried to the roadside. Only the front bumper and winch on the Jeep were visible, but something about it seemed familiar. Parked on the bend in the road like it was, Colt and Lily couldn't get a good look, so they darted to a thicker pack of trees and foliage on the other side. Colt had practiced moving through the woods in stealth mode since he was in grade school, but Lily hadn't mastered even the basics of moving quietly outdoors. He stopped behind a clump of bushes and pulled her down into a crouch. "Wait here. I'm going to get closer and take a look." He started to leave but turned back and dropped to one knee. "I'll come back here for you, so whatever you do, don't move from this spot. Okay?"

She turned trusting eyes toward him and nodded. He planned to do the responsible thing by rising to his feet and leaving to investigate their visitor, but instead he cupped her face in both his hands and kissed her. He deepened the kiss, almost forgetting about the red Jeep and the mystery person, who was probably now investigating the white Ford Ranger. Lily's hands found his arms and he felt her fingernails brush his skin. She moved one hand to his chest and pushed him away. She said only one word, and the tone of her voice hinted at confusion, but thankfully not anger. "Colt."

An apology hung on the tip of his tongue, but he couldn't bring himself to say he was sorry when in truth he wasn't. "I'll be back."

Colt moved across the hillside, careful not to make a sound or be in the open. When he was probably less than a hundred feet from the crash site, three gunshots sounded in quick succession. He moved closer and finally got a look at the shooter, a well-built man of average height, with reddish-blond hair. Colt couldn't be certain from this distance, but the guy was probably in his thirties. He picked up the tent and set it next to some of the other scattered camping gear. Was he the Camo Bandit, or just some drunken redneck who had happened onto the scene? With his gun raised, the man shot the left front tire of the Ranger. He scanned the surrounding woods, and Colt felt the man's eyes passing over his hiding place. "Lily Vanasche! I know you're here," the man bellowed in a raspy voice.

Colt froze, his suspicions confirmed. Other than the breeze rustling through the branches above him, an eerie quiet had settled over the mountain. Suddenly, the man yelled out a string of foul language and began firing rounds from his weapon. Colt backed away, hoping the man's noise would mask any sounds of his escape. His exit route took him lower on the hillside than he expected, and he ended up circling a thick stand of sticker brush to reach the place where he'd left Lily. Colt nearly swore himself when he realized she was gone. *Why didn't she listen? I told her to wait.* Frustrated, he spun in a circle, trying to figure out where she might've gone. *Of all the times to lose her . . .*

Behind Colt, the man yelled about the money, fired another round, and then invited Lily to come out and make a deal. Colt had no idea what she was thinking, but to either escape or make a deal involving the money, she would need to go back to the ATV. Retracing their tracks, he followed the faint trail of crushed grass and then vaulted over a downed tree as he raced up the hill toward the road.

Moments later, he burst through the thick foliage and onto the dirt road. He glanced at the Jeep and saw no one, so he continued running toward the four-wheeler. A sick feeling spread through his gut as he remembered Lily didn't know where he had hidden the ATV. She could be anywhere. Taking a chance, Colt quietly said her name, but heard no response. He reached the four-wheeler and pulled out his ax, wishing he had a gun. Lily hadn't made it back, so either he'd passed her without knowing it, or she'd gone the other direction—closer to the crash site and the gun-toting maniac.

The sun stood directly overhead, and the weather was uncommonly warm for early fall. Colt closed the lid on the rack compartment. Sweat dripped from his forehead as he turned toward the crash site. Time was running out.

He followed a zigzag pattern as he searched the woods, forcing himself to move slowly enough that he wouldn't be heard. Fortunately, the Camo Bandit had created enough ruckus to cover any sounds Colt may have made on his dash to the ATV.

Now, he passed the place where he'd kissed Lily. A twig snapped and branches rustled above him on the hillside. He changed course, aiming to intercept whoever it was. When his boot dislodged a rock and sent it tumbling down the mountain, Colt cringed, hoping a bullet wouldn't find his heart.

He scrambled the rest of the way up the rocky ledge and into the dense foliage above. Lily's voice brought him to a stop. "Colt!"

He turned to see her climbing out from between two large elderberry bushes. He grabbed her arm and helped her to her feet. "I told you to wait for me—not to move," he said angrily and propelled her toward the road.

She pulled back, wrenching her arm free. By the look of terror on her face, a person would think she'd just stepped out of her worst nightmare. "Wait for a dead man? I heard gunshots. He yelled my name. I thought he'd killed you, or maybe you were bleeding to death somewhere." Lily's eyes glistened with tears. She shook her head and walked away.

Colt glanced over his shoulder, then hurried to catch her. He reached out and caught her hand in his. "I'm sorry. I was scared spitless when I couldn't find you. I don't know what I'd do if that guy got his hands on you."

She wiped a tear from her cheek. "I saw him—the man who robbed the bank—and I recognize him. Lewis Henderson is his name. He applied for a loan, but we had to turn him down. He was furious when I told him."

After another glance over his shoulder, Colt nudged Lily forward. "We need to keep moving," he said as they continued up the hill.

At the road, he broke into a jog. A sharp gasp from Lily brought him to a stop. He turned and saw the Camo Bandit carrying an armful of salvaged gear toward his Jeep. Colt reached back and grabbed Lily's hand, forcing her to move her feet faster as he began running for the ATV.

A loud yell sounded behind Colt. He glanced over his shoulder and saw the man climbing into the Jeep. Colt's heart raced, and not just from sprinting. The Jeep's engine fired to life as he and Lily left the small meadow where they'd eaten and entered the trees. He dropped the ax into the ATV's largest storage compartment and closed the lid, then straddled the four-wheeler and started the motor. Lily's hands found his waist as she climbed behind him. "What are we going to do, Colt?"

He moved the gearshift into reverse and backed out of the trees. Then he turned the ATV so it faced the road, as well as the Jeep approaching from the left. "I don't know yet," Colt said, putting the machine into high gear. The terrain and foliage wouldn't allow him to drive very far without a trail, so he needed to get to the road. But to cross this meadow and reach the road, he might have to play chicken with the red Jeep and an armed robber.

Lewis Henderson slowed the Jeep and aimed a pistol through his passenger window. *A moving target is harder to hit,* Colt thought. He gunned the engine and angled to the right—the direction he didn't really want to go. As it was, the gunman blocked the route back to Colt's truck. Taking the old Jeep road farther into the mountains could be risky. Colt hadn't studied the maps well enough to know if he could reach his truck going that way. Plus, even one downed tree blocking the road could spell disaster. He doubted he could saw through another trunk before Henderson caught up to them. If they came upon another tree fall, Colt and Lily would be making a run for it on foot.

Henderson fired two rounds at them. Lily screamed and burrowed her face in Colt's back, tightening her grip on him. The vehicle moved forward. Clearly Henderson meant to cut them off, but his maneuver opened a path from the meadow onto the road behind the Jeep. Colt smiled when Henderson tried to fire a third round and nothing happened. The man dropped the gun and turned into the meadow as if he meant to ram the ATV. "Hold on!" Colt told Lily.

At the last second, he cranked the wheels to the left, turning the four-wheeler so sharply it tipped onto two wheels. He leaned to the inside and straightened the wheels enough that the machine didn't flip. His fender scraped the passenger side of the Jeep as they bounced onto the road. Colt pressed the gas, sending up a cloud of dust as the ATV fishtailed in the loose dirt and gravel. Lily leaned away from him and then said, "He's turning around!"

Colt blinked at the rush of air blowing past his face. He pushed the ATV, going as fast as he dared on the winding, rutted road. Once, negotiating a sharp bend, he had to brake hard, and the four-wheeler went into a skid. He didn't want the Camo Bandit right on his tail when he reached the truck, and theoretically Colt should be able to put some distance between them. Periodically, he felt Lily turn to look behind them. When they neared Colt's truck at the intersection with the Forest Service road, he asked, "Do you see him?"

"No. I think you lost him."

"I doubt we've lost him for good." Colt slowed the ATV and reached into his pocket. "Here are my keys. You start the truck while I get the duffle bag."

Lily took the key ring and again turned to look over her shoulder. Colt's Dodge, parked with two tires off the road in the tall grass, came into view. Something wasn't right. He hit the brakes and slid to a stop in the loose gravel. A plume of dust filled the air. "What the—" He jumped to the ground and ran to the vehicle, with Lily behind him. Using the toe of his boot, he nudged the rear tire. It was flat as a pancake. He pulled on the door handle and it opened. He hadn't seen Lily unlock it, yet she must have. He dug behind the back seat for the lug wrench, thinking this would have to be the fastest tire change in history, or they'd be sitting ducks.

"Colt, we have a problem." Lily sounded panicked.

He stepped back with the wrench in hand. "I know. I'm working on it."

Frowning, she pointed at the front tire. "Look."

His gaze shot to the tire. The side of the rubber bulged with a gaping hole. It had been slashed. He ran to the other side of the vehicle. Those tires were flat as well, and lying in the grass was his red gas can. There was no mistaking it, with his dad's neat block lettering spelling out the name Murdock in black Sharpie ink. The loose cap dangled from the extended nozzle as Colt picked up the can—completely empty. Shaking his head, he tossed the can and the wrench into the truck bed.

Lily's eyes met his from the other side of the truck. "Get back on the four-wheeler," he yelled, then ran around the truck and slammed the door. It was time for Plan B.

Twenty-Four

Lily had a sinking feeling things were about to go from bad to worse. When Colt had looked at her from across the bed of the truck, she'd seen fear in those blue-green eyes, like a sudden squall at sea.

She scrambled onto the four-wheeler and moved back, giving him room to climb on in front of her. Even before he sat down, the machine shot ahead, leaving a trail of dust behind them. Lily looked back once before leaning forward and wrapping her arms around his waist.

"We're going to run out of gas," he said a few minutes later. "Try your phone. See if you have any bars."

Lily's fingers trembled as she dug her phone out of her pocket. She squeezed the protective plastic case, not wanting to drop the phone as the four-wheeler bounced over the rough road. The screen lit up. One bar.

She dialed and pressed "Call," but the call failed. Frowning, she tucked the phone back into her pocket and said above the noise of the motor, "Only one bar. I tried 9-1-1, but it didn't go through. How much gas do we have?"

"At this speed, it won't last long. I switched on the reserve just before we got to the truck."

An SUV barreled around the corner in front of them, and Colt swerved and slowed down. The man driving wore pinstriped blue overalls and had a tuft of white hair that looked like it hadn't seen a comb in at least a week. With one hand maintaining control of the ATV, Colt stood and waved, trying to flag the man down. "Hey! Stop," he yelled. "We need help."

Lily raised her hands and yelled, "Wait!" But the old-timer stared straight ahead, acknowledging Colt with nothing more than a flick of his fingers as he lifted them off the steering wheel. A cloud of dust, as thick as smoke, followed the vehicle. Colt must have considered trying to catch the SUV, because he swerved into the middle of the road like he might make a U-turn. Suddenly, though, he continued down the mountain. That was fine with Lily. She wanted to go one direction—away from the man who had terrorized her during the bank robbery and then kidnapped her.

As the ATV gained speed, Lily clamped her stinging eyes shut and coughed, while Colt muttered under his breath in front of her. The air soon cleared, and Lily wondered how much farther they would need to go before they found help. Early that morning, toward the base of the mountain, they had passed several RVs parked in the grassy meadows off the side of the road. By the look of the current scenery, she guessed they were getting closer.

Barbed-wire fencing held up by weather-beaten round poles came into sight. Most of the land in the lower elevations was fenced for cattle, with gates to allow for hikers and horseback riders. Colt had taken Lily through one such gate on their way out of the mountains with Duke and Charger. The road snaked through a meadow, dotted with wild flowers and cattle. In the middle of that stretch, the four-wheeler engine sputtered and died.

"Shoot!" Colt said. He turned the wheels and let the ATV coast off the road to a standstill in the grass. Then, he jumped to the ground and dug the duffle bag out of the storage compartment. "Come on," he said, offering Lily his hand. "Let's keep moving."

She shuddered to think of the two of them out in the open, with nothing but a skinny fence post to hide behind should Henderson decide to add a drive-by shooting to his rap sheet. She slid her hand into Colt's, and when they reached the road, they started running. About a quarter mile later, when the tree line intersected the road, Colt slowed to a walk. He looked over his shoulder once, and Lily followed his gaze. Behind them, the mountain meadow was a picture of serenity.

Her phone pinged in her pocket, telling her she had messages. "Do you think he's still following us?" she asked, grabbing for her phone.

Colt pulled out his own phone. "Without a doubt. He knows we've got the money, and that dirt bag already slashed all four of my tires. He's not going to give up that easy."

Lily glanced down at her display. Three missed calls from Nick, and one from Angela. She tucked away her phone and watched as Colt dialed 9-1-1 and then raised the phone to his ear. Looking at where the road disappeared around a bend, she asked, "How did he know we came up here?"

"I don't know. I didn't see anyone following—" Suddenly, Colt's voice rose a notch. "We need the police up Fairview Canyon. We found the money from the bank robbery in Lehi, and now the man known as the Camo Bandit is chasing us." Colt paused. "No, ma'am, this is not a prank call. My name is Colt Murdock and I'm with Lily Vanasche, the hostage victim in the robbery. She received a threatening note from the robber last night, and now he's hunting us down. His name is Lewis Henderson. He's armed with a handgun, and shots have been fired."

Lily waited anxiously as Colt began giving the operator directions. Before he could finish, the hum of a vehicle's engine caught her attention. She looked behind her, then grabbed Colt's arm. "There's a car coming."

He spun around and they ran for the trees. "Gotta go," he barked into the phone. "Send someone up here. Quick!" He ended the call and put his phone in his pocket.

Three strands of barbed wire blocked their escape. Colt stepped on the middle one, pushing it down, and lifted the top one. Lily climbed through and then held the wire for him. He tossed the duffle bag onto the ground at her feet and eased through the fence. The vehicle approached slowly. Colt grabbed Lily's hand and pulled her into the bushes. A sticky line of spider webbing circled her neck, making her cringe. When Colt placed a hand on her shoulder and pushed her into a crouch next to him, she came face to face with the likely perpetrator of the webbed gauntlet. Lily tried to stand, but a firm hand gripped her elbow.

"Shh, hold still."

Her neck and arms began to itch. She glanced down, expecting to see an eight-legged culprit exploring her skin. The spider in front of her wrapped its long legs around a mummified fly and spun it a few more times. Lily grimaced, feeling the forest close in around her. Something crawled beneath her pant leg and she swatted at it, only to realize it was a stalk of grass. She brushed at her arms, then checked the location of the spider. With a shudder, she whispered, "I can't do this."

Colt took his eyes off the road and looked at her, then wrapped his arms around her and pulled her into his chest. "I'm sorry. This is my fault. I never should have brought you up here. But I promise I won't let him hurt you."

Lily took a deep breath, focusing on the firmness of the muscles beneath her cheek and the safety she felt in those strong arms. From his comment, he probably thought the likely arrival of the robber was the sole cause of her fear.

She felt Colt's body stiffen and his head lift. "It's him," he said softly.

Lily leaned back and peered through the gap in the leaves. The red Jeep came closer, with Lewis Henderson searching both sides of the road. Colt's voice came out in barely a whisper. "Don't move."

When she felt the man's gaze pass over their location, she clamped her eyes shut and concentrated on holding still. Colt's embrace had pulled her off balance and onto her knees. Now the rock-hard dirt clods dug into her skin. Colt's hand slid down her back and rested at her waist. She focused on the warmth of his skin radiating through her shirt. A cell-phone chime sounded loudly. With a gasp, Lily opened her eyes. Colt's face paled, both of his hands going to his pockets. He silenced his phone and then looked back to the road. The Jeep was about to round the corner and disappear from sight. The hum of the engine moved into the distance, and Lily sighed. Colt stood, bringing his finger to his mouth, "Shh." Then he pointed in the direction the Jeep had gone. "As carefully as we can, let's follow the road."

Lily nodded and they hiked away. When they could no longer hear the crunch of the Jeep's tires on the gravel, Colt retrieved his cell phone. "It looks like dispatch called me back, and I have two missed calls from Agent Dawson." Colt returned the call to the 9-1-1 operator, and from his side of the conversation, Lily thought it sounded like they believed his story and were sending officers. He repeated the directions to their location and described the 1980s Jeep Renegade that Lewis Henderson was driving.

The next call was to Agent Dawson. Colt explained the situation and then fell silent as if listening closely. "That's okay. Yeah, she's fine. We're both fine. And congratulations, man!" After ending the call, Colt said, "He's already on his way. Said he's almost to Fairview and the local sheriff is ahead of him. Hopefully they spot the red Jeep on their drive up here and catch the guy."

"What was the congratulations about?"

"Dawson's wife had a baby last night—a girl named Ella. There were complications and she had an emergency C-section. That's why he didn't get my call."

Lily and Colt continued down the mountain, keeping to the woods and walking parallel to the road. At times it was slow going, with patches of thistle and stickers. In places the terrain was so steep their feet slid, unable to gain traction. A wall of rock jutting out in front of them forced them down onto the road. Colt stopped and tilted his head as if listening for something before he set foot onto the gravel.

He broke into a jog and crossed the road. Lily followed and they both looked over the edge where the land dropped off sharply. There was no way they could safely walk off-road over there. Colt must have come to the same conclusion because he continued running along the road's edge, slowly pulling ahead of her. Maybe it was the lack of sleep catching up to her, or the stress, but Lily's legs felt like dead weight and she had no energy. By the time Colt glanced over his shoulder again, she was probably a hundred feet behind. He stopped and waited, repositioning the strap of the bag on his shoulder. "You okay?" he said as she jogged toward him.

She pasted a smile on her face. "I'm tired is all."

Before Lily reached his side, they heard the crunch of tires on gravel. Terror struck her heart as the red Jeep burst around the corner and barreled down on them. Colt spun to face the vehicle as the driver locked up the brakes. The Jeep skidded to a stop, blocking their escape and sending a billow of dust into their faces.

Twenty-Five

The man Lily had hoped to never lay eyes on again—Lewis Henderson, dressed in a camouflage T-shirt that perfectly suited his media-given nickname—stepped out of the Jeep. He waved his gun and yelled at Colt. Four-letter expletives flew from his mouth, and Lily recalled the same thing happening at her desk a few weeks ago, when she had informed Henderson that his small business loan could not be approved. He had already maxed out three credit cards and had little in the way of assets to secure the loan. A locksmith by trade, he wanted the loan to start his own company. Over the past decade, he had worked for a string of different employers, and Lily wouldn't have been surprised if he'd been fired more than once. His volatile temper and erratic personality reminded her of an ex-boyfriend from college who had gotten involved with drugs.

"Stay back, Lily," Colt said as he stepped off the road toward the edge of a cliff. He held his hands out in front of him, as if to pacify the gunman.

Lily inched away, praying the guy wouldn't shoot Colt.

Henderson moved a step closer. "You stole my bag."

Colt took the bag off his shoulder. "I found this back yonder, when I cleared some downed timber. You got your name on it anywhere?" He loosened the top of the bag and looked inside.

Henderson laughed, a grating sound that was overly loud in the still of the forest. Suddenly turning serious, he leveled his weapon at Colt. "Since I have the gun, I get the last word. And I say it's my bag, so toss that thing over here. Now!"

Colt scratched his head and repositioned his ball cap. "You've got a good point there. I just have one question for you first. How did you know we came up here? I didn't see anyone following me last night, or this morning."

Again Henderson laughed. "Since you ain't gonna be alive much longer, I'll tell ya. You ever heard of the Find My iPhone app? I hid my phone in your truck last night, then used my girlfriend's phone to track it down." As if supremely proud of himself, he pulled an iPhone from his pocket and waved it in the air. "I lost the signal when you went in the mountains, but by then I guessed where you were headed. Once I found your truck, it was easy to jimmy the lock and take this back."

While the man talked, Colt had inched even closer to the edge of the steep cliff that dropped away, making Lily fear he might fall. Colt nodded. "You're right, Henderson. That was pretty clever. I don't know if I would have thought of that. But I'm wondering if that was before or after you slashed all four of my new tires."

"Toss that bag over here. I'm tired of waiting."

Colt stretched his arm to the side, letting the canvas bag dangle over the cliff. "Hang on a second. Let's talk this through. You let Lily go, and I'll give you the bag."

Henderson's face turned bright red. "Wrong! Now give me the money," he yelled. Apparently, Colt wasn't moving fast enough, because the man waved the gun in Lily's direction. "Throw it here, before I shoot somebody."

"You shoot and I drop the bag."

Lily felt her chest tighten. Obviously Colt was stalling—she just hoped he didn't take it too far. Without help, they wouldn't make it off this mountain alive. Searching for her faith, Lily lifted her eyes and sent up a prayer. *Father, please help us.*

Henderson swiveled the gun between her and Colt.

"Whoa there," Colt said. "Easy, dude. I'll do it. I promise. But first you have to let her go."

Henderson nodded at her. "Get outta here."

She looked at Colt, saying his name once before he cut her off. "Run, Lily." She watched over her shoulder as Colt gathered the duffle bag. "Here it comes."

Henderson's gaze never left the bag as Colt lifted the bundle, like a pitcher winding up for the throw. But instead of sending the wad of canvas toward the robber, Colt let it fly off to the left and away from Lily. The bag hit the road and rolled, sending bundles of cash and loose currency into the dirt. Henderson lowered his weapon and swore as he hurried toward the dollar bills fluttering in the breeze, turning his back on Colt.

As if the ball had been hiked on a football play, Colt bolted forward. A gunshot rang out, followed by a grunt as he tackled Henderson. The two men hit the gravel and rolled—arms and legs flying like something from a round of mixed martial arts on ESPN. Again the weapon fired, and Lily's hand flew to her mouth as she screamed.

A car careened around the corner, red and blue lights flashing. The police cruiser stopped behind the Jeep. The driver's-side door flew open as the wrestling match continued in the gravel. A third shot fired from Henderson's weapon, punching a hole in the passenger side of the Jeep.

Lily's eyes darted between the fight and the officer. Colt seemed oblivious to the fact a policeman had arrived. Henderson was on his back, with Colt straddling him. Colt had one hand on the gun barrel and the other balled in a fist, pummeling the Camo Bandit in the face. A moment later, Henderson let go of his weapon and used both hands to try to protect his face. Colt scrambled to his feet and pointed the gun at the robber.

The officer, wearing a cowboy hat and boots, aimed his gun from behind his car door. "Drop your weapon and get down on the ground." In the background, the officer's radio crackled as he yelled, "Down on your knees! Drop your weapon! Both of you get face down on the ground. Hands behind your heads."

Colt jerked his head in the direction of the commanding voice. Breathing heavily, he quickly let the pistol dangle from one finger as he followed orders. He set the gun on the ground, pushed it away, and wiped the trickle of blood from below his nose with the back of his wrist. He winced and shifted his weight as his knees and then his chest touched the rocky surface.

Lily saw all of this unfold in a state of shock, more like watching a completely unexpected scene in a movie than a real part of her own life. The officer glanced between Henderson and Colt. Both of them were on the ground with their hands in plain sight. Lily thought it was over, but the cop moved warily to the side, most likely putting himself in a position to keep his eye and his gun on both men.

When Henderson rose to his knees and placed a hand on his Jeep as if to stand up, the cop raised his weapon. "You there! Don't move! Stay down on the ground or I'll shoot."

Henderson looked at the officer's gun through swelling eyelids and dropped back to the ground.

At the sound of approaching vehicles, Lily glanced to the road. A black unmarked car and two county vehicles pulled up behind the Fairview sheriff's car. Officers swarmed the scene, some aiming guns and others Tasers at the two men on the ground. The Fairview sheriff issued orders to the arriving officers. "You two take that one," he said, pointing at Colt. A deputy pulled out handcuffs as he moved toward Colt and kicked the gun out of reach.

Lily hurried forward. "You're arresting the wrong guy," she said to the sheriff and pointed at Henderson. "He's the man who robbed One National Bank in Lehi. He tried to shoot us."

"Miss, I'll ask you to stand back," said the sheriff, using his left hand to wave her away.

The deputy apprehending Colt knelt and cuffed him before pulling him to his feet, while the other officers stood guard, guns drawn.

A familiar-looking officer told Lily, "Sit tight, Miss Vanasche. Someone will take your statement soon." While she wasn't positive, she thought he might be one of the officers who had arrested Colt at the restaurant.

Two cops dragged an unhappy Henderson to their car and locked him in the backseat. The Camo Bandit threw out complaints the entire way, especially the four-letter variety.

The officers who took Colt didn't end up putting him in their cruiser. Agent Dawson stepped out of the unmarked car and, after identifying himself, took Colt aside. When the FBI agent finished talking with Colt, Dawson motioned for one of the deputies, who then stepped behind Colt and unlocked the cuffs. Walking toward them, Lily heard the deputy laugh and say, "Colton Murdock, that's twice I've used my handcuffs to take you into custody in the last week. Dude, let's try not to make it a third, all right?"

Colt chuckled. "Yes, sir. I'll try to steer clear of your county for a while."

Agent Dawson turned to Lily. "Miss Vanasche, may I speak with you?"

Lily followed him away from the others, anxious to explain what had happened at the bank, now that she finally remembered. While she told Dawson the story, a couple of the other officers pulled on gray latex gloves and worked the scene, collecting the money and canvas duffle bag, along with Henderson's gun. They stored each item in an evidence bag labeled with a black marker.

When Lily had finished her statement and answered all of Agent Dawson's questions, he thanked her and said he would be in touch. She could expect a subpoena to testify when Lewis Henderson's case went to court.

Colt grinned as Lily joined him. He wrapped both arms around her waist and asked, "Are you okay?"

"Of course. But what about you?" She touched the bright-red spot on his cheek that would soon be a dark bruise. Dirt and blood streaked his sweaty face.

He turned his arm and Lily could see gravel embedded in his forearm and elbow, and several small cuts clogged with dried blood. He chuckled. "I'm fine. Nothing a hot shower won't fix."

Lily shook her head and pulled away from him. They'd just survived a dangerous experience and he was making jokes? "What on earth were you thinking, running at him like that? He could have shot you."

Smiling, Colt closed the gap between them. "Better me than you."

She raised her eyebrows. *Men!*

His voice turned serious. "With his back to me and his gun lowered, it seemed like good timing. You heard what he said. Once he got his hands on the money, what would stop him from shooting both of us? Henderson doesn't seem like the type to leave witnesses. That guy's got a few loose screws. He looked ten years older than me, so I figured I had a good chance at taking him. More than anything, if someone was going to get shot, I didn't want it to be you. I wanted to keep his attention on me, to give you time to get away. I knew the police were close." Colt's expression changed. "Plus, after what I saw in that surveillance video, Henderson had it coming. He had no right to hit you."

Lily's breath caught in her throat and her eyes filled with tears. Not trusting her voice, she simply hugged Colt. When his arms tightened around her and she felt his solid chest against her cheek, she exhaled and relaxed. Then she murmured, "Thank you. I've never had anyone risk his life for me before."

He tipped her chin up and looked intently into her eyes. "Lily Vanasche, I'd die for you any day."

Before she could get over the shock of what he'd said, he kissed her. His lips caressed hers, sending a tingle all the way to her toes that made her knees go weak. If he hadn't been holding her so tightly, her legs might have buckled. She ran her fingers across the nape of his neck as they embraced.

Someone cleared his throat from behind Colt. "Excuse me," an officer said. "We'd like to take you both down to the station to answer a few more questions."

Twenty-Six

Colt sat on an uncomfortable chair in the hall, waiting for Lily to finish with the detective. He peeked through the hole in his pants as he pulled the fabric away from the bloody scrape on his knee. He was paying the price for that tackle on the gravel. Noticing his knuckles looked swollen, he flexed his fingers. But bringing that guy down had felt really good.

Detective Hansen had taken Colt's statement. The exact spot of the wreckage was marked on a topographical map so they could recover the vehicle. When Colt had left Hansen's office, he had found Lily in the chair he now occupied. She'd been talking on her phone until the detective held his door open and motioned for her to enter his office.

Lily's interview with Hansen was taking far longer than Colt's had, which made sense because she now remembered more about the day of the robbery. Colt pulled his hat down over his eyes, then leaned back, crossed his arms, and stretched out his legs.

Sometime later, in that fuzzy place between reality and dreamland, he heard the office manager say, "She might still be in with the detective, but come right this way and you can wait for her if you'd like."

"Yes, thank you. I'll wait." Recognizing the voice, Colt looked up as Nick Borino lowered himself onto a chair. After sending Colt a cursory nod, Lily's fiancé rested his elbows on his dark-washed designer jeans and started tapping the screen of his smart phone. An oversized silver watch caught a glint of sunlight and reflected a bouncing beam onto the opposite wall. The collar on Nick's white-and-blue-striped polo shirt still had its fresh-from-the store crease.

Colt would bet a hundred bucks this guy was the other half of the phone call Lily had been so wrapped up in when Colt left the detective's office. So much for grabbing that bite to eat with Lily after they were done here. Then again, following through on the invite he had issued on their drive to the station might be iffy, with good old Duke currently being his only functioning form of transportation. And of course, the horse was miles away.

Immediately after his interview with Detective Hansen, Colt had called some towing companies. He'd found a guy familiar with the area that could haul the truck and four-wheeler to the nearest tire shop. Colt had arranged for a new set of tires, but it would be several hours before he could pick them up.

He shook his head, trying not to think about the city slicker across the room who had won Lily's heart. With the resolution of this case, he might as well resign himself to the fact that she was about to step out of his life for good.

Hansen's door clicked open and Lily emerged from his office. Colt met her gaze. Just as she smiled at him, Nick stood and said, "Lily, are you all right?"

Clearly, she hadn't noticed her fiancé until he spoke. "I'm fine," she told him. Her gaze shifted between the two men. "Uh, Nick, have you met Colt? He's the guy who rescued me."

Colt stood, gritting his teeth when his knee didn't want to straighten all the way. He limped the first two steps and then reached out.

Nick shook his hand. "Nice to meet you. I'm Nick Borino — Lily's fiancé."

Not bothering to smile, Colt put extra force behind his squeeze of Nick's hand. "That's what I hear. Congratulations."

"Thanks."

Lily fidgeted with the sweatshirt and phone she held in front of her, then said, "Colt, do you need a ride? We could give him ride home, couldn't we, Nick?"

Her fiancé looked Colt over from top to bottom and grimaced. To a slick-dressing TV personality, Colt probably looked like a rough and rowdy redneck. Nick said, "Of course," but his expression made it clear this was the last thing he wanted to do.

"No thanks, I've already called a tow truck," Colt replied.

Nick wrapped an arm around Lily. "I'm going to ask the detective a couple of questions and then we'll get going. Just hang tight. This will only take a minute." He pressed his lips to hers in a quick kiss. Her cheeks blushed as he disappeared into Hansen's office.

Colt knew he should leave. The tow-truck driver currently had no plans to stop by the police station and pick up a passenger. But the last person Colt wanted to bum a ride off was Nick Borino.

"Thanks for helping me last night," Lily said. "You're like a regular knight in shining armor."

Colt chuckled as he met her gaze, remembering his little sister saying the same thing about Lily's fiancé. The natural blush looked good on her. Too bad it wasn't his kiss that had triggered it. "You're welcome. Anytime." He stepped closer, knowing Nick might exit the detective's office at any second. "Lily," Colt whispered. "Don't marry that guy. He's not right for you."

She opened her mouth, but before she could respond, the door opened and Nick emerged with a notepad and pen. He shook Hansen's hand, a happy grin on his face. "Thank you for your time, Detective. I appreciate the information and the statement about the case."

Colt pulled his phone out as he stepped away. "Goodbye, Lily. You take care of yourself." He walked down the hall before touching redial on his phone. Terry the tow truck guy answered on the first ring with a cheerful hello.

"This is Colt Murdock again. I'm stuck at the police station. Is there any chance you could swing by here once you've got my truck?"

The streetlight turned green, and Colt hit the accelerator. The Cummins diesel engine rumbled as the truck gathered speed on the way out of town. Four new tires hummed beneath the vehicle on the asphalt. Colt tuned the radio to the local country music station and settled in for the drive home. While he had waited for his truck, he'd grabbed a burger and shake at a fast-food joint down the street from the tire store.

The ringer sounded on his cell phone. Colt didn't recognize the number as he said hello.

A woman's voice, clear and pleasant, said, "Hi, I'm Cassidy Pearson with Fox News. We're in Juab County covering the developing story of the Camo Bandit. Detective Hansen referenced you as the individual who assisted in apprehending the man responsible for robbing the One National Bank and kidnapping employee Lily Vanasche. Is that correct?"

Colt smiled. He'd always liked Fox News, and he had no trouble imagining Cassidy Pearson on the other end of the line. A good-looking, tall brunette, with a down-to-earth kind of personality—or at least that was the impression she gave from behind the camera. More than once he'd seen her cover sporting events and interview sports celebrities, although he didn't think she was Fox's regular sports reporter. Her sweet smile probably got her through doors that were closed to the Nick Borinos of newscasting. "Yes, ma'am. That's right," Colt said.

"Would you be available for an interview?"

"Uh, when?"

"Now, if possible. My camera crew is just packing up. We're leaving the county jail. Is there someplace we could meet you?"

Colt turned on his blinker and eased off the road. "Sure, I'll give you an interview. I'm only a couple of blocks away, so why don't I just meet you at the jail."

"Awesome," Cassidy replied. Then her muffled yell came through in the background, as if she'd held the phone away from her. "Hey, you guys, set everything back up. He's meeting us here." He imagined her pulling the phone back to her mouth. "Thank you, Mr. Murdock. Our van is parked by the front entrance."

"Sounds good. I'll see you in five." He smiled to himself as he made a U-turn. Nick Borino wasn't the only guy who'd be on the news tonight.

Twenty-Seven

Lily massaged her forehead with her fingertips and leaned back against the kitchen chair. "Thanks, Angela. I really appreciate your parents letting me stay here."

Angela stood to clear away their empty bowls. "No problem. You can stay as long as you like. It will be like old times."

When they'd shared an apartment in college and then later the townhouse, ice cream had always been their go-to food after one of them had a bad day. The fact that Lily's best friend pulled it out tonight was a testimony to how well she knew her.

A mournful meow filled the room. Lily looked down at the calico twitching her tail and rubbing her shoulder across Lily's leg. "I know, Juliet. I miss him too." She scooped the cat into her arms and cradled the small feline against her neck. Someone from the police department had called on the drive home to tell her they found Juliet at Henderson's apartment and that Lily could pick her up at the local animal shelter. Of course she had asked Nick to drive her there first thing.

"I can't believe what that guy did to your cat ... and your house," Angela said. "What kind of sick, twisted person does that?"

"The cops said he has a history of mental illness and drug addiction, as well as two prior arrests for animal abuse when he was a juvenile." Lily shuddered. "I'm sick at the thought of what might have happened if Henderson had been the one who found me after that crash instead of Colt. Or what if I would have been home last night when he broke into my house?"

"Stop!" Angela said. "You can't think like that."

Lily couldn't hold back the tears that pricked her eyes and trickled onto her cheeks. As if peering through a rain-covered windshield, she looked at the blurry image of her friend. "I can't get it out of my head—the picture of Colt tackling him. Henderson tried over and over again to shoot him. Colt never wavered; he attacked like a pit bull."

Angela smiled. "What did you say Colt told you? I mean, to me he sounds more like a German shepherd protection dog than a pit bull."

Lily pulled a tissue from the box on the table, then wiped her eyes and took a deep breath. "He said he'd die for me anytime. But who says stuff like that nowadays?"

Angela put her hand to her heart and let out a romantic sigh. "Someone who hasn't let chivalry die in the face of the women's rights movement."

"Maybe."

"Maybe? Girl, you better know I'm right," Angela said. "I met your cowboy for one minute and figured out he's a good guy and a gentleman. Now what you need to ask yourself is, are you engaged to the right guy?"

Lily lifted her brows. "Nick and I have been friends forever, and we've dated for almost a year. It's only natural to take the next step . . ." Her voice faded as she contemplated her future.

Angela folded her arms across her chest and waited.

"Earlier today, when I got the messages from you and Nick saying you'd seen my house and were notifying the police, I called Nick back to tell him I was fine. As soon as he found out where I was and what had happened, he said he was on his way to pick me up. Do you know how I felt? Disappointed. Colt and I were planning to get something to eat after we finished at the police station. Even now, I wish I had done that instead of walking out the door with Nick. All I can think about is Colt. Where is he? How is he feeling? Did he get some antibacterial ointment on those cuts and scratches? What's wrong with me that I'm not even excited to see my soon-to-be husband? You always seem excited to see Damian."

"That's because I *am* always excited to see him," Angela replied.

"All Nick could talk about today was the news angle of my story. It's great that he loves his job, and I'm proud of how far he's come, but sometimes I feel like our relationship takes a back seat to his career. Like he's more excited about the next big story than about anything I have to say."

"Honestly, Lil, if you can't stop thinking about Colt, maybe you should look into it, before it's too late."

Lily breathed out a loud sigh and covered her face with her hands. "What about Nick? After that fiasco last week, the whole state knows we're engaged."

A smile lit Angela's face. "You know how it is—front-page news one day, forgotten the next. They'll get over it. What's important now is your happiness. Who is going to make you happy today, tomorrow, and forever?"

Lily thought for a moment. "I'm not sure yet."

"Girlfriend, you better figure it out, and soon."

Lily stood in front of the mirror, brushing her damp hair. After all the dust she'd eaten on that dirt road, a hot shower had never felt better. Her mind kept questioning how she and Colt had survived on the mountain in such dangerous circumstances.

Had her prayer been answered, or were they just lucky? To discount it as luck felt wrong. Perhaps Colt had also prayed, and God had answered his petition, not Lily's. But that didn't feel right either. Warmth spread through her soul and tears of gratitude filled her eyes as she realized God *had* heard and answered her prayer. Perhaps she could again find the faith to believe in Him and trust in His timing.

Lily spread a line of paste on her toothbrush and had it poised in front of her mouth when Angela's youngest sister pounded on the door. "Lily, come quick! Angela says your cowboy's on TV."

"Colt?" Lily gasped. She dropped her toothbrush on the counter, yanked the door open, and rushed into the family room. Angela sat perched on the edge of the couch, the remote poised for action in her right hand, and the TV paused. The image frozen on the screen showed Colt standing in front of his truck with a Fox News reporter. Angela patted the spot next to her. "I'll rewind it so you can see from the beginning."

The female reporter pushed her dark, wavy hair back and adjusted her earpiece. She made eye contact with the camera and sent a supermodel smile into the homes of thousands of viewers. "Good evening, I'm Cassidy Pearson reporting from Juab County, where the Camo Bandit, now identified as Lewis Henderson of Lehi, Utah, was apprehended earlier today. Henderson is being charged in the robbery of the One National Bank. He will also face charges of attempted murder, assault and battery, and aggravated kidnapping." The camera view widened, and Cassidy turned her winning smile on Colt as she moved closer to him. So close, in fact, her shoulder touched his. "Here with me is Colton Murdock, the man who heroically captured and disarmed Henderson. Tell us the events leading up to your encounter with the Camo Bandit."

The microphone moved in front of Colt, who showed Cassidy that mischievous half grin that had endeared him to Lily. "I don't know if I'd go so far as to call it heroic, Miss Pearson. I just did what I had to." He gave a brief synopsis of what led them to find the money and how Henderson had tracked them down and threatened to shoot both him and Lily.

When he finished, Cassidy reached out and touched his shirt, pulling it away from his waist. Lily leaned forward, her mouth opening as she watched Cassidy's smile turn flirtatious.

"Jumping between a gunman and a girl. If that's not heroic, I don't know what is. I highly doubt I'm the only girl out there with that opinion." The camera zoomed in on Colt's T-shirt, where Cassidy slipped a manicured fingernail through a small round hole. "Looks like you came awfully close to taking a bullet protecting Lily Vanasche."

Colt glanced down and chuckled. "I guess so, but close only counts in horseshoes and hand grenades."

Cassidy laughed. Lily tapped Angela and pointed to the screen. "Is she flirting with him?"

"She's definitely flirting with him."

"This is Cassidy Pearson with Fox News, reporting from the county jail," the reporter said. "Back to you, Caleb."

Angela shut off the TV and looked at Lily. "What should worry you is that he was flirting back."

Heat flared inside Lily. She didn't care much for Cassidy Pearson at the moment. "She's not Colt's type."

"I doubt he cares about that right now. Look at it from his perspective. The guy is nearly shot, and then he goes a round of boxing with an armed madman only to have the girl he fought to protect run off with another guy. That cowboy's on the rebound. If you don't do something quick, you won't get a second chance."

Lily groaned. "You make it sound so dramatic, Angela. What was I supposed to do? Nick insisted on picking me up. I couldn't tell him no. After all, he is my fiancé."

Angela put her arm around Lily. "You're my best friend and I just want you to be happy. But from what I can see, I don't think Nick is your match."

"You've never even liked him all that much."

"I know, but I held my tongue because I didn't have anyone to compare him to before now. Did you know your face lit up like a Christmas tree when Colt walked into the bank yesterday? I've never seen that with you and Nick."

Lily bit down on her lower lip and stared at her fingernails. Angela linked her arm around Lily's and started to stand. "I'll bet you're tired. Everything always looks better after a good night's sleep. Just promise me you'll think about what I said."

Twenty-Eight

Colt let the warm water cascade over his shoulders and down his back. For the third time he touched his side and glanced down. A two-inch pink welt marked his skin above his hip. At the time he attacked Lewis Henderson, he hadn't realized how close he'd come to being seriously injured, or even killed.

Hours after the fight, while in the restroom at a fast-food joint, he had scratched an itch on his side, only to have the skin sting. That was when he found the two holes in his shirt and the pink welt above his hipbone where the bullet must have grazed him. As Colt had poked his finger through the holes in his shirt, he thought he might lose his meal right there in the men's room. He hadn't really felt nervous or scared when he'd faced Henderson on that remote mountain road. But leaning over the porcelain sink with air conditioning blowing from the vent overhead, he knew those suppressed emotions had caught up with him. His pulse throbbed in his ears, and he started to sweat.

Colt turned off the shower. No doubt God had watched over him—protected him and Lily. Colt needed to focus on that, instead of the nagging "what if" thoughts that had plagued him

230

since he had finished talking to Cassidy Pearson. During the interview, he never would have mentioned the bullet's near miss and the holes it left in his clothing, but she had a real eye for detail and had noticed them herself. In front of the camera, she had sensationalized the whole incident, and it got Colt thinking more than he would have otherwise.

With a towel wrapped around his waist, he walked into his bedroom. His boxers were in the top drawer, and his wallet lay on the dresser. Next to his wallet, he'd dropped a business card featuring the blue Fox News logo in the top left corner. Colt picked it up and read the name and number, then flipped it over to glance at the back. After Cassidy had put the microphone away and the crew had cut the power to the cameras, she had hung out next to Colt's truck, asking him questions completely unrelated to the Camo Bandit incident. If it weren't for her crew's not-so-subtle hints that it was time to go, who knows how long the two of them might have kept talking.

Colt tapped the card against his fingers. He just might have to give her a call this weekend.

His cell phone rang. The display showed his mother's name. He smiled. "Hello, Mama. How are you?"

"How am I?"

Colt recognized that tone. Exasperation. Disbelief. Definitely the you-are-in-trouble-with-your-mother voice.

"Colt, honey, I swear, you are going to be the death of me. My son's in a brawl with a notorious outlaw, he's nearly shot in the belly, he helps the cops arrest said outlaw, and then he's the top story on the ten o'clock news. But does he tell his mama any of this? No! I'm in Tennessee and I get a call on my cell phone from Deb, my nosey next-door neighbor."

Hearing his mother's native Southern accent, which always became more prominent when she was angry, made him smile. "Mama, don't worry. Everything is fine. That reporter exaggerated the whole story. It wasn't that dramatic."

"I don't believe you. I reckon if my boy has a bullet hole in his shirt, then something big happened. And Sam said you brought a girl to sleep at the house late last night."

"That was Lily Vanasche. The lady who was—"

"Honey, everyone knows who Lily Vanasche is—Nick Borino's fiancé. I want to know why you're sneaking her into my house in the middle of the night when I'm out of town."

"I'm sorry, but we had to get an early start on looking for that lost money."

"Most people in your shoes call the police. Didn't I teach you about 9-1-1 in kindergarten? I can't believe you started a fight with that man when he had a gun. How many times have I told you boys to just walk away? No good ever comes from fighting."

Colt laughed. "Mama, I was walking away. In fact, I was running away, but Lewis Henderson was crazy. He might not have let Lily and me leave that mountain alive."

His mother let out a long sigh, and Colt imagined her rubbing her forehead, a sign that she was about to cave. "Can you at least promise me you'll let the police handle things from now on?"

"Yes, the police can take it from here."

"You're sure you don't need to see the doctor?"

"Yes, Mama. I do not need to see a doctor."

"Well, all right then. You stop by the house on Friday after I get home and let me have a look at you. I need to see for myself, and I want to hear all the details from you, not some reporter."

"I can do that."

"I'll see you then, honey. I love you."

Early the next morning, Colt climbed into his truck. He planned to return the four-wheeler to his dad's shop and then get to work. He couldn't expect Jared to cover for him indefinitely. Things had piled up after being gone for the hunt, and the unexpected absence the day before had put him even more behind. He moved the gearshift into reverse and placed his arm over the passenger seat. He looked over his shoulder. Lily's bag still lay on the back seat where she'd tossed it the day before.

Colt returned the gearshift to park and leaned onto his elbow to reach under the passenger seat. Suddenly, things didn't look so bleak. Before he and Lily had taken the four-wheeler up the mountain, she had tucked her purse beneath the seat. If nothing else, he'd at least see her once more.

The goodbye he uttered the day before had come out sounding curter than he had intended. But as much as he might want to, he could never take it back. He wouldn't stoop to begging. Her phone call to her fiancé to come pick her up had been Colt's cue to step aside. She must love the guy—she was engaged to him after all. Colt would stay out of her way and she could enjoy her life . . . after he returned her purse.

The drive to his parents' house was an inconvenience when he had a full schedule of work ahead of him, but he didn't want to haul the ATV around town all day, either. Colt parked next to the shop and lowered the tailgate on his pickup.

His sister, shading her eyes from the sun, walked toward him as he straddled the four-wheeler. "Well, you appear to be moving around just fine."

Colt grinned back at her as he fired up the engine. "Never felt better, Lizzy." He backed down the ramp and drove through the open door into the shop.

As he walked back to get the ramp, she intercepted him. "Mama told me to look you over, make sure you're okay." He rolled his eyes as she studied his face. She touched his cheek. "Does that hurt?"

Colt shook his head and told a little white lie. "Nah, it's fine."

Lizzy pointed to his white polo shirt. "And your side?"

He pulled it up and peered down. The pink welt was not as prominent as the night before. "See? It's just a scratch."

"Good, I'll tell Mama she can stop worrying. You wanna come eat pancakes with me and Sam?"

"No, I just ate. I gotta get to work before Dad fires me."

Colt put away the ramp and closed the garage door on the shop. He waved to his sister as he drove away.

Colt finished up with the Alpine School District representative over new construction projects as the lunch hour rolled around. He had made the requested revisions to the contract and things were moving along with the new elementary school. If all went according to plan, they should be able to break ground within the next eight weeks.

For the hundredth time that day, Colt's thoughts turned to Lily. One National Bank wasn't far from where he was. He pulled the purse from beneath the seat and set it next to him. The thought of seeing another man's fiancé shouldn't bring a smile to his face and send the blood rushing through his veins, but it did.

Colt parked in the same spot as Monday night and pulled the straps of Lily's purse and bag over his shoulder. When he stepped out of the noonday sun into the bank's lobby, he paused to let his eyes adjust. The teller behind the counter smiled at him. His gaze skimmed over her toward the small collection of desks. The one he'd seen Lily occupying on his previous visit was empty, but the curly-haired, dark-skinned woman whom Lily had introduced as Angela met his gaze.

He took a step in her direction and asked, "Is Lily here?"

Angela shook her head. "No, she's talking with Nick. They left to pick up lunch. You can wait. I know she'd want you to."

So much for seeing her. He crossed the lobby to Angela's desk in a few long strides. "Sounds like she's busy, so I'll be on my way. But these belong to her. Can you make sure she gets them?"

Angela stood and picked up her phone. "You can give them to her yourself. I'll send her a text to let her know you're here."

Colt dropped the purse and bag behind her desk and leaned toward Angela. "Keep a close eye on the purse," he said in exaggeratedly soft whisper. "Her engagement ring is in there. We wouldn't want that to get lost." He knew his voice dripped with sarcasm. He walked toward the door.

"Colt, wait!" Angela called.

He glanced over his shoulder and wondered at the distraught look on Lily's friend's face. But obviously none of this was any of his business. "I've gotta get back to work. Make sure she gets her purse. Okay?"

"Sure, but please don't leave until after you see her."

"No thanks," Colt replied after turning back toward the door. *I've seen all I need to see.*

Twenty-Nine

Lily's phone vibrated in her pocket with an incoming text message. But this was hardly the time to take her attention away from Nick to answer it. His eyes looked darker than normal, and his facial expression had gone from relaxed to tense and pinched within seconds. "You let me announce our engagement to the whole state and now you're breaking up with me?"

Lily felt her body stiffen at his harsh tone. "Nick, all I'm saying is I don't know. After everything that happened last week, I need some space and a little time to sort things out."

He slammed his palm against the steering wheel. "Everything that happened? Is this about that hunter? Lily, what happened during those four days in the mountains?"

"Nothing happened—"

Nick let out a grunt followed by his favorite expletive. "First everything happens, and then you say nothing happened. Well, I'm not buying it. Something happened with that guy, and I want to know about it."

Lily clenched her trembling fingers in her lap. Adrenaline flooded her system, and she recognized the fear. Far too many times in the past week she had been forced to keep company with fear. And she wanted no more of it. Her eyes filled with tears. "Nick, just take me back to the bank. We'll talk more later."

"No! We'll talk now. This isn't the kind of conversation you can leave for later, Lil."

"I did kiss him, and through the whole ordeal we became close friends, but that's all."

"What can you possibly see in some redneck hunter?"

The first tears spilled over Lily's lower lids and dampened her cheeks. "I don't want to talk about this when you're upset. Just take me back."

Nick took a deep breath and glared at her. "I can't believe you'd cheat on me like that."

"At the time I didn't remember you, our engagement, or even my name. I'm sorry."

Although Nick wasn't yelling, the anger directed at her was too much. Lily grabbed the door handle and tugged. The door swung open, and she touched her toe to the asphalt of the parking lot. Nick caught her left wrist in his hand before she could get out. "Sit down. We're not done here. I want to understand exactly what's going on."

Lily yanked her arm out of his grasp and stumbled from the vehicle. "Don't you dare tell me what to do." She took a step back, rubbing her sore wrist. The joint had popped when she pulled away from him. Silence filled the gap between them. "You would never take a bullet for me, would you?" Lily asked finally.

Nick leaned back and let out a laugh. "What does that have to do with anything?"

Lily stuck her head into the car. "You'd know if you kept an eye on what the competition is reporting."

"You're not making sense. I don't have time for riddles."

"Just leave, Nick. I'm walking."

Lily slammed the door, and Nick cringed as if she had damaged his precious car. At that moment, she realized he probably loved his car more than he loved her. Through the blur of tears, she hurried toward the street. It couldn't be more than a mile to the bank. She wiped her eyes. At least the walk would give her time to get her emotions under control.

As she stepped through the bushes separating the parking lot from the sidewalk, the image of Nick wouldn't leave her mind. She had no idea he had such a temper, and his bad temper made him ugly. Each time his words echoed in her thoughts, she fought to hold back the river of tears. She cared for Nick, but could a successful marriage be built on the kind of foundation they had? She didn't think so.

Lily hadn't gone more than a block before a car slowed behind her. She glanced over her shoulder. At the sight of Nick's BMW she stared straight ahead. "Lil, I'm sorry," he said. "Get in the car and I'll drive you to the bank."

His apology didn't sound particularly genuine. Lily put out her hand to wave him away and shook her head. "It's not that far. Just let me walk. I need some time alone."

"Come on, Lily. Don't be stubborn."

Traffic was too heavy to allow the car behind Nick to easily pass, and the driver honked. "Just go. I'll call you later," she said. Nick glanced in his rearview mirror and then rolled up the window. She watched as he accelerated away from her. Exhaust tainted the air, making Lily long for the sweet mountain breeze. Fresh tears trickled down her cheeks. This time she didn't bother trying to dry her eyes. The hurt went too deep.

The hum of engines and tires kept Lily from noticing the truck that slowed behind her a few minutes later. "Lily?"

At the sound of the familiar voice, she spun to face the white Dodge. She wiped her eyes, bringing into focus the red, triangular J. M. & Sons logo. The door lock on the passenger side popped up. Colt glanced in his rearview mirror and Lily followed his gaze. Two cars were slowing behind him, their left blinkers flashing as they looked for an opening in the neighboring lane.

His eyes traveled from her face to her high-heeled dress shoes, and his brow furrowed. "Hop in. I'll give you a lift."

Without hesitation, Lily practically catapulted herself into the cab of his truck. She knew someday she would look back on this moment and smile. The tenderness in Colt's eyes drew her to him now, just like it had when he'd found her lost in the woods. Lily pulled the passenger door closed, and the exhaust pipe spewed a cloud of black smoke as Colt accelerated. He darted glances at her but didn't say anything.

During the short drive to the bank, Lily tried to dry her eyes, but the tears never let up. She felt like a train wreck. Nothing had gone right for her in the last week.

"Your friend said you were out to lunch with your fiancé."

"I was." Lily choked back a sob at the realization that he *was* her fiancé, as in past tense. At one time she had been engaged and looking forward to her future, but that was all gone now. Once again, she found herself picking up the pieces of a broken life.

"I dropped your purse off at the bank, and as I drove away it looked like you were getting harassed by a guy in a Beemer." Colt paused to grin at her, and Lily felt the heaviness in her heart dissipate a little. "I thought I'd better turn around and see if you needed me to beat up any more guys for you. You know, since I'm all practiced up after yesterday."

"That's okay. He's not worth it."

The streetlight went from yellow to red, and the truck came to a stop. Colt turned his head and lifted his eyebrows. "Do you know that guy?"

"Apparently not as well as I thought I did. That was Nick."

"Your fiancé?"

Lily heard the frustration in her voice. "Technically, yes. But right now, he's the last person I want to be engaged to."

The light turned green, allowing Colt to turn left into the strip mall that housed the bank. After he parked, he draped his arm over the back of the seat, looking smug. He leaned closer.

"I should say I'm sorry, but truthfully I'm not. Or maybe I could say I told you so."

Lily pushed him away, smiling for the first time since she had left Nick. "Colt, you big tease." She took a deep breath and pulled down the visor in front of her. Mascara streaked her cheeks. Her blue eyes looked bloodshot, and her lids were puffy. "What a mess. I look awful."

Colt reached over and touched her shoulder. "Did he hurt you?"

The seriousness in his voice made her feel self-conscious and she looked down, touching her wrist. "Not really."

"Let me see," he said, holding out his hand.

Lily's gaze traveled from his outstretched hand, up his muscled arm, across the square jaw, and met his sea-green eyes. He waited, never taking his eyes off of her. She moved her hand into his. Her voice came out closer to a whisper. "Nick didn't want me to get out of the car. He grabbed my wrist."

Colt looked down and turned her hand over to examine the reddened skin. "I am sorry about this." His calloused fingers moved over her palm, caressed her wrist, and paused on her light blue vein. He brought her wrist to his mouth and kissed it.

Then, he released her hand and touched her face, his thumb tracing the damp spot above her cheekbone. His eyes roamed over hers, before dropping to her lips. Lily's heart raced, while the air caught in her lungs. The kiss she expected from him never materialized. He seemed frozen, as if something held him back, but the longing in his gaze was unmistakable.

As her mind flashed back to the times he had kissed her before, Lily knew it was what she was waiting for, what she needed. She cupped his cheek with her hand, closed the distance between them, and pressed her lips to his. All the stress and anxiety of the past twenty-four hours melted away as he gathered her into his arms and thoroughly kissed her.

Thirty

Colt draped his arm across the steering wheel and grinned at Lily. A pink blush highlighted her cheeks, making her look even more beautiful. "That far exceeded my expectations when I decided to drop off your purse during my lunch break today."

She laughed as she slid back in front of the mirror on the visor. "How can I go into work looking like this? But after how much time I've missed in the last week, how can I not?"

"Come get something to eat with me and we'll swing by your house. You can fix your makeup, or whatever."

Colt picked up a chicken teriyaki bowl to go and drove to Lily's house. He had tried to buy her one, but she insisted she had eaten earlier. He parked his truck in her driveway. Yellow police tape still blocked the entrance to the house. They ducked under and he followed her inside. "Looks like somebody started the cleanup," he said, noticing the cat wasn't where they had left it, and the tiled entryway had been scrubbed clean of any blood.

"That was Angela and me, last night. Is your offer to help me bury Romeo still open?"

"Of course, but where is he?"

"We put him in a box in the garage. We're ordering pizza after work, and she and her fiancé are hopefully going to help me finish cleaning this up tonight." Lily looked at Colt, her eyes bright. "You could stop by, if you wanted."

He smiled. "I'd love to help. Do I dare ask if Juliet is okay?"

Lily paused on the bottom step. "Oh, yes. She's at Angela's house. The police found her in the apartment Henderson shared with his girlfriend. Evidently, he told her they were pet-sitting for a couple of days."

"I'm glad everything worked out."

"I'll see if I can repair this mascara damage. Sorry it's still such a disaster in here, but make yourself at home, as much as possible at least."

Colt cleared a spot on the counter for his food. He bent to retrieve an unbroken glass from the tile floor. This one must have landed on the hot pads and towels that came out of the drawer Henderson had turned upside down. Colt rinsed it, then filled it with water and ice from the refrigerator. His metabolism was still running in high gear, because he felt like a bottomless pit. After scraping his Styrofoam container of the last speck of rice, he cleared the counter of his mess and went in search of the trashcan.

The distinct scent of decay greeted him when he opened the door to the garage. A trio of flies took flight, hovering over a cardboard Amazon box. The flaps were tucked beneath each other, holding the top closed. Another day in this heat and that cat would stink up the whole place. As Colt bent to retrieve it, his nostrils flared. Already the hot temperatures hadn't been kind to Romeo. He pulled a black garbage sack off the shelf and put the box inside while he carried it to the small chest freezer against the wall. Colt pressed the garage door opener to air out the place as he stepped back inside.

Still no sign of Lily, so he pulled the garbage can into the center of the kitchen and began tossing in shattered glassware. He replaced the drawers, noticing one of them had separated at the seam. A couple of finish nails should do the trick. He'd have to remember to throw a few in his truck before he came ~~back~~ tonight. Only a handful of glasses and plates had survived the encounter with the Camo Bandit. She would need to restock her kitchen.

"Wow, thanks," Lily said from behind him. "I didn't expect you to start working already."

Colt smiled back at her. Her silk top, in baby blue, clung to her perfect figure and made her eyes look brighter than he remembered. "You look beautiful. No one will ever guess you had a good cry for lunch."

Lily chuckled. "I guess we'd better go. I still haven't made it through all the emails that stacked up after last week."

Colt stooped to pick up another piece of glass and tossed it in the trash on his way out the door.

When Lily's cell phone chimed on the counter, Angela peered at the display and announced, "It's Mr. Hot Stuff again."

Lily let out a sigh and rolled her eyes. "He's the last person I want to talk to right now. Just ignore it."

Colt bent over the garbage sack and pulled the blue ties closed. Their work here was done. Lily's house had been put back together, and the majority of the mess cleaned up. With five of them working, it hadn't taken as long as Colt had expected. Angela was a ball of energy and she'd brought along her fiancé and her younger sister Abby. Angela's fiancé Damian was a down-to-earth, sports-loving kind of guy, the type Colt could easily relate to. Angela and Damian had everyone laughing so hard at one point, Colt thought he was going to fall over.

He doubted he had let Lily out of his sight the whole night, and it was no different now that her friends were leaving. She hugged Angela, then waved at Abby, who was already on the front porch.

"Thank you!" Lily said. "I don't know what I would've done without you guys. You're amazing."

"You're welcome," Angela said as she slipped her hand in Damian's and started out the door. "You call me if you need anything else, or if you change your mind and want to sleep at my house another night."

Lily waved. "I'm sure I'll be fine."

Colt walked up behind Lily and placed his hand on her waist. "Can I scoot past you?" he whispered in her ear.

Lily looked up into his face, then down to the garbage sack he held. "Sure. You can take the trash out any day."

When he stepped back inside a minute later and closed the front door, Lily stood in the entryway as if waiting for him. "What now?" he asked.

Her voice and expression were more somber than they had been earlier, when she said, "We still need to bury Romeo."

"We should take care of that sooner rather than later," Colt said, remembering the smell when he'd put the cat in the freezer. He didn't think Lily would appreciate moving that box around to get at her food. "Like tonight."

"You don't mind?"

He smiled at her. "Gives me a good excuse not to say goodbye to you yet."

Lily's eyes brightened and the somberness left her expression. "Where should we bury him?"

"Grab a jacket and come with me. It's a bit of a drive, but there is a good spot out at my parents' place."

She grabbed her purse and coat and followed Colt through the garage to his truck.

As soon as they hit the freeway heading south, he pulled out his phone. Colt grabbed his Bluetooth and then dialed his parents' home. His little sister answered. "Hey, Lizzy, I'm on my way home with Lily Vanasche. Is it okay if we bury her cat in your cat cemetery?"

Lizzy squealed. "Yes, but what is she doing with you? I thought she was engaged to Nick Borino."

Colt chuckled. "You'd have to ask her that. I'm not sure yet."

Stars twinkled overhead and the night breeze whistled out of the canyon as Colt stuck his shovel into the rocky soil. Lily stood next to him, looking as if she was fighting not to cry. He'd known the little black-and-white cat for less than a day, but still a pang of sorrow went through him as the animal quickly disappeared beneath a layer of dirt. Probably his empathy for Lily had triggered this sadness more than anything he felt for Romeo.

Lizzy wrapped an arm around Lily. "I'm so sorry."

As Colt compacted the dirt with his boot, Lily turned and hugged his sister. Her voice caught as she said, "It's just so awful how he died. He didn't deserve that."

His sister muttered words of comfort, while Colt mounded loose rocks over the grave. He found a smooth, round stone and pulled the Sharpie from his pocket. He wrote "ROMEO" in big block letters and held it up for Lily and Lizzy. "Look okay?"

Lily nodded and then crossed the small space between them. She flung her arms around his neck. "Thank you. It's perfect."

Colt pulled her closer and buried his nose in the hair behind her ear, thinking how perfect she felt in his arms.

Thirty-One

Lily brought the mug of hot cocoa to her lips. The sweet liquid slipped down her throat, warming her from the inside out. By the time they had finished outside, she was shivering. Colt never ceased to amaze her with his thoughtfulness. She couldn't imagine Nick driving nearly an hour to bury a cat after dark. He would have put poor Romeo in a Hefty bag and tossed him into the trash.

Colt handed Lizzy a mug and poured one for himself before he joined them at the table. Sam passed through the kitchen on his way to the basement but didn't want any cocoa.

"So," Lizzy said, looking at Lily. "What happened to Nick Borino? He said on TV you were his fiancée."

Colt shifted in his chair. Lily glanced to the left in time to see him glaring at his sister.

"What?" Lizzy frowned back at Colt. "You wouldn't tell me. You said I needed to ask her myself, so I did."

Colt stretched his arm across the back of Lily's chair and leaned forward. "I didn't mean you should ask her tonight!"

"That's okay." Lily met Lizzy's eyes. "I don't mind. The truth is, I'm not sure Nick is the right one for me, so I'm taking a break from him while I figure it out."

"Oh good! Maybe you can keep hanging out with Colt—he needs a girlfriend. It's been like forever since my brother's gone on a date."

Colt leaned against the back of his chair and pressed his hand to his forehead. "Shut up, Liz."

"Just because Mama's gone doesn't mean you can boss me around."

"Yes, I can. I'm the adult here. Mama asked me to stop by the house each day and look in on you and Sam."

Lizzy scowled at her brother. "I turn eighteen in nine days. I don't need a babysitter."

Lily laughed at their bantering.

"Don't you have school tomorrow?" Colt said. "You should run along to bed."

Lizzy pushed her chair back, and in a high-pitched mocking voice said, "Yes, Mama." She reached over and gave Lily a hug. "I hope you come back again. I really like you."

Lily took another swallow from her cup. "Thank you for making a spot for Romeo, and I really like you too."

As soon as Lizzy left the room, Colt leaned back in his chair and exhaled.

"Your sister's cute."

Colt downed the last of his cocoa. "I'm glad you think so."

Through the teasing, Lily still felt the love in their home. "Oh, be nice, Colt. It could be worse. At least you aren't an only child."

He stood and cleared their empty cups. "If you say so."

When Lily yawned despite her best efforts at stifling it, she suggested he take her home. Colt escorted her to his truck and opened her door without cracking a smile. Lily, on the other hand, couldn't help but grin at the memory of what his sister had said. As soon as he turned his truck out of the driveway, Lily had to join in on the fun. "So, you don't date much, huh? That's kind of hard to believe."

Colt looked at her, the glow of the streetlamps showing the lift of his eyebrows and the smirk on his face. "Not you too."

"Maybe you just have them all fooled. After the way Cassidy Pearson was flirting with you during that interview on TV, I'm surprised you were even available to help me tonight. I thought she'd snatch you up right there on the spot."

"She did give me her phone number. I was thinking about asking her out this weekend."

Lily gasped. "No way! I was totally joking about that."

Colt didn't say anything as he merged into the late-night freeway traffic.

Lily folded her arms. "Did she really give you her number?"

"Yeah, she wrote 'Call me' and drew a little heart on the back of her business card."

Lily turned sideways in the seat to get a better look at him. "For real?"

He nodded.

"Are you seriously thinking of going out with her?"

Colt shrugged his shoulders. "I thought I'd take her out to dinner on Friday, maybe a movie on Saturday, and then I'd invite her to church on Sunday. But why should you care? Don't you still have a fiancé?" He glanced over at her. "Wait, you're not jealous are you?"

While the grin on his face softened the effect, Lily knew he spoke the truth. "What if I told you I don't plan on having a fiancé by the time the weekend rolls around and that I'd love to go to church with you?" she said.

Colt scratched his head, making a show of thinking it over. "What about the movie and the dinner part?"

Lily laughed. "Yes, to all of it."

"In that case, I'd have to toss that business card in the trash. I won't have time for Cassidy Pearson, or anyone else — I'll be too busy trying to win your heart."

Epilogue

Eight Months Later

The judge brought the hammer down, signaling the end of Lewis Henderson's trial. Lily stood and slid her hand into Colt's as he moved into the aisle. She breathed a sigh of relief, grateful to close that chapter of her life. She was more than ready to start the next one.

They were moving with the crowd toward the exit when Agent Dawson with the FBI put his hand out to stop Colt and then nodded in Lily's direction. "I'm still not sure I'm buying that story you gave me during interrogation. Look at you two. For never having met each other a few months ago, you sure seem close." The agent stared at Colt with steely eyes.

Lily didn't know what he was talking about, but his stern tone of voice made her anxious. She pulled her eyes away from the agent and looked into Colt's face. He met Dawson's stare for a moment and then broke into a full-toothed grin and pulled Lily closer. "What can I say? Opportunity knocked, I answered. Like I told you before, she's very pretty."

Agent Dawson chuckled as he slapped Colt on the shoulder. "You're right about that. It looks like you scored big on the whole ordeal." He motioned toward Lily's left hand. "I saw the ring when you took the witness stand. Congratulations!" Lily's gaze dropped to the diamond ring on her finger and she felt herself smile. It was perfect—the shape and cut of the gemstone, the twist and curve of the white gold band, the array of sparkling diamonds.

Colt nodded. "Thanks, man."

"No, thank you," Agent Dawson said. "You did good bringing that guy down."

They exited the courtroom and soon stepped into the bright May sunshine. Lily put on her sunglasses and wrapped her hand around Colt's arm. "Only a month. I can't wait."

He gave her a blank look. "What happens in a month?"

Lily raised her chin and glanced away. "You big tease. I'm not even answering that question."

Colt spun her around to face him and flashed a crooked grin, the one that had endeared him to her at his elk camp all those months ago. He tipped her chin up and kissed her.

"How could I forget? June 1—our wedding. I love you, woman with no name."

About the Author

Kelly Nelson graduated from Brigham Young University with a bachelor's degree. She worked in public accounting for four years before starting a horse-boarding business so she could be more involved in raising her family. An avid book lover, she later decided to pursue a career in writing. Her published novels include the LDS romance *Love's Deception,* and a young-adult fantasy series called The Keeper's Saga. Kelly resides in Cornelius, Oregon, with her husband, children, and a herd of horses.

Learn more about Kelly and her books at kellynelsonauthor.com, or follow her on Twitter @kellynelsonauth. She loves hearing from readers and can be contacted at kellynelsonauthor@gmail.com.

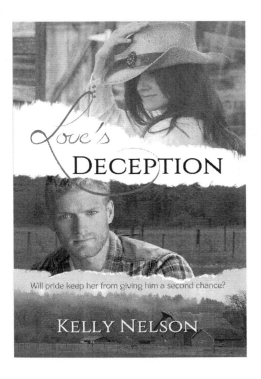

Catherine Lewis lost her husband to a roadside bomb in Baghdad shortly after discovering she was expecting their first child. Seven years later, Cat fears her chance at true happiness has slipped through her fingers.

After growing up the son of a humble Oregon farmer, Ty Bradford is climbing the corporate ladder at an accounting firm in California. But when his father suffers a heart attack, Ty returns home to help with the family farm. Rescuing a beautiful cowgirl stranded on a rural road transforms his previously miserable leave of absence into one of the happiest times of his life.

Ty isn't a member of the LDS Church, and normally Cat, an active Latter-day Saint, wouldn't give him a chance. Against her better judgment she falls for him, believing he is a farmer. Once she realizes he is leading a double life, will she shut the door on the relationship for good? Or could Mr. Wrong possibly be the right one for her after all?